THE FALLING GIRL

THE FALLING GIRL

THE FALLING GIRL

THOMAS FINCHAM

The Falling Girl
Thomas Fincham

AUTHOR'S NOTE
This book is a work of fiction. Names, characters, places and incidents are products of the author's imagination or are used fictitiously. Any resemblance to actual events or locales or persons, living or dead, is entirely coincidental.

The scanning, uploading and distribution of this book via the internet or any other means without the permission of the publisher is illegal and punishable by law. Please purchase only authorized electronic editions, and do not participate in or encourage electronic piracy of copyrighted materials. Your support of the author's rights is appreciated.

Visit the author's website:
www.finchambooks.com

Contact:
finchambooks@gmail.com

THE FALLING GIRL

ONE

One year ago

Gail Roberts was frowning as she got out of the taxi.

Gail was short, stocky, and she had shoulder-length auburn hair. She had graduated with a degree in creative writing. She dreamed of being a novelist, but after a couple of years spent toiling away on an unfinished manuscript, she decided to give screenwriting a try.

With two finished screenplays to her name, she took a job as an assistant in a movie production company. She figured it would give her access to agents, producers, and studio heads. Maybe an A-list actor would fall in love with one of her scripts and want to star in the film.

The assistant job was supposed to have been a stepping stone to bigger and better things. It was anything but that, proving to be a thankless job with long hours and no benefits.

She thought about quitting, but she gave herself another year until she could save enough money. She would then sit down and plan what she would do next with her life.

Her parents were always supportive of her decisions, but even her father had reservations when she had told him she wanted a career in writing. "Do something practical," he had warned her. "Do something that will give you a stable income."

She held out hope that someone might stumble upon her scripts and offer to buy them. Maybe someone would even hire her to write a script for them. There were a lot of maybes, and they were what held her in her current position.

Her plans changed when she came upon something that shook her to the core. It went against everything she believed in. It was vile, depraved, and criminal. She knew she could not stay silent. Her parents had raised her to speak out for the weak and helpless.

She had stormed into the offices of those responsible and told them what she was going to do. They did not take kindly to her decision. They threatened her with lawsuits. She had signed non-disclosure agreements. She didn't care. She was willing to face prison in order to do the right thing.

When they saw her resolve, they offered her money. But she refused. She was not going to change her mind.

She was scheduled to speak to a reporter the next day. The reporter did not know her name nor the details of what she was about to disclose, but her revelations would be explosive.

Gail hoped her whistleblowing would start a dialogue and that others like her would come forward. She would be the face of this new movement. Even if she was not, it didn't matter. She was not the victim. Others were. It was their voices she wanted heard.

Earlier in the day, she had gone out with her friends to ease her anxiety about what she was going to do. She had debated giving them a heads up, but she never saw the right opportunity. Her work required her to travel often, so she hardly saw her friends. The moment they were together, she was swept up in the excitement of spending time with them. They laughed. They drank. They told stories of their youth. One of her married friends even broke the news that she was pregnant. Her announcement brought joy to an already boisterous gathering.

Then Gail received the call. She hesitated answering, but she did. The caller pleaded to see her. All he wanted was for her to hear him out.

She finally agreed. What she was about to do the next day was going to be devastating to the parties involved. She had to give them a chance to explain themselves. She doubted very much that their words would change her mind, but what was one more meeting?

Her friends were not happy she was leaving the party early, but she assured them she would fill them in on the details the next time they met up. She knew full well it would be sooner than that. The moment the news broke, her phone would be ringing off the hook. In fact, her friends would be banging on her door to get all the juicy gossip.

After paying the taxi driver, she walked up to the front lobby of her apartment building. Her place was located in a rough and dangerous neighborhood. It was not uncommon to see gang-related shootings, people selling drugs around the corner, or the police raiding the building.

She could not wait to move out, but the rent was cheap, so she was staying put. It might not be for long, though. She might have to take refuge in her parents' house from all the attention she was about to put on herself. Luckily, her parents lived outside the city.

She unlocked her apartment door and entered. Warm air hit her, and she felt like she was walking into a sauna. The apartment was hot and stuffy, and she almost couldn't breathe.

She walked over to a wall and checked. For some strange reason, the thermostat was turned up high. She turned it down and moved to the glass doors that led out to the balcony. She slid them open. She would give the cool air a minute or two to circulate through the apartment before she went back inside.

She leaned over the balcony railing and stared down at the streets below. She was fifteen floors up, but she could still make out people. Down below, a man was walking his dog while he smoked a cigarette.

The view across from her balcony was terrible. She was surrounded by buildings just like hers. Sometimes when she couldn't sleep, she would come out to the balcony and stare into the living rooms and bedrooms of the people living in those buildings. It was voyeuristic, even creepy, but it helped pass the time.

She sensed movement behind her.

She was about to turn when something strong gripped her legs.

The next second, she was over the balcony.

She let out a loud scream as she fell to her death.

TWO

Present Day

The sun was up, shining from a clear sky as the Honda SUV moved down the narrow road. On either side of the road were tall trees and bushes. The view was idyllic, almost serene.

Dana Fisher was a detective with the Milton Police Department. She was five-foot-five, weighed one hundred and ten pounds, and had dark, shoulder-length hair. Her thin nose pointed upwards, and it moved whenever she opened her mouth.

Her large green eyes took in the surroundings, and she almost wished she didn't have to go where she was headed. There was a murder, and she was called in to investigate.

A part of her wanted to turn around and head in the opposite direction.

Fisher grew up in the city. She was constantly bombarded with noises from buses, garbage trucks, and drivers honking. This made her somewhat accustomed to the hustle and bustle of city life, but even so, she appreciated the beauty and tranquility of what nature provided.

She rolled down her window and inhaled the fresh air. It filled her lungs, giving her renewed energy.

She and her siblings were born a year apart from each other. After having two boys, her parents were grateful for a girl. They then wanted to give her a sister so that she too would have someone to play with. When the last child ended up being a boy as well, they stopped having kids.

Fisher and her siblings fought incessantly about everything. First they vied with each other to get their parents' attention, then they squabbled over toys, who got to watch their favorite shows, and who was best at sports. That competitive spirit stayed with her when she reached adulthood.

Fisher had joined the police force straight out of college. Her first year as a recruit was spent patrolling the streets. She dealt with drug addicts, prostitutes, and civil complaints. She then moved up from recruit to officer, where she was involved in police raids on drug manufacturers, shutting down human trafficking, and capturing gang leaders.

She was quickly promoted to detective, and now she had her eyes set on becoming sergeant. She hoped she would make captain by the time she retired. She was fully confident she would.

She slowed the SUV when she spotted a deer by the side of the road. A doe. The deer watched her for a second. When the doe was certain Fisher was not a threat, it darted across the road.

She sighed. The day had started with so much potential, but from her experience conducting murder investigations, days never ended that way. By the time she got home that night, she would be mentally and physically drained.

She accelerated the SUV and continued down the road.

THREE

Her destination was tucked away behind a row of massive oak trees. To reach it, you had to get off the road, pass through a brick entrance, and drive up a long gravel path.

The house had a gray exterior, a triangular roof, and French windows. A police cruiser was parked next to a black limousine.

Fisher pulled up next to the cruiser and got out when a uniformed officer approached her. He was tall, and he had blonde hair hidden underneath his police cap. His deep blue eyes were set, and he had a prominent chin.

Fisher had first seen Officer Lance McConnell at the annual police games. He had won the 100-meter dash. She then met him twice during her last major murder investigation.

Whenever she was around McConnell, she found she could not stop blushing.

"Detective Fisher," he said with a smile.

"Officer McConnell," she replied. Her face burned. She coughed to regain her composure. "I'm surprised to see you here."

"I don't normally patrol this area, but when someone called in sick, I was asked to come here," McConnell said with a shrug.

The Milton PD was restructuring the way it policed the city. Officers were constantly being redeployed to areas with urgent needs. They called it Modernization of Service, which was a fancy way of saying they had no money to hire new officers and were forcing existing officers to take over their colleagues' shifts. The police union was up in arms over this and had gone on a PR blitz. In their ads, they named the police chief, the head of the police services board, and the mayor as the people responsible for the thin-stretched service. It was going to be a bloody fight. Fisher hoped the union prevailed in the end.

"Will you be working solo on this?" McConnell asked.

Detective Greg Holt was her partner. After his nephew's brutal murder, Holt was encouraged to take some time off. Holt refused like he always did. He lived for the job. Nothing else mattered when he was in pursuit of a killer.

The department—under the direction of the Officer Assistant Program, which was set up to monitor officers' health—forced Holt to attend a law enforcement conference in Las Vegas. He was even allowed to bring his wife, Nancy, to this event. They figured, rightly, if Nancy was there, Holt would not put up a strong fight.

Nancy was Holt's Achilles' heel. He would do anything to make her happy, even if it meant sitting through long lectures and presentations, surrounded by thousands of strangers.

Fisher knew Holt deserved a break whether he liked it or not. He had been through so much in the past couple of years. Holt and Nancy had adopted a boy from Ukraine. The boy did not live to see his first birthday, dying from a rare form of cancer. And when his nephew was gunned down, Holt had reached the breaking point. Thankfully, they were able to find his murderer, and Holt was able to provide closure for his sister, Marjorie.

Fisher spotted a man next to the limousine. The man looked pale as he spoke into his cell phone.

"Who's that?" she asked.

"He called 9-1-1."

"Let's go take a look at who the victim is."

"I think you'll recognize him when you see him," McConnell said.

A knot formed in the pit of Fisher's stomach. It was the same feeling she had when she found out Holt's nephew was murdered. "I will?" she slowly said.

"It's Dillon Scott."

FOUR

Dillon Scott had starred in over thirty film productions. Ten of those had opened at number one at the box office. Scott had started in showbiz when he was sixteen years old. His first role was in a TV series, where he played a troubled kid with a heart of gold. He reminded viewers of a young James Dean. He became an overnight star and was named Most Likely to Win an Academy Award.

He spent three years on the short-lived TV series. In his public life, he mostly imitated his character on the show. He was caught on camera taking drugs, got charged with DUIs, and even spent a night in jail for assaulting an extra on set.

He then disappeared from the public eye. He cleaned up his act, and two years later, at the age of twenty-two, he starred in a remake of *Romeo and Juliet*. His portrayal of the tragic lead character made him a heartthrob for young girls. The movie was a smash hit.

His subsequent movies made him one of Hollywood's leading men. He dated starlets, young and old, but then he did something that surprised even his most die-hard fans. He married an unknown woman by the name of Rachel Poole. She worked as a real estate agent, and she had sold Scott a six-bedroom mansion in Beverly Hills. They ended up having two children—a boy and a girl—and Scott settled into being a bankable movie star.

At the height of his fame, he was commanding a salary of ten million dollars per movie. He was everywhere, starring in action-adventure, science fiction, romance, and even drama films. In one dramatic role, he played a quadriplegic detective, which got him his first Oscar nomination.

He parlayed his success into charitable work that focused on children in poor countries. He backed projects in Africa, India, and Latin America. He gave his time and money to set up orphanages in many parts of the world.

His last couple of movies had flopped at the box office, however, and his star had started to fade. Even then, audiences loved him for his roles. He was the all-American good guy who, against all odds, would still come out on top.

Fisher would never admit it to anyone—especially not Holt—but she had a crush on Scott when she was a teenager.

Like many girls her age, she had a poster of him playing Romeo. He had long hair, piercing blue eyes, a slight grin, and he looked like he was staring directly at her.

She dreamed of marrying him one day, even though he was much older than her. According to his date of birth, Scott was forty-five as of this year.

She had followed his career with the enthusiasm of an ardent fan. She knew Scott was on the verge of a major comeback. He was signed on to play Jean Valjean in the reproduction of *Les Miserables*. His performance would remind viewers of the time he had won them over as Romeo. Fisher was certain he would be back on top in no time.

She was shocked he was dead.

FIVE

The hula girl figurine wiggled her hips on top of the van's dashboard. The girl had a smile that he found enticing and also disturbing. He was not sure why. Maybe because whoever painted her face made her eyes bulge out and her lips three sizes too big.

He scanned the minivan's interior. The dashboard, handrest, and even the steering wheel were covered in colorful stickers. He looked down at the floor mats, and all he saw were cartoon characters.

Lee Callaway was tall, tanned, and he had strands of silver around his temples. He had also begun to get gray strands on the top of his head, but those were still unnoticeable.

Callaway felt out of place behind the wheel of the minivan. He was wearing a black coat, dark sunglasses, and he had stubble on his cheeks. Parents held their children closer as he drove past them. He looked like he was out to kidnap their children.

He missed his Dodge Charger. That car was pure muscle and power. Whenever he accelerated, he could feel the adrenaline course through his veins.

The Charger was the reason he was driving the minivan. It had suffered exterior damage when a client had gone at it with a baseball bat. At least that's what Callaway thought was used. The weapon could have been a tire iron or a wrench. Whatever was used had cracked the Charger's windshield, smashed the taillights, and dented the body.

The car had since been restored to its full glory, but Callaway did not have the money to pay for the work done. He rarely had money to begin with, but that was another story.

The auto shop's owner had done him favors before, and Callaway was not about to swindle him out of his hard work.

He offered to repay the owner by taking on small tasks at the shop. It would take months, maybe even years, but Callaway was adamant he would pay every penny he owed him.

Paying off the bill would be much easier and a lot quicker if Callaway landed a solid case. He was a private investigator who rarely investigated anything. He was desperate and broke. He was accustomed to following cheating spouses, but he was now even willing to find people's missing pets.

Boo Boo hasn't been seen in days? No problem. PI Lee Callaway will bring her home.

He turned on the radio. The speakers blared children's music. He pressed a button and another children's song came on. After failing to find an adult radio station, he let the children's music play.

Ten minutes later, he found himself singing along with the songs. They were kind of catchy, and also positive. They made him feel like he could do anything if he set his mind to it.

If this orphaned girl can become a princess, he thought, *why can't I get my Charger back?*

He reached his destination: a bungalow. He parked in the driveway. A woman holding a baby came out to meet him. He handed her the invoice. The minivan had come to the mechanic shop for an oil change, a wheel alignment, and a transmission fluid replacement. The woman did not have a second car, so the shop owner agreed to have one of his employees drive her van back to her. Fortunately, Callaway was at the shop, and he gladly took on the task.

The woman paid him the amount on the invoice, and then she handed him an additional ten dollars as a tip.

Lady, I'm not some pizza delivery guy, he wanted to say. But he pocketed the cash. He was not about to turn down a kind gesture.

He thanked her and left.

SIX

Dillon Scott lay on the living room carpet. His eyes were closed, and even in death, he was still handsome. He had aged gracefully in front of his audience. His face was slightly wrinkled, but it made him more distinguished. His hair was still thick with not a gray strand in sight. He had a small scar at the top of his chin. He had gotten it in a fight during his troubled youth. Someone had hit him with a beer bottle. The wound required over forty stitches to close up.

Fisher found the scar charming. She couldn't help but stare at it whenever she watched one of his movies. The scar gave him an air of danger, even when he was playing a helpless schmuck. As a viewer, you could never tell when he would rise up and save the day.

His arms rested by his sides as if he was asleep.

Did someone move his body? Fisher thought. *And was his death caused by falling on the table?*

She couldn't be sure.

The coffee table's glass top was in pieces. Shards of glass lay scattered around Scott.

She took a step back to get a better view of the scene. The sectional sofa took up most of the living room. Behind the sofa was a built-in bookshelf that held many books. The coffee table was in front of the sofa, and across from it was a fireplace. On top of the fireplace was a large LCD screen. It was not turned on, which told her Scott was not watching TV at the time of the attack.

He had been attacked; she was certain of that. She could not imagine him fainting on the coffee table. The body's positioning would be more... *natural*. The arms would be at different angles, the legs would be spread apart, the head would likely be turned left or right, and the probability of the body being on one of its sides would also be very high.

It looked like the scene was staged.

But why?

Even if it was, what did the killer gain by moving the body? And why not move the body completely, perhaps out of the house even? The house was in a secluded location. The next neighbor was half a mile away.

The only logical explanation was that the killer was cleaning up evidence that may have been left behind.

She walked around the room. She hoped one of the framed photos on the wall would give her an idea of what the room looked like before the murder. It was common to see families posing on a sofa or in front of the fireplace. She might detect what, if anything, had been altered by the killer.

She frowned when she saw that all the photos were of landscapes, architecture, and nature.

She did learn one thing as she moved around the living room. The house did not belong to Dillon Scott. There was nothing personal she could find anywhere. No photos of him or his wife and children. No posters of movies he had starred in.

She was told that actors were vain and insecure. They constantly needed to be reminded that they were movie stars and deserved the attention they received.

Maybe Scott was different. Maybe he didn't care for the adulation.

If that was the case, he would be a rarity in the profession.

SEVEN

Fisher left the house and walked up to the limousine parked in the driveway. A man was behind the wheel. He got out the moment he saw her approach. He was wearing a suit, tie, and polished shoes. He was clean-shaven, and his hair was gelled back.

"Officer McConnell told me you called 9-1-1," Fisher said.

The man swallowed. "Um, yeah, I did."

She could tell she would have to be gentle with him. The man looked like he was about to faint. "Your name?" she asked.

"David Gill."

"What were you doing here, Mr. Gill?"

"I was hired by the studio to drive Mr. Scott."

"When did Mr. Scott move into this property?"

"I picked him up from the airport two days ago."

"And you've been driving him around Milton ever since?"

"Yes."

"Okay, tell me what happened before you called 9-1-1."

He took a deep breath. "It's my job to also make sure Mr. Scott is ready before I pick him up. I've been a limo driver for almost ten years, and you wouldn't believe how many times I've showed up and the client was still in bed. A lot of actors aren't known for being punctual or considerate."

Fisher's brow furrowed. "Considerate?"

Gill's eyes widened. "I mean... um…"

She gave him a reassuring smile. "It's okay, I just want to understand what you are saying. That's all."

"Some of the actors treat us like we are their servants," Gill explained. "Like we're supposed to be at their beck and call twenty-four seven. There have been a dozen times when I've had to wait in my vehicle for hours while they got ready to go. There have also been times when I've shown up and they've disappeared."

"Disappeared?" she asked, curious.

"Yeah, they decided to go with someone else instead, and they didn't bother to notify me. I wouldn't find out until much later. Even though I'm still being paid, I think it's disrespectful."

Fisher sensed Gill was frustrated. "Okay, so you called him before you arrived at the property, is that correct?"

"Yes. I called the contact number I was provided for Mr. Scott, but he didn't pick up. I was concerned. I had to drive him for his rehearsals, and I didn't want him to be late. The studios blame us when it happens." He shook his head at the absurdity. "Most of these studio bosses don't have the power to make these stars do anything they don't want to, so how can *we* make them? We're just hired hands." He exhaled. "I then drove over here. I got out and knocked on the door. When I didn't get a response, I checked the door and it was unlocked."

This is interesting, she thought. "Unlocked?"

"Yeah."

"Does the house have an alarm system?"

"I believe it does. I saw Mr. Scott punch in the code."

"Do *you* know the code?"

Gill shook his head. "They don't share that information with us."

"Who would know then?"

"Mr. Scott, and I guess the production company."

Fisher made a mental note of this. "When you found the door unlocked, what happened?"

"I called out Mr. Scott's name. I thought maybe he was still asleep. I went inside, and that's when I saw—" Gill gulped for breath, "—his body in the living room."

"Did you touch anything?"

"I checked to see if he was okay."

"So, you did?"

"Um, yeah, I guess so."

"And then what did you do?"

"I ran out of the house and dialed 9-1-1."

Fisher pondered this.

"What did you do yesterday?"

"Yesterday?"

"Yes, and don't spare any of the details."

"Um, okay, sure. So, I woke up in the morning and I—"

"No, Mr. Gill, I mean from the time you picked up Mr. Scott from the studio."

"Oh, right. At exactly six o'clock, I was at the studio parking lot, waiting for Mr. Scott. He came out of the building and got in my limo."

"What was he wearing?"

Gill paused to think for a moment. "He had on a white T-shirt, a green jacket, blue jeans, and I think he was also wearing black boots," he said.

That's what he's wearing now, Fisher thought. *Minus the boots.*

"What was his demeanor like?"

Gill looked confused. "Demeanor?"

"Was he quiet? Talkative? Upset?"

"They don't really talk to us. Most of them don't even acknowledge that we exist. They are usually on their phones, or if they have company, they talk to them."

"Was Mr. Scott alone?"

"Oh, yes."

"So, you picked him up and you…"

Fisher let her words trail off.

"I drove him straight to the house," Gill said.

"And during the drive, did he call anyone?"

Gill pondered Fisher's question. "He kept checking his phone," he replied, "but I don't think he spoke to anyone. I mean, as drivers, we are supposed to be invisible, but it's easy to listen in on their conversations if they are talking loudly. The majority of the actors don't care what they are saying in the limo. They know we would never disclose what was said to anyone. If we did, we would never work in the industry again. These people value their privacy like it's the most precious thing in the world. I guess they have to because they are so famous. I know of a driver who mistakenly spoke up while the client was talking to someone on the phone. The client was confused about what day it was, and the driver was trying to be helpful. He was let go right after, when the client complained. The driver was hired to take the client from point A to point B, not to eavesdrop on her personal conversations."

"What time did you drop him off at the house?"

"Around six thirty."

"And did you wait around on the property?"

"I asked Mr. Scott if he wanted to go anywhere. Usually after a long day, they like to go to a club, a restaurant, a bar, somewhere to unwind, but Mr. Scott said he wanted to go over his script. I reminded him I would pick him up at nine thirty the next morning. He said that was fine. I then drove home."

Fisher's eyes narrowed. Up until six thirty the night before, Dillon Scott was still alive. Now she had to find out what he did after that, which led to his demise.

EIGHT

Callaway got off the bus. He was scowling. After dropping off the minivan, he didn't have enough money to take a taxi back. A cab would cost a lot more than the tip the customer had given him.

He had to walk four blocks before he found a bus stop, and then he had to wait a half hour for a bus to arrive. If that wasn't bad enough, he had to sit between a man whose large butt took up a section of his seat and a man who had fallen asleep with his head on Callaway's shoulder.

Callaway thought about moving to another seat, but he was sandwiched so tight he could barely move an inch. He was relieved when the sleeping man finally got off the bus. Callaway wasn't sure how the man knew it was his stop. He just stood up, wiped drool off his face, and disembarked.

Maybe this is his daily routine, Callaway thought, *and his body has an internal alarm clock.*

Callaway was grateful to be out of the hot and stinking bus. The bus had no ventilation, making Callaway feel like a piece of steak being cooked to medium-rare.

He walked straight to a mechanic shop down the street. A Hispanic man appeared from behind the hood of a car. He had smooth dark hair, a pencil-thin mustache above his upper lip, and whiskers on his chin. He was wearing blue overalls.

"Lee, you're back so early?" he asked with a smile, wiping grease off his hands with a small cloth.

"You call that early? It took me nearly an hour to get back here."

Julio shrugged. "I figured it might take you the entire day."

Callaway shook his head and pulled out the money the woman had given him.

Julio grabbed the cash and put it in his pocket.

"You're not going to count it?" Callaway asked.

"Should I?" Julio asked.

"I mean, what if I pocketed some of it?"

"You could have, but I'll eventually find out once I count it later."

24

"For your information, it's all there."

"Good," Julio said.

Callaway walked over to a black car in the back of the garage. His beloved Charger was good as new.

He moved his hand across the side of the car. He wanted his baby to know that he was doing everything he could to bring her home.

"Have you considered selling it?" Julio asked, coming up behind him.

Callaway glared at Julio as if he had called his mother fat and ugly. "It's not for sale," he growled.

"I know, I know," Julio said. "It's just that it will take you a very long time to pay me back if you keep doing these small jobs for me."

"I'm well aware of that, Julio. Say, are you sure you don't need *my* services?"

Julio looked confused. "What do you mean?"

"I mean, I can be very useful to you."

"Like how?"

"I can dig up dirt on your competition."

"My competition?"

"Yeah, the other garages in the neighborhood."

"You want to put them out of business?"

Callaway paused. "I didn't mean that, but I could find out if they are overcharging their customers. It would be a great boost for your business if they were."

Julio laughed. "All mechanics overcharge their customers, Lee. That's how they stay in business."

Callaway's eyes narrowed. "You didn't overcharge me for the Charger, did you?"

Julio's expression turned dead serious. He waved a finger at Callaway and said, "I did not charge you for labor, only for parts. I'm not making a penny off the Charger. I know how much it means to you, Lee."

Julio was a hardworking family man. For that reason, Callaway had left the Charger at the shop until he had enough money to take the car back. Plus, after Callaway had dropped off the Charger for repairs, Julio had lent him an older model Chevy Impala so he would have a mode of transportation. Julio didn't have to do that, but he did. Callaway had nothing but the utmost respect for him.

He leaned closer to the Charger and whispered, "I'll be back for you, darling."

He left the garage.

NINE

Fisher went back inside the house. She found a woman in a white lab coat leaning over the body.

Andrea Wakefield was petite with short, cropped hair, and she wore round prescription glasses. Her eyes were intently focused on the victim's face as she recorded and stored all pertinent information in the back of her mind.

Fisher noticed that the medical examiner was smiling. Fisher had rarely seen Wakefield smile before.

Fisher felt almost guilty for intruding on her moment of bliss. She slowly asked, "Did you find anything interesting?"

Wakefield coughed as if she had been caught with her hand in the proverbial cookie jar. "I... um... I was admiring the victim's skeletal structure."

Fisher blinked. "Skeletal structure?"

Wakefield blushed. "I meant to say the victim is still striking."

Fisher wasn't sure if that was a compliment or something more morbid. The medical examiner spent most of her waking hours with cadavers. Fisher's partner, Holt, always believed Wakefield had more affinity for the dead than the living.

"You're a fan?" Fisher asked.

Wakefield nodded. "When I saw him in *Romeo and Juliet,* I was smitten."

Fisher was surprised. There wasn't a lot she knew about Wakefield, even though she had worked with the woman on numerous murder investigations.

The relationship between detectives and the medical examiner was built on trust. Without the medical examiner's findings, the detectives had no case. The medical examiner was also called to testify in court, and the M.E.'s statements and the detectives' statements could not be divergent, or else a savvy defense lawyer would tear their opinions to shreds.

Fisher believed they now had something in common: they both admired Dillon Scott. "Did you have a poster of him on your bedroom wall as well?" Fisher asked.

Wakefield shook her head. "No, but I watched *Romeo and Juliet* thirty-four times."

That's an odd number, Fisher thought. "Why thirty-four?"

"Well, during the thirty-fifth viewing, the DVD player stopped working. I might have watched the movie over a dozen times in a twenty-four-hour period." She paused for a moment. "I had just come out of a long-term relationship, and I found the movie soothing, even though the lead characters met a tragic end."

Wakefield had a boyfriend? Fisher thought. *I had no idea she even dated.*

Wakefield turned back to the body and said, "I don't see any signs of a struggle. The fingernails are clean, and there is no visible bruising anywhere on the face, neck, or arms."

Fisher knew those areas of the body were more prone to attack. "Is the cause of death from falling on the coffee table?"

Wakefield leaned closer to Scott. With gloved hands, she turned his head to one side. "As you can see, there are shards of glass in the victim's hair, which would indicate he fell on the table and broke it, but I don't think he died from the impact." She moved her fingers around the top of the head and then parted the hair to reveal a visible gash on the dome of the skull. "Without a thorough examination, I can only give you my perfunctory opinion."

"Understood."

"It looks like the victim died from blunt force trauma. His attacker hit him on the head. He then fell on top of the coffee table and rolled onto the floor."

Fisher thought that made sense. "Did you notice anything else?"

"There is a stain on the carpet," Wakefield replied.

"I noticed that too," Fisher said. "I think the attacker cleaned the carpet with bleach. In fact, the entire crime scene looks like it has been restaged."

"No, not that stain... *that* one," Wakefield said, pointing at the foot of the sofa. There was a deep red splash on the white material.

How could I have missed it before? Fisher thought.

"Is that blood?" she asked

"I don't think so," Wakefield replied. "There doesn't appear to be any indication of much blood from the head wound. Also, I have a similar type of rug at home, and I've been clumsy a few times as well."

"So, what is it?"

"Red wine."

Fisher's eyes narrowed. "You believe the victim may have been drinking when he was attacked?"

"Yes."

Fisher had not seen a glass on the floor when she surveyed the crime scene. She spotted a small table in the corner. She walked over. The table held several bottles of liquor, but no wine bottles or glasses.

The only logical explanation was that the attacker must have removed them.

TEN

Fisher decided to take a quick tour of the house. The crime scene unit would conduct a thorough examination by taking photographs of the scene, dusting for fingerprints on all locks and doors, and making sure all crucial evidence was tagged and sent for further analysis.

Fisher's review was cursory. She just wanted to get a better idea of what might have transpired when the victim was murdered. She had a vague theory formulating in her mind. With Holt, she could toss ideas back and forth, trying to see if her theory was valid, but now that he was miles away, she had to figure things out by herself.

She knew Dillon Scott was not home alone the night before. He was having a get-together with someone over drinks. Perhaps during their get-together, they had a disagreement about something, and the other person hit him with a heavy object.

Fisher was certain the murder weapon was not in the house. If the attacker had cleaned up the crime scene, he or she would have definitely taken the weapon with them. The attacker would have been downright careless not to.

Even so, Fisher had to be certain.

She checked the kitchen. The fridge was stocked with bottled water and nothing else. She opened the lid of the garbage bin and found a Styrofoam box stuffed inside. She pried the box open and found a half-eaten sandwich, most likely from the day before.

She made her way upstairs. There were three bedrooms—two with beds and dressers, and one with a table and chair for an office. The first bedroom did not look like it had been touched. The master bedroom, however, had several pieces of luggage on the floor, and the bed sheets were in disarray.

A small blue case was on the nightstand next to the bed. She gently unzipped the case and found an insulin injection inside.

I didn't know Dillon Scott had diabetes, she thought. *That explains the bottles of water in the fridge.*

In diabetics, excess sugar builds up in the blood stream, forcing the kidneys to work overtime to filter and absorb the sugar. Diabetics drink plenty of water to ensure the kidneys flush out excess sugar. The fact that the disease is so common these days explains why no celebrity media outlets reported Scott's condition.

She spotted a folder on the bed. She picked the folder up and discovered it contained a movie script.

"*Memories of a Killer*," she read out loud. "A psychological thriller about an investigator in pursuit of a killer who may not remember he committed the crimes."

Fisher had stopped watching murder mysteries the moment she became a detective. Her work was already filled with dark and disturbing realities. She did not need to be reminded of them when she got home. She much preferred watching romantic comedies. Lately, though, she had found herself immersed in sci-fi and fantasy. There was something relaxing about watching people fight aliens or dragons. However, the script's premise sounded interesting. She would have loved to see what Scott did with the material, but now she would never get to.

Only one piece of luggage was open. Scott had arrived two days earlier, which explained why he did not have time to unpack.

She took one look around the bedroom and left.

As she made her way downstairs, she couldn't shake the feeling that she was missing something.

When she reached the main floor, she remembered what was missing.

Scott's cell phone!

She had not found the phone on his person, nor was it anywhere else in the house. The driver had clearly stated that Scott kept staring at his cell phone throughout the ride to the house.

Could Scott have been messaging his attacker?

Did the attacker take the phone when he or she cleaned up the crime scene?

Fisher was not a hundred percent sure, but her gut instinct was telling her that was why Scott's phone was nowhere to be seen.

ELEVEN

The Chevy Impala was a nineties model with over three hundred thousand miles on the odometer. The exterior was covered in rust spots and had a few dents. The interior was brown and ugly, and there were tears in the seat fabric. Even with all the imperfections, Callaway had come to enjoy driving the vehicle. Julio's loaner was reliable.

He would miss the Impala when he got his Charger back.

He pulled into a parking spot outside a restaurant. He found Joely behind the counter, serving a customer a plate full of eggs, toast, and bacon.

Callaway pulled up a stool and sat at the counter.

Joely Patterson filled the customer's cup with steaming coffee and then came over to him. She had blonde hair that she kept pulled back in a ponytail. She wore a white apron over her tight-fitting T-shirt. The necklace she wore had a pendant that read *Joshua*.

Joely was a single mother who had aspirations of becoming a singer. She thought she had finally caught her break when a music producer asked to hear her work. She soon realized the producer was interested in her body, not her voice.

"Nice to see you this morning, Lee," she said with a smile.

Callaway smiled back. "I figured I'd come and see you. How's Joshua, by the way?" he asked.

Joely beamed with motherly pride. "He's growing up fast. I signed him up in a pee-wee baseball league, and I tell you, Joshua is a natural. He can hit the ball farther than the older kids. When he makes it to the pros, I'll quit this job and never set foot in a diner again."

Joshua was only six years old, and the odds of making it to the major leagues were no better than winning the lottery.

"You can't give up on *your* dreams," Callaway said. "Sooner or later, someone will see your talent and offer you a big contract. Then you can quit this job and never set foot in another diner again."

Her ex-husband, Joshua's father, was an equipment manager for a rock band. While touring on the road with the band, he called Joely and told her he wanted a divorce. He last saw Joshua when he was two.

Joely's smile widened. "Thanks Lee, but flattery won't get you a free meal."

"I meant every word of it," he said, sticking his hand in his back pocket. He pulled out the ten-dollar tip the minivan's owner had given him and dropped it on the counter. "I'll have whatever that'll cover," he said.

Callaway had stopped asking Joely for favors. Bill, the restaurant owner, had warned her not to serve him if he did not bring cash. She was raising a child with her waitressing job, and Callaway was not about to jeopardize that.

She grabbed the bill. "Have you ever thought about getting a steady job? One that will leave you with money in your pocket?" She thought it was cool that he was a private investigator, but she knew the work was sporadic and the pay was negligible.

"I've been thinking about it," he confessed. He was getting tired of being broke. If he didn't get a case soon, he would have to face the hard truth that his chosen profession was nothing more than a fanciful hobby.

She leaned closer. "One of our cooks quit two days ago. Bill is looking to hire someone to replace him. I know Bill doesn't like you very much, but I could maybe try to convince him to take you on, you know."

"Thanks, I appreciate the gesture, but I'm not much of a cook." Callaway suddenly realized he did not have many skills to offer potential employers. He was not good with numbers, so a desk job was out of the question. Plus, sitting in a cubicle like a caged animal would make him gouge his eyes out with his fingers. He was not good with his hands, so a job in the trades was out of the question. Julio could not offer him a position in his garage because Callaway knew next to nothing about what was under a car's hood. Also, Callaway did not trust himself with someone else's vehicle. He would easily botch any repair job.

"I can serve customers," he said.

"That's my job," she said with a mock scowl. "And with your demeanor, you'll only drive customers away."

She was right, he knew. He could be salty and a jerk when he was having a bad day. Joely, on the other hand, had a gift for making customers feel special.

She held up the ten-dollar bill. "Let me get you the biggest meal we've got on the menu," she said with a smile.

TWELVE

The news of Dillon Scott's death had spread like wildfire. Someone had tipped off the press, and Fisher believed the limo driver, Mr. Gill, was doing so when she first arrived.

The press was the least of her worries. They understood the rules of an active crime scene. If they broke them, their access to future police briefings would be restricted. The police department rarely took such drastic actions—they did not want to appear to influence public opinion—but sometimes such actions were necessary.

Fisher was far more concerned about Scott's fans. Their love and devotion was so blind that it made them act irrationally. It was not uncommon to have someone get past the yellow police tape just to get close to their idols.

To prevent something like that from happening, the Milton PD had stationed additional officers at the scene. Police cruisers blocked off the entrance on the main road.

Fisher stood in front of the house, watching the chaos from a distance. She could see a row of vans lining the side of the main road. All major news outlets were there, but also amongst them were vans for tabloid magazines, entertainment channels, and even talk shows. The media circus was in full swing.

She felt immense weight on her chest. The world's eyes were on her as she searched for Scott's killer. She wished Holt was next to her. He would take some of the pressure off her. She knew he would gladly end his forced retreat and be on the next flight to Milton if she made the call.

She would not.

Holt was long overdue for a break.

She had already conducted a walk around the property. There were four security cameras—two in front, and two in back of the house. She noted the security company's information. She would pay them a visit later in the day. She hoped the cameras had caught what had happened the night before.

She still had no motive and no murder weapon.

Officers had searched the grounds for anything that could have been used as a weapon. They came up empty. She was not surprised, and the zero results further confirmed her belief that the attacker had taken the weapon with them after sanitizing the crime scene.

The commotion on the main road suddenly got louder. There was a large crowd around the entrance. She could see people holding their cell phones as they took photos and videos.

They are taking photos of me, she thought.

The media was waiting for a statement, but she was in no mood to get in front of the cameras. She knew very little about what happened, and as such, she had little to tell them. Scott's fans were anxious for word, but there was nothing she could do about that. The investigation was still in its infancy.

She turned back to the house and stopped. There were two marble lion statues on either side of the stairs leading up to the front door. The lions were seated with their heads held high, as if on high alert. What caught her attention was not the animals but how identical each statue was to the other.

Her eyes narrowed as something flashed in the back of her head.

She raced into the house. She found Wakefield was still with Scott's body, which was now in a black body bag.

"Are you okay?" Wakefield asked when she saw the look on Fisher's face.

Without responding, Fisher moved past her and headed for the bookshelf behind the sofa. She leaned over and picked up an object. The ivory bookend was carved in the shape of a Roman column.

Fisher turned to Wakefield. "Could this be used to harm someone?"

Wakefield came over and held the bookend in her hands. "It is sturdy and heavy. Yes, I do believe it could."

"When I was examining the living room, I noticed one bookend, but I paid no attention to it. It was when I saw the identical lion statues outside that I realized there had to have been another identical bookend."

Fisher pointed to an empty space on the shelf. She then took the bookend from Wakefield and placed it in the space. The bookend fit perfectly.

"The missing bookend is our murder weapon," Fisher said.

THIRTEEN

Becky Miller lay in bed with a blanket over her head. A chill went through her body, and she quickly hugged herself tight. Her eyes were red and puffy. She had been crying for hours. She was scared.

She was sixteen years old. She was five-foot-three, weighed less than a hundred pounds, and had curly brown hair that reached to her shoulders.

She should have been in school, but she was at home, hiding in her bedroom. Her friends had called her, texted her, and some had sent her messages on her social media page.

She thought about telling them she was sick, but what if they started asking her more questions? Like what was wrong with her? Did she have a virus? She was not ready to face the queries just yet.

Her cell phone was next to her, and she could see it blinking, but she didn't have the courage to check her messages. She was afraid of what she would see.

The last message she had read told her everything was fine and that she had nothing to worry about. The message made her feel good, but that lasted only a short moment. The reality was that everything was not fine—and might never be.

There was a knock at the door. Becky was so startled she almost jumped off the bed.

"Becky, are you okay, dear?" her mom asked.

"I'm fine, Mom," she replied, her voice cracking.

"You don't sound good."

"I am, honest."

"Can I come in?"

Becky knew if she protested, her mom would be even more concerned. She didn't want her mom to worry because of her.

"Okay," Becky finally said.

Sara Miller entered the room. She had curly brown hair, similar to her daughter's. Wrinkles had begun to appear on her face, making her look older than she was. The past year had been tough on her, and it had been even tougher for Becky. But things had started to look up. Becky had found someone who was suffering as much as her, maybe even worse. She needed someone to share her pain, and he was just the person.

She was hoping to introduce him to her mom, but then the world came crashing down on her.

Her mom came over and sat on the edge of the bed. "Baby, why are you crying?" she softly asked.

"I feel cold."

Her mom put her hand on her forehead. "You don't have a fever."

"I just don't feel good."

"Do you want me to take you to the doctor?"

"No. I just want to stay in bed today. Is that okay?"

"Of course it is. Do you want me to turn on the TV?"

"No!" Becky shouted.

Her mom was taken aback, but she said nothing.

"I just want to sleep," Becky said.

Her mom smiled. "I have to go to work, but there's meatloaf in the fridge. If you get hungry, you can microwave some for yourself."

"Okay, I will."

Her mom leaned over and kissed her on the forehead. "I love you, baby."

"I love you too, Mom."

When her mom closed the door, Becky pulled the blanket over her head.

She began to cry again.

FOURTEEN

The meal consisted of homemade pancakes covered in maple syrup, fried eggs, buttered toast, a side of oven-roasted potatoes, and a steaming cup of coffee. Way more food than the ten dollars Callaway had given Joely could cover, but she had gone out of her way to stuff his plate with just about everything.

Callaway enjoyed every bite.

He was bursting at the seams as he climbed a flight of narrow metal stairs. The Callaway Private Investigation Office was on the second floor of a building located above a soup and noodle restaurant. The office had no sign indicating its location, but it did have a telephone number taped to the black metal door.

Potential clients could either call him or get in touch via his website.

The lack of a sign was more of a safety precaution than anything else. His job required him to follow cheating spouses and catch them in compromising positions. Naturally, the spouses did not take too kindly once they found out. They threatened him with legal action, and some even threatened him with physical harm.

Callaway used to carry a registered firearm with him at all times, but during a heated dispute, he had pulled his gun and brandished it. He had scared away the guy who was giving him a hard time, but at the same time, he realized the ramifications of what he almost did. He could have pulled the trigger and ended the man's life. The responsibility was too much for him, so he started keeping the weapon locked up in his office. He only took his gun with him when he went into a dangerous situation. He would rather err on the side of caution in those circumstances.

So far, he had been lucky that no one had pulled a gun on him. He did, however, have an irate client break his nose and bruise his ego. Callaway deserved what he got. He had slept with his client's wife, whom he was supposed to have been following to gather evidence of her infidelities.

There was a more pressing reason for not having a sign out by the front door. Callaway was never good when it came to money. The moment he had some in his hand, he would gamble it away on one thing or another. There was always a sure bet out there that would make him instantly rich. All he had to do was be there at the right time. More often than not, it was not an opportunity but a scheme to sucker people out of their hard-earned dollars, and with a near-zero bank balance, Callaway would foolishly go to unsavory people to borrow the money for these get-rich-quick ventures. When it would all blow up in his face, he would spend the next couple of days or weeks hiding from these people until he could find a way to pay them back.

I should just play the lottery like most sensible people, he thought. *The odds may be stacked against me, but at least I would only be out a couple dollars, not my entire investment.*

He reached the top of the stairs and unbuckled his belt. The meal, albeit delicious, was now coming back up his throat. He should not have gorged himself as if he had been starving for days.

FIFTEEN

Callaway opened the door and entered the small, windowless space. There was no air conditioning, and the heating barely worked during the winter months, but the rent was the cheapest in the city.

He had considered closing down the office, but he liked the idea of having a place to go other than his home. Speaking of his home, with his finances in shambles, he was constantly moving. Sometimes he would sleep in his office until he found a place to stay.

He was lucky to crash at a beach house for months. His client was away traveling Europe, and she had let him use the property as a reward for catching her husband in the act. The divorce settlement was so substantial that she would never have to work another day in her life.

I need to get me a nice rich old lady, he thought. *She would surely rid me of my money problems.*

But he knew he would never go after someone because of their wealth. He had spent his professional life helping his clients get money out of their spouses, and he saw the damage first-hand. The clients would say and do anything to squeeze even an extra penny out of the other spouse. They would even involve their children in the divorce proceedings. Those children never asked for that. They only wanted a stable and loving home. They didn't want to have to choose between their parents.

He shut the door and sat at his desk. There was a sofa in the corner, and across from it was a flat-screen TV a client had bequeathed him. He grabbed the remote and turned on the TV, which was tuned to a twenty-four-hour news channel. He liked the sound of the TV running in the back. The sound made him feel like he was surrounded by people, not stuck in a confined space. The news also let him know what was happening in the city. This gave him a chance to search out potential clients.

He sat upright when he saw the headline at the bottom of the screen: MOVIE STAR DILLON SCOTT FOUND DEAD. CAUSE OF DEATH SUSPICIOUS. POLICE HAVE NO SUSPECTS OR MOTIVE YET.

Callaway had heard of Scott. Who hadn't? Unless you lived in a cave and didn't have access to a TV or internet. He had even watched some of his movies, and he found them entertaining. The characters Scott played were average Joes down on their luck who overcame all obstacles to defeat the bad guys and win the day.

If they made a movie about his own life, Callaway would have chosen Scott to play him. That dream had now faded like a movie's end credits.

Dana must be overwhelmed, he thought. He knew with Holt away, Fisher was likely running the show solo.

He turned on the laptop on his desk. He prayed someone had contacted him via his website. He desperately needed some work.

He once had a stable job and a steady source of income. Prior to becoming a private eye, he was a deputy sheriff for a small town. The job was uneventful, mind-numbing, and utterly dull. The most exciting thing that ever happened in Spokem County was when someone lit a firecracker and shot it in their neighbor's shed. The shed went up in flames, but the loss was a few gardening tools and a lawn mower. Callaway was so bored he could have slit his wrists.

The laptop took a good fifteen minutes to boot up. The computer was an older model he had bought secondhand. The laptop had an outdated operating system and an old processor, but it was good for checking emails and surfing the internet. Sometimes, though, he would turn the laptop on, leave the office to buy coffee, and when he returned, the computer would still be loading.

He decided to check his voicemail.

As he listened to his messages, a smile crossed his face.

SIXTEEN

The Roman-column-shaped bookend had been tagged and photographed. Even though it was not *the* murder weapon, they at least had an idea of what the weapon might look like.

Fisher watched as Scott's body was loaded into an ambulance. She heard a commotion in the distance, coming from the main road. A man was talking loudly to one of the officers. The officer was trying to calm the man down.

The officer turned toward her, and she realized it was McConnell. He waved to her and she made her way to them. Instantly, cameras were aimed in her direction and began to flash. The press thought she was about to make a statement. She was not. The communications officer would do so once Fisher had briefed her. She was planning to do that as soon as she had finished examining the crime scene.

McConnell met her halfway up the gravel road. "Sorry about this," he said, "but he wants to speak to you." He pointed to the man who was yelling at him a moment ago. "I told him you were busy, but he was adamant that he see you."

"Who is he?" she asked.

"He says he's a movie producer."

"Let him through," she said.

She moved further away from the crowd as McConnell escorted the man through the yellow police tape and toward her.

"I'm Detective Dana Fisher," she said.

"Sherman Grumbly," he replied. He was of medium height, medium build, wore thick prescription glasses, and had dark, unruly hair.

"You're the producer of *Memories of a Killer*?" she asked.

His eyes widened. "How did you know?"

"I saw a copy of the script in Mr. Scott's bedroom."

"I need to get that. It's confidential material."

"No one is allowed in the house until the investigation is over," she said.

"You don't understand," he said with exasperation. "If that script gets leaked online, the entire production will be jeopardized."

44

"I assure you, the script is safe. The property has been secured."

He didn't look convinced.

"How about this," she said. "You answer my questions, and I'll have an officer personally deliver the script to your office."

He mulled this over.

She added, "Unfortunately, no items can be removed from the crime scene at this moment."

He finally nodded in resignation. "Okay, what would you like to know?"

"Mr. Scott was in Milton to shoot a movie, is that correct?"

"Yes."

"And you or your production company rented the property for his use?"

"Yes, we did. Even though the studio is at the other end of the city, Dillon wanted a secluded area to rest and relax. I couldn't blame him. He was constantly hounded by the paparazzi."

"The property has a security alarm system. It was disabled when we arrived at the scene. Did you know the password?"

He paused to consider his response. "Of course I did," he said. "I was provided this information when I signed the rental agreement. But I was nowhere near here yesterday."

"Where were you?"

"In my office at the studio."

"Can anyone confirm this?"

"Absolutely. I was in meetings all day. My secretary can vouch for me."

Fisher made a mental note of this in case she needed to verify it later. "Do you know what Mr. Scott was doing last night?" she asked.

"I really don't. We had a read-through of the script yesterday. I wasn't there, but Barry was."

"Who?"

"Barry Rowe. He's the director of the film."

"Okay, I'll need to speak to him and whoever was with him at the reading."

"I've already informed Barry. He knows there is going to be an investigation." Grumbly pulled out his cell phone. "I have to call the insurance company and let them know our star actor is dead."

Fisher could tell it was a call he did not want to make. As he walked way, she didn't envy the position he was in.

SEVENTEEN

Callaway's heart sank the moment he set eyes on the house. It was a semi-detached with a small garden in front, no driveway, and a tiny porch.

He double-checked the address and confirmed it was the right one. Back at his office, he had contacted the woman who left him the voicemail. She believed her husband was cheating on her, and she was eager to retain his services.

On the drive over, he was hoping the woman had money to spare. He needed a well-paying case, one that would fix the current predicament he was in. His landlady had been inquiring about the rent, and he didn't want to resort to hiding from her.

He thought about turning the Impala around and going back to the office. In his experience, regular folks did not appreciate what he had to offer. They always tried to lowball him when it came to his fees.

The rich, on the other hand, were willing to pay to resolve their problems. They didn't like to get their hands dirty. Most were downright lazy. Money afforded them the luxury to have others do their bidding. If they needed someone followed, they called him. If they needed information on a competitor, they called him. If they needed an alibi, they called him.

Callaway was not the only PI in town. His client's spouses also hired their own private investigators. Sometimes Callaway would have to throw the other PI off his client's tail. It was not an easy feat, but with some ingenuity, he was able to manage it.

A client once came to him and told him he was being followed. Callaway asked him whether he was being unfaithful to his wife. The client said he was. Callaway then began following his own client. One night, as the client went to meet his mistress, Callaway caught the other PI tailing him. Callaway quickly approached the mistress's house and made it look like the client was in fact meeting a group of friends. Another time he spotted the other PI well in advance and warned the client not to proceed with his rendezvous. The other PI eventually lost interest when he could not catch the client alone with his mistress.

As Callaway debated whether to ring the doorbell, the front door opened. A woman came out on the porch. She was wearing a patterned dress, stockings, and she had short dark hair. The woman was on the heavier side, and she was wearing makeup.

She smiled and waved at him.

He reluctantly got out of the Impala and approached her.

"You're the private investigator, right?" she said, still smiling.

"I am."

"I saw you sitting in your car. I thought maybe you had forgotten my address."

I hadn't forgotten it, he thought. *I was thinking of driving away from it.*

"Please come inside," she said.

They sat in a small living room filled with children's toys. In the hall, he had almost slipped on a remote-control car.

"After speaking to you," she said, sitting across from him, "I sent the children to my neighbor's house. I didn't want them to listen in on our conversation. I don't want them to know their father is..." She stopped, looking as if saying the words aloud would hurt.

"How old are your children?" he asked.

"Jackson is seven, David and Suzie are five, and Kim is two."

His eyes shot up. "Four! Wow."

She smiled. "My husband and I came from big families, so we wanted one ourselves."

Right, he thought. "How long have you been married?" he asked.

"Our eight-year anniversary is coming up."

Callaway noticed a wheelchair in the corner. "Does someone else live with you and your husband?"

"No, that was actually for me. It was during last winter, and I was unloading groceries from the car when I slipped on ice, broke my leg, and fractured my hip. I couldn't stand or walk for months. My husband took care of me and the children."

He nodded. "Sorry, I didn't catch your name on the phone."

"Oh, how rude of me. It's Betty Henderson. My husband's name is Frank."

"Okay, I'm Lee Callaway."

"I know. I read about you in the newspapers when you worked for Paul Gardener."

He had gained some notoriety from that case, but unfortunately, it had not resulted in many jobs like he expected.

"Can I offer you coffee or tea?" she asked.

"Thank you, I'm fine," he replied. "Now, let's get to why I'm here. On the phone you said you believed your husband was having an affair."

Her eyes welled up. She bit her bottom lip and nodded.

"I know this is tough, but you will have to tell me all the details. That is the only way I will be able to help you."

She inhaled deeply and then exhaled slowly. "Frank does deliveries for a large department store. He works long hours, but the pay is good, and it comes with benefits. Anyway, Frank likes to laugh, and he likes to have fun. The children adore him. But he has been acting like a different man the past couple of months. He is withdrawn, and he looks unhappy. Even the children have noticed a difference. I asked him what's wrong, and he said it was stuff at work. One day I decided to surprise him. I dropped the children at the neighbors', and I bought tickets to a superhero movie he had been waiting to see, and I drove to his workplace. While I was waiting in the parking lot, I saw him and another woman coming out together. The way they were talking was like they knew each other really well."

"Maybe they are co-workers," Callaway suggested.

"They are," she agreed. "I found out she works in the company's shipping department. I was about to go up to him when they both got in his truck and drove away."

She covered her face and broke down in tears.

Callaway wanted to console her, but he wasn't sure how. He was never good at that stuff.

When Betty was done, she said, "I want him to leave this other woman, and I need your help."

Callaway blinked. "That's not how it works," he said. "My job is to prove your suspicions that he is being unfaithful, not to convince him to do something he shouldn't be doing."

"I want my husband back, Mr. Callaway."

"I understand, but sometimes it's not as simple as that. If your husband is being unfaithful, then I can get you material evidence to convince a judge that you deserve more of the family assets at the time of the divorce. You are the devastated spouse in this relationship."

"But I don't want to divorce Frank. He is the only man I've ever loved. And he is the father of our children."

Callaway stood up to leave. "Unfortunately, I don't think you need a private investigator. You need a marriage counselor."

She pulled an envelope from her purse and held it out for him. "It's five hundred dollars. I've been saving it for a rainy day, but this is far more important. We need our old Frank back."

Callaway stared at the envelope. Five hundred was not a lot of money, but he was desperate. Something was better than nothing.

"Please," she pleaded. "Just talk to him. He needs to know how much he means to his family."

"What if I can't convince him?"

"Then I'll focus my attention on my children and move on."

Callaway reluctantly took the envelope.

EIGHTEEN

Barry Rowe, director of *Memories of a Killer*, was tall and lanky with a full head of gray hair and a heavy British accent. He was wearing a checkered shirt, blue jeans, and black boots.

Fisher was in Rowe's makeshift office at the movie studio. The room was not spacious, and the amount of material scattered around made it look and feel even smaller. Fisher saw large storyboards on the walls, along with mock-up posters for the film. Pieces of fabric lay on a table, likely from the costume department. Camera equipment was stacked in the corner, and there were even props in the middle of the room.

Barry shook his head. "When Sherman called and told me what happened, I thought he was playing a movie joke on me," he said.

"A movie joke?" Fisher asked.

"Sorry, that didn't come out right. What I meant was that in our films, we come up with creative ways for a victim to die so that the hero can solve their murder. When Dillon died, I thought it was a cruel joke, because his character in the film was an investigator, you know?"

"I see," she said. "And have you worked with Mr. Scott before?"

"No, this was the first time," Rowe replied. "My background is in stage production, but I have directed TV series and films for the BBC. This was actually my first big picture, even though the budget is relatively small."

"How so?" she asked, curious. Fisher loved movies, but she had never met a director before.

"It's only ten million dollars. And the only reason we were able to get that was because of Dillon. We were certain with his name attached to the film, we could sell it to a distributor."

"How was it working with Mr. Scott?" she asked.

"I only spent a few days with him, but I could tell he was excited about the role. He had so many ideas he wanted to explore, and we discussed all the different directions we could take the part in."

"It's my understanding he was at a script reading with you yesterday," she said.

"Yes, he and our lead actress, Leslie."

"Leslie?"

"Leslie Tillman."

"Okay."

"With a tight budget, you don't get many days of rehearsal, so I wanted to squeeze in as much time with Dillon and Leslie as possible. Both of them have to carry the movie."

"And how was Ms. Tillman and Mr. Scott's relationship? I mean, did they get along?" Fisher asked.

"They got along fabulously. Dillon immediately took her under his wing. Her role is more intense than his, so he wanted her to feel comfortable around him."

"Intense?" she asked.

Rowe paused, looking unsure.

"Don't worry," Fisher said. "Whatever you tell me won't leave this room."

He nodded and said, "Leslie plays a victim who survives a brutal attack in the film."

Fisher squinted. "And why does she have to be comfortable around Mr. Scott?"

"He plays the attacker."

She blinked. "He does what?"

Rowe smiled with glee. "That was the twist of the entire movie. Dillon's character is an investigator who is harboring a secret. He is the killer who suffers from episodic amnesia."

Fisher's mouth dropped. "So the killer he is searching for is in fact *him*?"

"Yes, but he doesn't remember committing the crimes, which makes the movie all the more intriguing."

Fisher wished Scott was still alive. She would have loved to see his performance in such a complex part.

"How did you get Mr. Scott to take the role?" she wondered aloud. "I mean, the money was a pittance compared to what he got in previous roles."

"Dillon waived his usual fees," Rowe said. "It was a challenging role, and one against his type."

"His type?"

"He was known for playing the clean-cut guys, the guys who may have made mistakes in their lives but who upheld good values. In this film, no one would have suspected him as the serial killer, you know?"

I wouldn't have, Fisher thought. *That's for sure.*

"Can you tell me where I can find Ms. Tillman?" she asked. "I need to speak to her."

NINETEEN

Callaway drove to the address his client had provided him. Betty Henderson had become his client, even though he was hesitant to take her on as one. The money was nowhere near enough to compensate him for the job she wanted him to do.

How can I convince a guy to stop cheating on his wife? he thought.

Callaway had been with many women, but he was never unfaithful while he was married. He had, however, been intimate with women who were married. It was not something he was proud of, it was just something that happened.

The women were mostly clients whose husbands were cheating on them. While Callaway was trying to catch the husbands in the act, he was also comforting their wives. The wives saw their flings with Callaway as an act of revenge on their cheating husbands, and Callaway was more than happy to oblige their requests.

As he stared at the department store's warehouse, he could not help but wonder how he was supposed to accomplish the task before him.

He sighed. *I should have driven off the moment I saw the house*, he thought. *But the woman caught me before I could do that.*

He did feel bad for her, though. She came across as a housewife whose entire world revolved around her husband and her children. The prospect of losing someone who was such an integral part of her life was devastating to her.

Callaway was once central in his wife and daughter's lives, but he much preferred the freedom to disappear whenever and wherever he wanted. His restlessness had spelled the end of his marriage.

He still harbored feelings for his ex-wife, even if he refused to admit it, and he was forever feeling guilty about not spending quality time with his little girl. He vowed to get his act together one day and make more of an impact in his daughter's life, but somehow he always managed to mess that up.

Is Frank Henderson like me? he thought. *He seems like he has a wife who loves him, and from what his wife says, his children adore him too. Is that why he is willing to throw it all away? Because he is not content with what he has?*

Callaway was not content.

He wanted more out of life. The problem was that he just wasn't sure what he wanted. If it was money, then being a private eye was the wrong profession. If it was fame, then so far he had not made enough of a name for himself so that people were knocking on his door to hire him.

Then what was it?

He knew the answer: He wanted excitement. He could not see himself spending the rest of his life in a small town like Spokem, where there was nothing to do but sit on the front porch with a cold beer in his hand and stare at the neighbor's dog as it chased its tail around the front yard.

A man appeared through a set of doors at the store's shipping center. Callaway recognized him from the photos he had seen at the Henderson residence.

Frank Henderson was a large man. He had big arms, a big belly, and even a big head. His beard was an unruly bush, covering his entire chin.

He kind of looks like Grizzly Adams, Callaway thought.

Callaway broke into a cold sweat at the mere thought of trying to convince a man Frank's size to stop what he was doing.

I am a dead man, Callaway thought. *This guy can have me for lunch.*

Frank got behind the wheel of an eighteen-wheeler truck and drove away.

Callaway swallowed, put the Impala in gear, and followed Frank.

TWENTY

Leslie Tillman was hysterical when Fisher met her at her hotel room not far from the movie studio. Tillman was originally from Texas. She moved to Los Angeles when she turned eighteen. She landed a few commercials and then found her way into minor parts on television.

The lead in *Memories of a Killer* was her big role. She was twenty-two with flawless skin—which made Fisher a little envious—perfect teeth, and eyes that could emote a variety of feelings. In short, she was made for the big screen.

She sat on a chair with her legs crossed. She wiped her eyes and said, "I'm sorry, but this came as a shock."

"I understand," Fisher said.

"I mean, he was alive yesterday, and today..." She covered her face with her hands and began to cry even more.

Fisher gave Tillman a moment to grieve.

"Were you a fan of Mr. Scott?" Fisher asked, hoping the question might distract her.

Tillman nodded. "I saw all his movies."

"And what did you think of his take on *Romeo and Juliet*?"

She shrugged. "It was okay, I guess. I mean, he was still learning his craft, you know?"

Sure, Fisher thought. *You're too young to appreciate a classic like that.*

"I understand you got to spend a couple of days with him?" Fisher asked.

"I did," Tillman replied, "and even in that short time, I learned a lot from him."

"Like what?"

"How to deliver your lines the right way. How to move around a camera. How to interact in a scene. I mean, I've taken acting classes, but when you get a chance to work with someone like Dillon, you don't want to mess it up."

"I heard from your director that he took you under his wing."

"He was so gentle with me. He knew this was my first lead, and he told me he would not let me fail. I can't believe I won't get to work with him."

Before Tillman could break down in tears, Fisher said, "What was it like working with him yesterday?"

"You mean during the rehearsals?"

"Yes."

Tillman thought for a moment. "He was full of ideas and bursting with energy. He even asked me if I wanted to join him at his home later that night to go over the script."

"And did you?" Fisher asked almost too quickly.

Tillman's eyes moistened. "I was so excited and overwhelmed by the role that at the end of the day, I had a severe migraine, which I occasionally get, and so I had to say no to him." She shook her head. "I now have to live with the knowledge that I turned down Dillon Scott. How stupid could I be?"

Fisher knew she was being overly dramatic, but she was an actress, so it was understandable. "Is it normal for an actor to ask another actor to come to their home late at night, especially one who is married?" Fisher asked.

"Sure, I guess," Tillman replied. "I mean, it's a big part, and I also play his love interest, so our chemistry has to be just right for it to be believable on the screen."

"I thought he played a serial killer who attacks you in the film?" Fisher asked.

"You know about that?" Tillman asked, surprised.

"The director told me."

"Okay, yes, he does, but I don't fall in love with him as a killer, I fall in love with him as the investigator."

Now I really wish this movie had been made, Fisher thought.

There was a pause before Fisher said, "Is there anything you can tell me that might help me find out what happened to Mr. Scott?"

Tillman thought for a moment. "Dillon kept looking at his cell phone all day. He would even stop in the middle of a scene to check it."

That's what the limo driver said too, Fisher thought. *But that is nothing significant. Scott was famous. He must have had people reach out to him all the time.*

Fisher stood up to leave, but a thought occurred to her. "What time did Mr. Scott ask you to meet him at his home?"

"What time?" Tillman asked, confused.

"You said he asked you to meet him later that night."

"Oh, yes, he asked me what I was doing around nine."

"And your rehearsal ended at six, is that correct?"

"It did."

Fisher's eyes narrowed. If the rehearsals ended at six, and Scott asked Tillman to meet at nine, there was still a gap of three hours that was unaccounted for.

TWENTY-ONE

Callaway tailed Frank Henderson as he made deliveries to the company's retail stores in the city. Frank would pull up to the back of the stores, wait for the store's employees to unload the goods, then head to the next location.

Once he was done, Frank returned to the company's distribution center, and after parking the eighteen-wheeler, he got in his pickup truck. He then sat there for twenty minutes.

Callaway was across the street, watching Frank.

What are you waiting for? Callaway thought.

A woman emerged from one of the doors in the back of the building. Her blonde hair was tied in a bun. She had on a jacket, a skirt that went down to her knees, and ankle-high boots with heels. She shoved her hand in her purse and pulled out a cigarette and lighter. She lit the cigarette and took a long drag. She blew thick smoke and then walked across the back lot to the pickup truck. The woman didn't look like she was in any hurry.

She got in the pickup's passenger seat.

Without saying a word, Frank started the pickup and eased out of the parking lot. After they drove past the Impala, Callaway put the car in gear and followed them.

The pickup turned left, then right, and then it got onto the main highway. The truck roared down the lane at speeds well above the limit. Callaway pressed down hard on the accelerator. The Impala jerked once as it fought to go faster. Julio had assured Callaway the Impala had been serviced and that the engine was in good condition. So far, the Impala had not disappointed him. The car gradually began to gain speed, to the point where Callaway could keep pace with the pickup.

After a couple of miles, the pickup got off at the next exit. Callaway quickly did the same.

Henderson and the woman drove for another ten minutes, weaving through smaller streets until they pulled into the driveway of a two-story house and stopped behind a station wagon.

Frank and the woman got out. Callaway pulled out his camera and snapped photos of them as they walked up to the house and disappeared through the front door.

Cindy Henderson was right, Callaway thought. *Her husband was spending time with another woman.*

Almost an hour later, Frank came out of the house. His face was drawn as he made his way to the pickup. He got behind the wheel and pulled out of the driveway.

The drive back to his house was close to thirty-five minutes. Callaway did not let him out of his sight once. Only when Frank was inside his home did Callaway decide to discontinue the tail. There was nothing more to be gained. He had concrete proof Frank was cheating on his wife.

Now came the hard part. He had to somehow convince Frank to give up his affair.

TWENTY-TWO

Becky was curled up on the sofa. A movie was playing on the TV. She had spent the day avoiding reading, watching, or listening to the news. She didn't want to know what was happening in the city.

Her mom was still at work. She used to work as a payroll administrator for a large packaging company, but after the company was bought by a rival, she was let go. The rival company already had an in-house payroll administrator.

She was now a full-time receptionist for a food processing company, and on the weekends, she worked as a cashier at a grocery store. Becky knew how hard her mom was working just to put a roof over their heads.

Things were not always like this. When her father was still alive, they were a happy family. Her father worked for a small construction company, and one day he was drilling a hole next to a concrete wall when the wall collapsed on him. He died on the spot.

The construction company refused to pay compensation. Her father was taking medical marijuana for an old back injury, and he had neglected to inform his employer. They took this as an opportunity not to pay his family. They argued the marijuana had impaired his judgment.

Her mom thought about hiring a lawyer, but no one wanted to take the case. They knew even if they won, the possibility of actually recouping the money would be very low. The construction company owners would declare bankruptcy or shut down the business just to avoid paying. Then they would reopen under another name and continue operation.

The lawyers could file a personal lawsuit against the individual owners, but the owners were clever not to keep any assets under their name. The chance of getting money out of them would turn into a long, drawn-out process.

There was also the option of a settlement, but that only worked if the construction company agreed they had done something wrong, which they had refused to do. They stuck to their conclusion that it was human error that caused the death.

What weakened their case even more was that OSHA, or the Occupational Safety and Health Administration, could not find anything to indicate the company was at fault.

Becky knew her dad would have never put his safety at risk if he believed the medication was affecting his ability to work. There were many days he would not go into work if he was not a hundred percent well.

Right after her dad died, her mom lost her payroll job. Her mom's positivity and resilience was what kept them from falling apart.

Then there was someone who had seemingly appeared out of nowhere. He had become her guardian angel. He had assured Becky that he would take care of her, and she believed him.

Everything was getting better, but then it abruptly fell apart.

Becky wanted to cry again, but she had no more tears left. Her eyes were dry and itchy. She had already gone through a full box of tissues.

She checked her cell phone for the umpteenth time. There were messages from her friends. They asked how she was feeling. She finally told them she was sick. One friend offered to come to her house to give her company. Becky refused, claiming she wasn't sure what she had and that it could be contagious.

Becky was not suffering from anything except the fear that at any moment, someone would knock at the door and take her away.

TWENTY-THREE

The morgue was in an old government building that had not been renovated in years. The building's exterior façade was cold and ominous. The interior was no better. The walls were painted in dark colors, and the floor tiles had turned an ugly shade of yellow. Fluorescent light bulbs flickered in the hallways, sending a threatening vibe to anyone who passed under them.

Fisher stood next to Rachel Scott. She had flown from Bayview to see her dead husband. She was dressed all in black—black coat, black heels, even her nails and lips were painted black. It was as if she came prepared to look the part of a grieving widow.

Fisher couldn't blame her. The press had gathered outside the morgue. They wanted a photo of *the* Mrs. Dillon Scott. After years of being married to a star, she knew what a perfect photo op could mean.

Her skin was without a blemish or wrinkle, almost too smooth for a woman her age. According to the newspapers, she was five years younger than Scott, which would make her forty. But even with all the Botox, Fisher could see dark circles around her eyes. She had been crying prior to arriving at the morgue. The stress of losing a loved one was hitting her hard.

Scott's body lay on a gurney in the cold room, covered in a green sheet. Wakefield stood on the other side of the gurney. As the medical examiner, she was preparing for the autopsy, but she could not proceed until the victim's next of kin performed the standard procedure of formally identifying the victim.

Rachel Scott shivered. Fisher placed her hand on her arm. "Are you okay?" Fisher asked, concerned.

Rachel bit her bottom lip and nodded. "Please show me."

Wakefield pulled the sheet back to reveal the face. It was gray and frozen. Even in death, Scott had left a beautiful corpse.

Rachel put a hand over her mouth. "It's him."

"Can you say it for the record?" Fisher said.

"It's my husband, Dillon Jeffrey Scott."

Wakefield would note Rachel's identification in her report.

"How did he die?" Rachel asked.

"We believe it was from being hit on the head with a heavy object," Fisher replied.

Rachel was confused. "A heavy object?"

"There was a bookend in the house, and we believe it may have been used to hurt him."

"Who would do such a thing?"

"We are in the early stages of our investigation. We will let you know once we make any progress."

Rachel nodded.

Wakefield covered the body.

Fisher and Rachel moved into the hall.

"I know this must be a difficult time for you," Fisher said, "but do you mind if I ask you a few questions?"

"Okay, I guess," Rachel replied.

"When was the last time you spoke to your husband?"

"Yesterday."

"Around what time?"

Rachel thought for a moment. "I think around six."

"Did he tell you what he was doing?" Fisher asked.

"We spoke briefly. He said he was leaving rehearsals and heading home."

"Was he meeting someone later that night, do you know?"

Rachel shook her head. "He never mentioned anything to me." She paused. "You have to understand, Dillon was a star and he relished being one. It gave him a free card to do whatever he wanted. This meant he didn't seek my permission to do something, even though I was his wife. I knew this before I married him, so I couldn't hold it against him. I'm used to him keeping me in the dark because he's always been away, shooting one movie after another." She sighed. "I'm sorry, I shouldn't be complaining. My husband is dead, and my children are without a father, but the man who was at home was not the man who was on the big screen."

"Can you elaborate?" Fisher asked, "I just want to know who could have done this to him."

"Being married to an actor is not easy. I mean, the money is good, and sometimes even the fame is too, but you are constantly in the public eye, and that can be difficult for a marriage."

"You and Mr. Scott were having marital problems?" Fisher asked.

"We had our disagreements. What married couple doesn't?" Rachel replied. "What I'm trying to say is that even if Dillon was somewhere last night, he would not bother to tell me."

TWENTY-FOUR

Callaway took the stairs to the hotel's third floor. After constantly moving from one place to another, he had booked a room for a month. Nothing permanent, but it was much cheaper than renting an apartment. He didn't have to provide first and last month's rent or sign a long-term lease, and with landlords becoming more cautious, he didn't have to give them access to his credit report. If he did, it would show him as a delinquent, which would not impress a potential landlord. Also, if he fell behind in his payments, he didn't have to worry about being evicted. He would put all his stuff in his one suitcase and go someplace else.

The hotel was not a five-star, it was more like a two-star. He wasn't sure why they didn't just call it a motel.

What's the difference between the two? he wondered.

He wasn't complaining, though. The monthly rate was far more affordable than most places in the city. His room had hot water, functioning plumbing, and the heating worked.

He once stayed in a basement apartment where the water was ice cold, the toilet didn't flush all the way, and there was a strong draft coming through the windows, which were not properly insulated. The apartment was tolerable for a couple of days, until his toes started to tingle and go numb from the near negative temperature. He packed up and left that very night, forgoing the remainder of the month's rent.

The landlord was a cranky old man who thought he was doing Callaway a favor for even renting his luxurious suite to him. Callaway had very little money, and the rent was very little as well, so he did not see a point in arguing with the old man for not providing the basic necessities.

The hotel room had a few cockroaches and other multi-legged critters, but no rats, thank goodness. If he saw even one, he would haul his butt out of there in no time. Rodents gave him the shivers.

He entered the cramped room. There was a bed on the right with a futon next to it. A TV sat across from the futon. He grabbed the remote and turned the TV on. Like the one in his office, it was set to a twenty-four-hour news channel. He pulled off his jacket and dropped it on the bed.

The room had a small bathroom but no kitchen. Callaway always ate out, so a kitchen would have served no purpose. The room came with a tiny microwave, which was useful for reheating leftovers.

Callaway had managed to squeeze in a minifridge he had found lying on the sidewalk. He had carried the fridge up to his room—something he later regretted doing because he was in terrible shape—but when he plugged the fridge in, to his surprise, the thing worked. He had stuffed it with cold drinks and microwave dinners.

He pulled out a bottle from the fridge and sat up on the bed. The reporters on TV were still talking about Dillon Scott's murder. It was not every day a movie star was murdered in the city. But Callaway's mind was not on Scott's murder. It was on Frank Henderson.

Callaway took a sip from the bottle and wondered how he was going to confront Frank the next day. It was not going to be pleasant, but it was something he could not avoid forever.

TWENTY-FIVE

The apartment building was in dire need of repairs. The lobby had not had a facelift in years. Not all the elevators were operational at the same time. The heat and cooling systems were known to stop working during the cold and hot months, respectively. The fire alarms were likely not up to code, and the hot water sometimes shut off at the most inopportune times.

Fisher had considered moving out on multiple occasions, but with rent so high in the city, and without a promotion in years, the place was the most she could afford at the moment.

Fisher was in excellent shape. She ran a mile each morning. Whenever the elevators were taking too long, she would race up the stairs to her apartment on the sixth floor.

That day, however, she was spent.

After meeting Rachel Scott at the morgue, she decided to pay a visit to the security alarm company. They were displeased to see her. The moment they saw her badge and heard what she was looking for, however, they were eager to assist her in her investigation. It seemed everyone had an opinion about what happened to Dillon Scott.

Unfortunately, the footage was of no use.

The camera was sensor-activated, turning on and off whenever there was any movement. The camera caught the limo driver dropping Scott off at the house at around six thirty in the evening, but the moment Scott disabled the alarm with his password, the camera was never reactivated.

Maybe he forgot to turn it back on, she thought. *Or maybe he didn't want anyone to know what he was up to.*

An elevator arrived, and she took it up to her floor.

Her apartment was brightly colored. When she had moved in, the beige walls had turned yellowish after years of accumulating dirt and grime. She took it upon herself to give her place a new coat of paint.

The bedroom was on the right, with the kitchen and living room on the left. The previous tenants had enclosed the balcony, and she now used it as a meditation room.

The walls of the apartment were covered in family photos. They were mostly of her and her three brothers posing with their parents. Some of the photos still made her cringe. There was one where her parents decided to dress up all the children the same. In another one, Fisher looked like a boy. Her father cut all her brothers' hair, so her mom figured she could do the same. This was a big mistake. Her mom ended up almost shaving her head entirely. Fisher wore a scarf over her head until her hair grew back to a decent length. Most of the kids in school thought she was Muslim.

Fisher dropped on the sofa and put her feet up on the coffee table. She shut her eyes. It had been a long and exhausting day. With Holt not available, she had to carry the load.

She stayed still for a couple of minutes before getting up and walking over to a DVD stand in the corner. She searched through the movies and pulled one out. On the front was a photo of a youthful-looking Dillon Scott.

She had suddenly felt the urge to watch *Romeo and Juliet* again. She wanted to be reminded of why she had fallen in love with Scott all those years ago.

TWENTY-SIX

He made his way down the street late at night. Osman Maxwell was wearing a hoodie, a baseball cap, and baggy clothes. The only thing flashy on him were his gold sneakers. They were an exclusive edition, and he had paid a steep price to acquire them.

He didn't care how much they cost, not when he just had a big windfall.

The people who he hung around with were suspicious. They asked where he had gotten the money.

"It's none of your damn business," he told them.

He owed nobody an explanation.

The first time he received a big payout, he had gone to Vegas and foolishly splurged on girls, booze, and drugs, but he had grown up poor and wanted to live a little.

This time, though, he was going to take it easy. He would not draw any unwanted attention.

Osman was a low-level drug dealer and, on occasion, a pimp. The girls needed someone to escort them to and from the client's place, and he was more than happy to oblige—for a fee, of course. But he was seriously considering doing something else with his life. He had seen way too many people get shot and killed in his line of work, and Osman didn't want to be another casualty.

Drugs and prostitution were a mean business that made you hard and cruel. In order to survive, you lied, cheated, and hurt people. Osman had no qualms about doing either of those.

He was just tired of hustling for scraps.

He had bigger plans.

The first time he received the money, he had spent it. This time he was going to invest his cold, hard windfall.

That night, however, he wanted to have fun and blow off some steam. The last couple of days were really stressful. Everything had to be just right or else it could have backfired on him. He could end up in prison doing ten to fifteen years.

Fortunately, everything went smoothly, and he came away a richer man.

He approached a building with no sign. There was a long line out by the front. A huge man stood behind velvet ropes. The man could crush Osman with his bare hands if he wanted to.

Osman pulled out a hundred-dollar bill. If the man refused to let him in, Osman would try his luck somewhere else.

The man revealed a toothy smile and snatched the bill from his hand. He removed the rope as Osman entered the club.

The music was loud. Lights flashed all around him. The club was packed, and Osman had to push his way past a group of people before he made his way to the bar.

He ordered a drink.

A girl came up next to him.

"You wanna buy me a drink?" she asked.

Osman eyed her from top to bottom. She wore revealing clothes, along with extra makeup and fake eyelashes.

"Sure," he replied with a smile. He ordered whatever she wanted.

"My name's Maya."

It was likely not her real name, he thought.

"What's yours?" she asked.

Two can play that game. "It's C.J," Osman said.

"You come here often, C.J.?" she asked.

He shrugged. "Whenever I get the chance."

He knew why she was chatting him up. To get in the club, you had to have money, and once in, you had to have more money to have fun. The drinks were expensive, and so were the girls.

Maya was not some regular girl out for a good night. She was an escort. And judging by her age, she had so far been unsuccessful in hooking a client.

Osman would string her along until he found someone younger. If he did not, she would do for the night.

He saw that a man sitting next to him was staring at his cell phone, engrossed in a news article.

"What's that?" Osman asked.

"Oh, you don't know?"

"Know what?"

"Dillon Scott is dead."

Osman's eyes widened in disbelief. "When?"

"Yesterday. They found his body in a house in Milton."

Osman pulled out a wad of cash and paid the bartender.

"I gotta go," he said to Maya.
"You need company?" she asked with a smile.
"Maybe next time."
He hurried out of the club.

TWENTY-SEVEN

The next morning, Fisher was back at her desk at the Milton PD. She had a fitful night. She couldn't help but feel like she was missing something. She wasn't sure what it was, but she knew it had to do with the three hours between the time Scott left the studio and the time he asked Tillman to meet him at his house.

If he was so eager to work with Tillman on the script, then why not stay late at the studio? Also, why not just go straight from the studio to his house with Tillman? Why ask her to come later that night?

Fisher leaned back in her chair and stared at the ceiling.

Tillman was drained from a long rehearsal, so she had declined the offer. Maybe Scott figured after some rest, she would be ready to get back to work a few hours later.

But then why did Scott constantly check his cell phone? And why did she not find it when she searched the house?

Fisher had a feeling Scott was meeting someone that night. It would explain the gap between the end of rehearsals and the time he invited Tillman over to his house.

Did this person arrive shortly after the limo driver had left? And did they take the cell phone after they had murdered Scott?

She wasn't sure about any of those answers.

She knew from her training that if something didn't make sense, go back to the scene of the crime.

She turned her attention to the folder on her desk, which contained detailed photographs of the living room, the hallway, the entrance to the house, the kitchen, the bedroom, and even the main-floor bathroom. They were taken so that the prosecutor could lead a jury through a tour of the house when the case went to trial.

She went through the photos and frowned. There was nothing in particular that stood out to her. She had combed every inch of the house when she was there, and it was still fresh in her mind.

After ten minutes, she dropped the photos and put her face in her hands. She rubbed her temples and gritted her teeth.

What am I not seeing? she wondered. *What am I overlooking?*

Her thoughts were broken by a conversation two desks over. A male detective was telling a female detective a story from years earlier.

"So, I'm in the car, right?" the male detective said. "And it's pouring like no one's business. I mean, it's so bad that I can't see five feet in front of me. Now, it's also late at night, so visibility is already low, and with the rain, I have no idea where I'm going. My wipers are on full, but all they are doing is moving the rain from one end of the windshield to the other. I'm pretty much driving blind. My wife's in the backseat, and the baby is about to come out any minute."

"So what did you do?" the female detective asked earnestly.

The male detective shrugged. "What could I do? I parked the car by the side of the road and jumped into action. It was a scene straight out of a movie. I've never experienced anything like it. I was so scared that I nearly blacked out from the stress."

"Oh my god!" the female detective exclaimed.

"But I'll tell you this: The moment I held my son in my arms, all that stress melted away in an instant. That kid was a miracle. He was a sign from Heaven that no matter how tough things get, they will eventually get better if you push your way through."

Fisher smiled. She had heard the detective tell that story to every new member of the unit, and he had told it with the same gusto when he told Fisher years ago.

She turned back to the photos. She wasn't sure if going through them again was worthwhile.

She was examining them one by one when something flashed in the back of her mind. She opened her desk drawer, searched through the contents inside, found the magnifying glass, and held it up to the photo.

She turned to her laptop, typed on the keyboard, and confirmed her suspicion.

She grabbed her jacket and left the station.

TWENTY-EIGHT

Callaway was back at the department store's shipping center. He had followed Frank Henderson from his home to his place of work. Frank was inside the building, likely getting ready for the scheduled deliveries for the day.

Callaway knew he would have to confront Frank sooner or later. He debated doing it when Frank left his house, but he worried his children might see his reaction. Frank was not going to appreciate a stranger meddling in his personal life. No man would. Then there was the matter of his wife. How would he act toward her knowing she had hired a private investigator to follow him?

The house was out of the question.

What about the shipping center? Their discussion would likely cause a scene, which could even affect Frank's employment. Callaway was not sure if management knew of his relationship with the other woman. Did they have a policy against workplace romance? Callaway didn't know, and he was not going to risk it.

What he was about to do required delicacy. It was a personal matter between a husband and wife. Callaway was not here to get between them, he was only here to convey a message. If Frank refused to heed his advice, there was nothing he could do about it. He could not very well force him to continue in his marriage if there were irreparable differences.

He would tread carefully.

Frank appeared from behind the building. He got in the eighteen-wheeler and pulled out of the lot.

Callaway followed behind.

The first two deliveries were routine stops from the day before, but the third stop was new.

The truck entered a vacant parking lot and came to a stop. Callaway parked on a side street with a clear view of the lot.

A white cargo van drove up and parked next to the truck. Two men got out of the van just as Frank emerged from the eighteen-wheeler. Frank unhinged the trailer's rear door and slid it up. The two men hurried inside and began moving goods from the trailer to the van. When they were done, one of them handed Frank an envelope. Frank put the envelope in his pocket without looking inside.

Callaway had photographed everything.

The men got back inside the van and drove away. Frank stood there for a moment before he got back in the eighteen-wheeler and pulled away.

Callaway wasn't sure what had just happened, but something did not feel right about what he saw.

He put the Impala in gear and continued following Frank.

Frank made two more drops before Callaway finally decided to make his move. There was no point in delaying it. He either completed what he was hired to do, or he did not. If he quit, he would have to face Betty Henderson again and return the five hundred dollars, along with an apology.

Frank had just unloaded goods and was making his way back to the eighteen-wheeler when Callaway approached. "Frank Henderson?" Callaway asked.

Frank turned to him.

"My name is Lee Callaway. I'm a private investigator."

Callaway held up his business card.

Frank paused and then looked at it. "What do you want with me?" Frank asked, concerned.

Up close, Frank was an imposing man. He could snap Callaway in half with his two fingers. Callaway's weapon was tucked behind his back in case things got out of hand.

"Your wife hired me to follow you."

Frank's face turned red. "She did what?"

"She knows you're cheating on her."

Frank grunted.

"She doesn't care if you are," Callaway quickly said, wanting to keep their conversation from escalating. "All she cares about is *you.*"

Frank stood still.

"She hired me not to spy on you, but to convince you that she loves you, and that your children need you."

Frank grimaced. "I love my wife, and I adore my children," he said.

"I'm sure you do, but I have photos of you and another woman going into a house together."

"It's not what you think."

"It doesn't matter what I think, it's what your *wife* thinks."

Frank's eyes moistened. This was not the reaction Callaway was expecting. He figured Frank would threaten him, or lunge at him, but he looked like a wounded animal.

"Betty's been through a lot," Frank said. "If you show her those photos, you'll be killing her."

He got in his eighteen-wheeler and drove away.

TWENTY-NINE

Fisher noticed that an even larger crowd had gathered outside the residence from the last time she was here. The press had not left the property, for obvious reasons. The house was still an active crime scene, and if there were any major discoveries, it would happen here.

The press, however, was now outnumbered by the fans who were arriving by the dozens. The outpouring of grief was palpable. They wept openly, held movie posters, lit candles, and offered prayers for the deceased movie star. There was even a bus with tourists who had likely taken a detour just to be here to pay their respects.

As Fisher got closer, she noticed a memorial had been set up for Scott. A large photo of his smiling face was stuck on a two-by-four, which was planted next to the entrance. Flowers piled two feet up were placed all around the photo.

Fisher had called in advance. The officers at the scene had already cleared a path for her as she drove through the crowd. Even then, the press snapped photos of her SUV. The cameras recorded her every move. Some fans even reached over and touched her vehicle as if they were trying to connect with their fallen idol. They didn't realize she was not related to Scott.

She moved past the yellow police tape and drove up the gravel road. A uniformed officer was standing by the front door. To her dismay, it was not Officer McConnell.

Why am I thinking about him now? she wondered.

The officer unlocked the front door and held it for her.

She entered and shut the door behind her.

Back at the station, when the male detective had regaled the female detective about the birth of his son, something had flashed in Fisher's mind.

She pulled out a photo that showed the house's hallway. With a magnifying glass, she had narrowed her focus on a pair of boots. They were black, and one of the pair had fallen on its side, exposing the soles. Fisher had spotted mud on the soles.

She walked down the hall. The boots were in the exact same position as in the photo. They were a size nine, and they had belonged to Scott. She leaned down and took a closer look. Mud and dirt had dried under the boots. With a gloved hand, she scraped some of the dirt away to make sure.

When she was walking up to the house, she noticed the area around the front steps was covered in dirt. The mud could have come from there.

She already confirmed that on the night Scott was murdered, it had rained between nine and eleven o'clock. When the limo driver had dropped Scott off, the dirt was still dry.

So how did Scott's boots get mud on them? He was not a smoker, so he wouldn't have gone out to light a cigarette. He could have gone for a walk, but Fisher doubted he would have done so in the rain. Plus, the next neighbor was a mile away, so there was nowhere else to go.

The only logical conclusion was that Scott had left the house right after the limo driver had dropped him off. And when he returned, it was raining, and that's how he got mud on his boots.

Her theory was supported by the fact that Scott had asked Leslie Tillman to meet him at nine, not before. Also, Scott had been checking his phone constantly. This could only mean that Scott was scheduled to be someplace.

Who were you meeting? Fisher thought. *And did they have something to do with what happened to you?*

THIRTY

Becky grabbed a slice of pizza, a cup of mixed fruit, and a carton of chocolate milk. She moved down the line, paid for her lunch, and took the tray to the corner of the school cafeteria.

A girl was already seated at the table when Becky sat next to her. Becky had known Ester Chow since they were in sixth grade. Ester had long, smooth hair, a few acne blemishes on her cheeks, and she wore braces. Her lunch was nachos with cheese, chicken nuggets, corn, and a bottle of water.

"How are you feeling now?" Ester asked, concerned.

"Better," Becky replied.

"I messaged you like forty times yesterday."

"Sorry about that. My mom gave me medication and I passed out all day." Becky hated lying to her best friend, but she couldn't tell her the truth. It wasn't that she didn't trust her to not tell anyone, it was just that she wasn't sure how she would react. Would she stop talking to her? Would she judge her? Would she be repulsed by her?

Becky couldn't imagine not being friends with Ester. Ester had been with her through thick and thin. She was there when Becky had her heart broken for the first time. She was there when Becky lost out on becoming class president. She was even there when Becky's dad passed away.

Becky hoped their friendship would last forever, but this could only happen if Becky never told her secret to anyone—not even Ester.

"It's okay," Ester said. "I forgive you."

Becky smiled. "So what happened while I was away?"

"You know Amber, right?"

"The girl with the freckles?"

"Yeah, her. She was bawling her eyes out yesterday."

"Why?"

Ester rolled her eyes. "She was sad because Dillon Scott died."

Becky froze. "Who?" she asked a second later.

"He's some actor. Apparently, Amber's mom had a crush on him when she was younger, and when she found out he was dead, she broke down. So, when Amber saw her mom crying, she got all emotional too."

"That's so sad," Becky said, unsure of what else to say.

Ester shrugged. "I guess so, but you know what I really think? Amber is a drama queen. She just needs an excuse to get attention. Last year she told everyone she had throat cancer. Everyone felt sorry for her. It was really a swollen lymph node. The doctor didn't even prescribe her anything for it. It went away on its own. The worst part was that she complained about it *after* the doctor had already told her it was nothing to worry about."

"Really?" Becky asked, surprised. "How come I don't remember this?"

"I think it was during the time you were away because of your dad."

"Oh, right."

"How's your mom doing, by the way?"

"She says she's okay, but I know she's not. Sometimes I can hear her crying in bed. I want to go into her room and hug her, but I don't want to embarrass her. She feels that as a parent, she has to be strong for the both of us. I want to tell her it's okay if she's not, but I'm not sure how to do it."

They ate in silence.

Ester smiled and said, "Guess who's been asking about you?"

"Who?"

"Daniel Bailey." Daniel was in all of Becky's classes. He was tall, dark, and handsome. Becky had caught him staring at her.

She blushed. "Get out."

"Really. He asked me twice if you were coming to school today."

"And what did you say?"

"I'm not telling."

"Come on," Becky squealed.

They both laughed.

THIRTY-ONE

Callaway was back at his office. He could not get Frank's words out of his mind.

It's not what you think.

What did he mean by that? Callaway had caught him red-handed with another woman. He had seen this woman get in his pickup truck and go with him to her house. How else could Callaway interpret this?

In his years as a private eye, he had captured on camera hundreds of people doing the exact same thing, and they were all cheating on their spouses.

He pulled the digital camera from his pocket. He preferred using film because negatives could not be easily altered, but with fewer and fewer photo locations developing film these days, switching to digital was done out of necessity.

He clicked on the images of Frank and the woman. He noticed the woman was smiling throughout their walk up to the house, but there was a hint of sadness on Frank's face. Maybe Frank knew that what he was doing was wrong. During their brief conversation, Callaway had sensed remorse from him.

If that was true, then why not stop doing what he was doing?

Callaway stopped at a photo. It was a full shot of the woman's house. There was a station wagon parked in the driveway, and the lights inside the house were on.

Did the woman live with a roommate or a friend? If so, was the location even practical for a rendezvous?

Something did not add up.

He clicked through the photos and stopped at the one where the men from the cargo van were unloading goods from Frank's truck.

Callaway zoomed in on Frank as he watched the men drive away. Callaway could clearly see distain on his face.

What is going on? he thought.

He went back to the earlier photos, where the woman had first appeared, smoking a cigarette. Something caught his attention that time. When the woman had gotten in Frank's pickup, they did not embrace. He thought it was odd, but he rationalized this by thinking they did not want their co-workers to find out about their relationship.

He then skipped to the photos of them getting out of the pickup and making their way up to her house. They were still not holding hands or even talking to each other. The woman was in front. Frank trailed behind her. He didn't look like a man who was looking forward to spending time with his mistress. He looked like he wanted to be anywhere but there.

Did Frank get himself into something he should not have?

He did say he loved his wife and his children, and from his tone of voice, Callaway knew he was telling the truth. Callaway thought it was odd that he would throw it all away for another woman.

He turned his laptop on. While it loaded, he left the office and went down to the variety store around the block. He bought a granola bar from the vending machine—the only thing he could afford with the loose change in his pocket.

He returned to his office and sat down behind the laptop. He punched the woman's address into the online phone directory. The name that came back was Sandra Wolkoff. There was a second name under the same address: Carl Wolkoff.

What the hell? Callaway thought. *Is this woman married?*

That explained the sedan parked in the driveway.

He conducted an online search and discovered that three years back, someone named Sandra Wolkoff and her husband, Carl, had been indicted for fraud and theft in the state of Michigan. They were both given a suspended sentence.

Callaway pulled up the department store's website. There was a Search button in the top corner. He decided to try his luck. He punched in *Sandra Wolkoff*. There were no hits. He then punched in *Sandra*.

Several names popped up. There was a Sandra Baker, a Sandra Levin, a Sandra Hoffman—and then there was a Sandra Ledford.

Why does that name sound familiar?

He went back to the articles from Michigan, and after searching for a moment, he found what he was looking for.

Sandra Wolkoff's maiden name was Ledford.

He clicked back to the department store's website. Sandra Ledford was the account manager at the shipping department.

Isn't that the department Frank works in?

Callaway suddenly had a feeling this was not about a man cheating on his wife. This was something far worse.

THIRTY-TWO

The boots were tagged and ready to be sent to the lab for further testing. Fisher was certain the mud on the soles could have only come from the dirt outside the house. She couldn't see any matching boot prints in the dirt, however. After Scott's body was discovered, over a dozen people had searched the area.

She spent an hour scouring the house again. She hoped she might find something that would explain why Scott had left on that fateful night. If she had Scott's cell phone, things would be easier. She wasn't worried, though. She had contacted Scott's cell phone provider, and they were going to courier her the call logs within a day.

When she was satisfied that she had checked every nook and cranny, she stopped by the front door and stared at the crowd by the entrance.

The press was waiting on her to give them an update. The fans were waiting on her to make sense of why their idol was gone.

She sighed. She was as much in the dark as them. She had no idea why someone would hurt a beloved movie star. She had no motive and no suspects.

She was turning to shut the door when her eyes caught something. There was a large potted plant next to the door. Inside the clay planter was a white piece of paper. She reached down and picked it up.

It was a taxi receipt. The amount was forty dollars, but with a tip, the total came to fifty. Her eyes widened when she saw the date and time at the top. The date was two days earlier, and the time was seven twenty PM.

The receipt had to have belonged to Scott. He must have taken a taxi from the house, and when he was dropped off, the driver must have given him a receipt.

But how did it end up in the planter? she wondered. The only explanation she could think of was that Scott had the house keys and the taxi receipt in the same pocket. When he reached to pull out the keys, the receipt must have fallen into the planter.

The receipt was a customer copy, and it showed that it was paid with cash. The receipt did not have the name of the taxi company, but it did have the medallion number and the driver number. It wouldn't be hard to find out who had picked up Scott and where he had been taken.

She realized it was her first big break in the case.

THIRTY-THREE

Callaway considered everything he had just discovered. The woman with Frank Henderson was Sandra Wolkoff. Sandra was going by her maiden name of Ledford. This explained why the department store had not picked up on her past when they had conducted a background check.

Now that he knew who she was, he couldn't understand how Frank was involved with her.

He could tell Frank was not happy with the arrangement. Whenever he was around her, his posture was that of a defeated man. He was being forced to do something he was not proud of. Callaway had a feeling it involved the men in the cargo van.

His ears perked up when he heard a noise coming from outside. Someone was making their way up the stairs.

I'm not expecting company, he thought.

He opened the desk drawer and removed his gun. As a responsible gun owner, he always locked up his weapon upon returning to the office. He was fortunate he didn't need it when he had met Frank, but now his weapon could be very useful.

He got up and slowly made his way to the closed door. There was no window for him to know who could be outside.

He cocked the hammer.

"You're not going to shoot me, are you, kid?" a man on the other side of the door said.

Callaway's mouth dropped. He blinked. He had not heard that voice in years. "Jimmy? Is that you?"

"Of course it's me. Who else would it be?"

Callaway returned the gun to the drawer. He tucked his shirt in his pants. He patted his hair down and then opened the door.

Jimmy Keith was five-ten with a protruding belly and broad shoulders. He had deep wrinkles on his face, a handlebar mustache, and a white mane that was slicked back. His dull gray eyes were focused on Callaway, and his face was sporting a grin.

"Kid," he said.

"Jimmy," Callaway replied with a big smile.

Jimmy took in the office. "Small but cozy. I like it."

Callaway's mouth was dry. "What… what are you doing here?"

"I came to see how you were doing," Jimmy replied.

Jimmy Keith was the reason Callaway had become a private investigator. As a deputy sheriff, he was bored out of his mind when he stumbled upon an article about Jimmy.

Jimmy was hired by a family to investigate the murder of their daughter and son-in-law while they vacationed in the Dominican Republic. The couple had been found bludgeoned to death inside their rental property. The Dominican police believed the murders were a result of a robbery gone horribly wrong. The house had been ransacked of all money and jewelry.

When there were no leads for over a year, Jimmy was brought in to find out what happened. He flew to the Dominican Republic and began his own investigation. He started with the local police, who were not too happy to see a private investigator poking his nose into their business. But after lining their pockets with American greenbacks, they were more than willing to let him at least see what they had on the case. To his horror, no work had been done on the couple's murder. The police had in fact closed the case as unsolvable. It was another statistic of tourists caught in the country's high crime rate.

He spoke to the couple's neighbors. They said they hadn't heard or seen anything. He even spoke to low-level criminals, but none of them had anything of value to add. After months of hitting walls, and with money running out, he returned to the United States, deeply dismayed.

But Jimmy never gave up.

On the second anniversary of the deaths, he caught a break. Someone had filed a claim on a life insurance policy for the daughter. When Jimmy investigated, he found it was her ex-boyfriend. He was the beneficiary on her insurance policy. But the ex-boyfriend was in the States at the time of the murders. He had a solid alibi.

Jimmy spoke to the family who had hired him, and they had nothing but positive things to say about the ex-boyfriend. The breakup was amicable, and the ex-boyfriend had even spoken at the couple's wedding. In fact, he had also purchased the trip to the Dominican Republic as a wedding gift.

This was all Jimmy needed to hear.

He dug deeper and found out the ex-boyfriend had visited the country twice before the wedding. Jimmy spent money out of his own pocket and found out that the ex-boyfriend had also visited the local police. In particular, he met the officer who ended up investigating the murders.

Jimmy then discovered that a large sum of money had been transferred from the ex-boyfriend's account to an account in the Dominican Republic.

Armed with this information, the family flew down to the country. With the help of the American consulate, they pressured the state police to look into the case. They found that the officer had indeed received the large sum of money. He had also been spotted at the scene around the time of the murder. No witnesses had come forward because they feared retribution from the officer, but with the state police's assurances, they spoke up.

Meanwhile, back in the United States, the FBI brought in the ex-boyfriend for questioning. With all the evidence piled up against him, he confessed. He was bitter about being dumped, and he decided to kill the daughter and cash in her life insurance. He paid the officer in the Dominican Republic to carry out the crime.

The ex-boyfriend was now serving life in prison for conspiracy to commit murder. The officer was sentenced to prison in the Dominican Republic, but two months later, he was found with his throat slashed. Apparently, there were criminals who could not wait to get their hands on an ex-police officer, even if he was a crooked cop.

In Callaway's eyes, Jimmy was a legend. He was also his mentor.

"Aren't you going to buy an old man a drink?" Jimmy asked.

"Yeah, sure, absolutely," Callaway quickly replied. "I know a great place around the corner."

THIRTY-FOUR

Fisher parked the SUV and got out. She was at Yonge Avenue, one of the busiest downtown streets in Milton. Businesses and retail stores lined both sides of the street.

After finding the taxi receipt at Scott's house, she was able to track down the driver. He was a new immigrant to the country, and in broken English, he confirmed he had picked up Scott at his home after six thirty in the evening. Fisher had pushed him for the exact time, but he wasn't sure.

The security cameras confirmed that Scott was dropped off at his house at precisely 6:32 PM by the limo driver. The time printed on the taxi receipt read 7:20 PM, which meant the taxi driver had arrived at Scott's house shortly after 6:45 PM in order to make the twenty-minute drive to Yonge Avenue.

Why was this timing so important? It explained that right after the limo driver had driven away, Scott had called a taxi. This raised a couple of questions: Why didn't Scott just have the limo driver bring him to Yonge Avenue? And why did he leave his house right after he had just arrived?

The answers were simple. He did not want anyone to know where he was going, and he was meeting someone at a precise time.

She was able to get the taxi driver to show her the footage from his taxi cab. The latest CCTV systems were equipped to store footage up to five days.

In the footage, as Scott got into the cab, he was wearing the clothes he had been found in. He was also wearing large aviator shades. He was carrying a backpack, which he placed next to him. Fisher had not found any backpack in the house. The way Scott held the backpack close told her it contained something of value to him.

The driver tried to engage in small talk, but Scott was not interested. He kept staring at his cell phone. It looked like he was waiting for a call or a text message. Fisher couldn't be certain. The footage was black and white and had no audio.

At his destination, Scott paid with cash, and the driver handed him a receipt. Scott stuck it in his jacket pocket and got out of the cab.

Fisher looked around the busy intersection. She saw a bar, a fish-and-chips shop, a cell phone store, and many other businesses. Yonge Avenue was like any other downtown street in America.

She could not understand why Scott would go through all that trouble to come here.

THIRTY-FIVE

Callaway and Jimmy found a booth in the corner of the bar. Callaway ordered a beer, and Jimmy had whiskey.

"You're beaming like a little school girl," Jimmy said, taking a sip from his drink. Callaway could still not believe the great Jimmy Keith was in Milton.

"I'm so happy to see you, Jimmy," Callaway replied.

"I haven't seen you in... what? Three years?"

"Five years."

Jimmy's eyebrows shot up. "That long, huh?"

"I called you many times, but I got no answer," Callaway said.

"You did? Well, you should have left a message."

"I left one each time."

"Oh, right, sure." Jimmy shrugged. "You know how it is in our line of work. We go where the job is."

The truth was that Jimmy was not the type to stick with a relationship for too long. His motto was *I'm here for a good time, not a long time*. When Callaway called him, he never expected Jimmy to reply. Callaway did it because he wanted to see if the old man had changed. He had not.

Jimmy was one of the best, if not *the* best, private investigators Callaway had ever met. The man was possessed when he was working on a case. Nothing else mattered. Not family, not friends, not anyone or anything.

He had never been married, but he fathered a child with a woman he had met only briefly. He never spoke about the son or daughter—Callaway wasn't sure which one it was—and Callaway never pushed him on it either. It was none of his business.

Jimmy was a hard-drinking, hard-living kind of man. He could drink anyone under the table and not get drunk. He had been with countless women, and he had tried every imaginable drug out there. If there was an example of a man squeezing every inch out of life, it was Jimmy.

92

The lifestyle eventually caught up with him. Jimmy rarely had any money in his pockets, and the last Callaway heard was that he had suffered a heart attack. Callaway tried to get in touch with him at the time, but it seemed like Jimmy was avoiding him. Callaway didn't blame him. Jimmy was a proud man. He didn't want Callaway to see him in a hospital bed, hooked up to tubes and machines.

Jimmy owned a rental property and a cabin boat. Whenever work dried up, he would rent out the main floor of the property and live in the basement. When things got even worse, he would rent out the entire house and live on the boat.

Jimmy was a fighter and a survivor. If he found himself in a hole, he would find a way out of it.

Callaway had taken a page out of Jimmy's handbook. He was always broke. He had also been with multiple women, and he always found himself in trouble. But unlike Jimmy, who had his rental property and boat, Callaway had no assets to his name.

But when it came to gambling, both men thought they were one opportunity away from hitting the jackpot.

Jimmy took another sip and laughed.

"What's so funny?" Callaway asked.

"I just remembered the time when that husband chased me out of his house with a chainsaw."

"You did sleep with his wife, so what did you expect him to do? Buy you a drink?"

"True, true, but the husband was a good runner. I was in my shorts and had no shoes on when I bolted out of there. Had you not shown up in the Charger, I would have been chopped up like firewood."

Callaway chuckled. "I had never seen a man with a beer belly jump through a window and into the passenger seat like you did."

"I was running for my life, kid. I would have jumped on a moving train to save my butt."

They both laughed hard.

"How's Nina?" Jimmy asked next.

"She's growing up fast."

"Do you see her often?"

"Not as often as I would like to," Callaway replied somberly.

They were silent for a moment, then Callaway said, "Who needs family anyway? They're only there to weigh you down. Isn't that what you used to say?"

"I did, but…"

"So, what're you doing in Milton?" Callaway asked.

"I'll tell you, but first you tell me what's bothering *you*."

Callaway shrugged. "Who said anything's bothering me?"

"You were all jumpy when I showed up at your office. If I had not announced myself, I might have caught a bullet through the door."

"I wasn't going to shoot," Callaway said.

"Okay, sure, but I can always tell when something's on your mind."

Callaway spent five minutes telling Jimmy about the Frank Henderson situation.

"You took on a case for *only* five hundred bucks?" Jimmy asked.

"I'm kind of desperate. I need the money."

"Don't we all," Jimmy said wistfully.

Callaway nodded and stared at his empty bottle.

"Okay, kid," Jimmy said. "I'll help you."

Callaway looked up, surprised. "You will?"

Jimmy smiled. "Sure. It'll be like the good old days. Just the two of us against the world."

Callaway liked the sound of that.

THIRTY-SIX

Becky opened the door and found the house smelling of food. Her mom was usually not home at this time of day, so she was surprised when she saw her in front of the stove.

"What're you doing?" Becky asked.

"I thought I'd make my baby her favorite meal."

"Okay," Becky said, still not believing what was going on. Ever since her dad died, her mom had been working around the clock. Becky had gotten used to eating out or putting together a meal of her own.

When she looked back on the past year, before her dad's accident, Becky lived a sheltered life. She had parents who doted on her. They had each other to lean on, and this helped them protect their only child. Now that one of them was gone, the other was barely holding on by a thread.

Becky had a lot of growing up to do the moment her dad was gone. She had to be the anchor for her mom.

Her parents had met on a train. He used to take the train each morning when he was apprenticing as a woodworker. She took the train as a student on her way to earning a diploma in sociology. The woodworking never took off, so her dad got into construction. The sociology diploma never opened many doors for her mom, so she took any job available. But during the time when they were each building toward a career, they saw each other regularly on the same platform.

Becky's dad dropped out of school at a very young age to help his mother pay the bills, which meant he never got a formal education. When he saw Becky's mom waiting for the train, clutching a textbook in her hand, he was instantly attracted to her. When he approached her, he was shaking. He said something incoherent and then quickly walked away, feeling ashamed. She found his awkward approach charming, and the next time they were at the same platform, she approached him. She saw a man who was big and strong but also had kind eyes and an easy smile.

They got married soon after, and they had a little girl. They wanted more children, but Becky was born after several miscarriages. In fact, the pregnancy was fraught with so many health issues that Becky's birth was a miracle.

Her parents had created a beautiful and happy life, until it all came crashing down one terrible day. Becky was in class when the school principal called her to his office. What he told her pulled the ground from underneath her. She thought it was a cruel prank, but the look on the principal's face told her it was not.

Becky knew things would never be the same from that day on.

"What're you cooking?" Becky asked.

"Cheese and spinach lasagna," her mom replied. She cut a piece and placed it on a plate. "I know it doesn't compare to how your dad used to make it, but I gave it my best shot." Her mom was eager to know what she thought.

Becky took a bite. The lasagna was moist and full of flavor. "It's perfect, Mom."

Her mom smiled. "That's a relief. You don't know how long I've been trying to get it just right."

She went to the stove to fill her own plate.

Becky took another mouthful and said, "So what are you *really* doing home so early?"

"There was a water issue in our building. It wasn't safe, so they let us go home."

"With pay?" Becky asked.

"No, unfortunately. I'm just an hourly worker, so it's without pay."

There was silence between them. Becky knew they were struggling financially. Any time her mom didn't work, they would fall behind on the bills.

"Mom?" Becky said.

"Yes, dear?"

"I miss dad."

Her mom stared at her and she began to shake.

Becky went over and hugged her. Her mom held her tight. "I know, baby," she said. I miss your dad too."

They both cried at losing someone who meant the world to them.

THIRTY-SEVEN

Osman was on the phone as he hurried down the street. He had called all his contacts, and after two hours, someone had the information he was looking for.

The crack house was above a tattoo parlor. To get to it, you had to go through a narrow alley next to the parlor, turn right, and then go up a flight of stairs. Osman would have never known the house existed had his contact not told him.

He raced down the street, found the tattoo parlor, and then proceeded to find his way to the crack house. He grimaced as he tiptoed over syringes and drug paraphernalia. This was another reason he could not wait to leave the business behind.

He sold drugs to just about everyone, but he disliked seeing them as they jacked up. He feared getting poked by one of the contaminated needles. He didn't believe you had to try your product in order to sell it. This was not some car, computer, or kitchen appliance he was promoting. This stuff already had an established market. The buyers wanted to get their hands on his products as soon as they could.

In his experience, it was not the addicts who made good customers, it was the casual or recreational users. The addicts were certainly repeat customers, but they were usually without money. They would beg, steal, and sell themselves to raise the cash needed to satisfy their addiction, but their money was only enough for that one hit. Afterwards, they were back on the streets hustling to get more money.

The casual or recreational users didn't know what the drugs went for on the open market. They never haggled with him, and they always paid what was charged. They also came from a variety of backgrounds. Osman sold drugs to executives, lawyers, and even politicians. Once they had their drugs, they couldn't wait to get far away from him. They didn't want anyone to see them associating with a drug dealer.

Osman was not offended. He never liked these people to begin with. They thought they were so high and mighty, but in reality, they were weak and pathetic. They thought the drugs gave them super abilities in order to function at a high level, but their addiction made them dependent on the drugs instead.

Osman was able to resist the siren call of drugs, which made him far tougher than all those people combined, even if they never realized it.

He made his way up the stairs and to a weather-beaten door. With his gloved hand, he turned the handle, and as he expected, the door was locked.

He banged his fist on the door and waited.

The door opened an inch a minute later. A young man with shaggy hair and glassy eyes said, "Can I help you?"

Osman shoved the man back and entered the crack house. The man tried to protest, but he didn't put up much of a fight.

The interior was dark. Heavy curtains were placed over the windows. The only source of light was from the yellow lamp in the corner.

As he moved from room to room, he saw garbage and debris everywhere. There were mattresses and worn-out cushions on the floor. People were lying on them with needles sticking out of their arms and legs. Their eyes told him they were in a place far, far away.

He scanned their faces until he saw who he was looking for. She was on the floor next to the bathtub. The bathroom was grimy, and the putrid smell made him cover his nose. He fought his gag reflex as he stood in the confined space.

Tamara Davis was wearing tattered clothes and dirty shoes. Her hair was coarse, looking like it had not been washed in months. Her nails were long and yellow.

As he stared at her, he could feel anger rise up in him. "Tamara, what the hell you doing here?"

She turned her head in his direction. Her eyes were distant, but a smile broke across her face, revealing stained and chipped teeth. "Hey Osman, whatch you doin' here?" she asked.

"I've been searching the entire city for you," he replied.

"I was right here the whole time," she said.

He could tell she was high. "What's wrong with you?" he growled. "I give you money, and the first thing you do is get all jacked up."

"A girl gotta have some fun, right?"

"I should have left you where I found you."

She was still smiling when she said, "If you did that, then how would you have gotten all that money, huh?"

"Shut your mouth!" he said, raising his voice. He looked around. There was no one else in the bathroom.

She was not deterred. "I am your ATM. Isn't that what you said? You have to be nice to me, or else I will go to the police and tell them I didn't really see Dillon Scott that night. I really saw—"

"Shut your trap," he snapped. "Someone could hear you."

She put her finger to her lips. "Shhhhh… I won't tell no one. Your secret is safe with me."

She burst out laughing.

He balled his fists. He wanted to make her stop laughing, but instead he walked out of the bathroom and left the crack house.

THIRTY-EIGHT

Jimmy eyed the Impala's interior and frowned. "What happened to the Charger?"

Callaway was behind the wheel. He let out a long sigh and told him.

Jimmy shook his head. "Kid, you never put something irreplaceable at risk." Jimmy was fully aware of how much the car meant to Callaway. He had many opportunities to sell or lose the car, but he always managed to hold on to it. The Charger was the one constant thing in his otherwise unstable life.

They pulled up to a house.

Jimmy said, "You sure it's the right place?"

It was a detached two-story with a long driveway and a double garage. "It's the right address. And take a look." Callaway pointed to a cargo van parked by the front of the house. "It's the same van that pulled up next to Frank's eighteen-wheeler."

Callaway had snapped a photo of the van's license plate number. Once he had that, it was easy to locate the van's owner.

"It's registered to a Boban Milodovic," Callaway said.

Jimmy stuck his hand in his coat pocket and pulled out a shiny police badge. Prior to getting into the PI business, Jimmy worked for the Miami Police Department. Jimmy had pissed off his superiors so much that they made his life so difficult, he was forced to quit.

"They let you keep it?" Callaway asked, surprised.

"Of course not. I know a guy who can make exact replicas. He's so good he can get you a passport that will fool any Transport Security Officer. Now let's go and talk to this guy."

They got out and approached the house. Callaway knocked on the door and waited. A minute later, a tall, skinny man answered. His head was shaved, and he had tattoos going up his arms.

"Who are you?" the man asked with a scowl.

Jimmy said, "Boban Milodovic?"

"I don't know that name," he shot back.

Jimmy held up his badge. "Lying to a police officer is against the law."

The moment Boban saw the badge, his bravado evaporated. "Hey man, I was just playing. What can I do for you, officer?"

Jimmy turned to Callaway. He pulled out a photo and held it for Boban. "Do you mind explaining what's going on here?"

Boban grimaced. "Oh man," he said.

"Are you selling narcotics or illegal drugs?" Callaway asked.

Boban waved his hands. "No, no, no. It's nothing like that. I'm a wholesaler."

Callaway was confused. "Wholesaler?"

"Yeah, let me show you."

He opened the garage door. Inside were boxes upon boxes of goods. Callaway and Jimmy spotted a TV in the corner, stereo systems, DVD players, jackets, shoes, even razor blades and deodorants.

Boban said, "People sell me stuff, and I then resell it to small businesses."

"They sell you *stolen* goods, don't they?" Callaway said.

Boban shrugged. "I don't ask them where they get it from."

"So you were meeting Frank Henderson to buy goods?" Callaway asked.

"I don't know who that is, but my contact told me to go meet the guy with the truck. I take my cousin with me to help me load the stuff in my van."

"Who's your contact?"

"A lady."

"Is her name Sandra Ledford?"

"I don't know her last name, but she told me to call her Sandra."

Callaway turned to Jimmy. "It's the woman with Frank."

Jimmy nodded. He turned to Boban and said, "Boban, tell us everything you know, and we may consider not charging you with profiting from stolen property."

THIRTY-NINE

Fisher hung up the phone and shook her head. Holt was on the other end. He was going insane listening to all the speeches at the law enforcement conference in Vegas. It was supposed to have been a retreat for him, but all he did was complain about how bored he was. Nancy was having a great time. While he was at the conference, she was spending her day at the spa or shopping. They would go to dinner in the evening, and they had even caught a few musicals. Seeing Nancy happy made the conference tolerable for him, or else he would have been on the next available flight back to Milton.

Holt adored his wife, and he was devoted to her. They had endured a lot as a couple.
Tragedy can tear a couple apart, but in their case, tragedy made their relationship much stronger.

They were an odd couple. Holt was tough and gruff, and Nancy was tiny and pleasant. What they each lacked, the other made up for. They complemented each other like no one Fisher had seen before.

Holt wanted details on the Dillon Scott case. He had a TV and internet in his hotel suite, so he was following the murder case with great interest. Did she have a suspect in sight? Had she found a motive? Was the department pressuring her to solve the case quickly?

After making some excuse, she finally had to end the call. She didn't want him getting too involved at this stage of the investigation. He would turn into an armchair detective and call her every hour for an update.

If she didn't solve the case by the time he returned, she would fill him in on everything—he was her partner, after all—but until then, she was on her own.

She turned her attention back to a piece of paper on her desk. Prior to Holt's telephone call, she was studying Dillon Scott's phone logs.

Unfortunately, they were of no use to her.

Scott had made several calls on the day he died. One was to his wife, another to his agent, and a couple were to a prepaid number that was not registered to anyone. Fisher had considered trying to trace that number, but she doubted it would be much help. The Milton PD did not have access to the same technology that perhaps the National Security Agency or the Department of Homeland Security might have. They couldn't pinpoint a target's exact location or listen in on their conversations. The most the Milton PD could do was triangulate which cell tower the signal had pinged from. This was unnecessary because she already had an idea of where these calls originated from.

They were made between six thirty and seven thirty PM. The first one was at six forty, a few minutes before the taxi picked Scott up. The last and final call was at seven twenty-two, a few minutes after the taxi driver had dropped Scott off at Yonge Avenue.

This further reinforced Fisher's belief that Scott had taken the taxi to meet someone and that this person had guided him to where they were supposed to meet. It explained why Scott had constantly checked his phone throughout the day.

But what about the backpack he was seen carrying in the taxi's CCTV camera? What did he do with that?

Fisher sighed. She almost wished the department had sent her to the conference in Vegas as well. Unlike Holt, she didn't mind listening to people share their experiences in law enforcement. Their stories might have given her ideas about how to solve Scott's murder.

FORTY

The station wagon was parked in the driveway. Callaway and Jimmy waited outside while Frank and Ledford went inside the house.

Callaway believed Frank was taking detours during his routine deliveries where people were handing him envelopes of monies for goods they took off his eighteen-wheeler. At the end of the day, he would drive Ledford to her house, where she and her husband would count the money. Once they were satisfied it was all there, Frank would then head home to his wife and children.

Callaway was still not sure how Frank was involved in all of this, but he could tell by his demeanor it was not by choice.

He watched as Frank came out of the house, got in his pickup, and drove off. Callaway turned to Jimmy and said, "Let me handle this."

"You sure?" Jimmy asked.

"I am," Callaway replied. If things went south, he did not want Jimmy involved. Plus, he had brought his weapon as backup.

He got out, walked up to the house, and knocked on the front door.

The door swung open and he was face-to-face with Sandra. She was wearing a jacket and skirt, and she reeked of cigarettes.

"Yes?" she said.

"Sandra *Wolkoff*?" Callaway asked.

She blinked. Callaway knew why. She had not heard anyone call her by that name since she left Michigan as a felon.

"I… don't… know who…?" she stammered.

"Or do you prefer I call you Sandra Ledford?" Callaway said.

A man appeared behind her. He was tall, skinny, and he had on a sweatshirt and dirty jeans. "What's going on?" he asked.

"Carl Wolkoff, I presume," Callaway replied. "Or do you prefer I call you Carl Wibley?"

He froze just like his wife had.

Callaway pulled out his business card, the one that read *Gator Peckerwood*—a fake name Callaway used whenever he wanted to shield his identity—and held it out. "I've been hired by your employer to investigate the theft of their property."

"Theft?" Carl and Sandra said in unison, trying to act surprised.

"Yes, and my investigation has led me to you both."

"Us?" Again, they resorted to mock surprise.

Callaway produced photos of Frank with Boban and his cousin. He also produced photos of Frank with Sandra.

"What does this have to do with us?" Sandra asked. "This looks like Frank is responsible for the theft in our company. You should have him arrested."

"The photos may show that, but Boban Milodovic—" Callaway pointed him out just in case they tried to deny it, "—doesn't know who Frank Henderson is, but he does know a woman named Sandra. I'm sure if I played a recording of your voice to him, he would confirm you are his contact. I also checked your company's records. You are the account manager for their shipping department." Callaway turned to Carl. "I also found out that a Carl Wibley works at the company's loading dock."

Carl averted his eyes.

"This is what I think happens," Callaway said. "You, Sandra, have access to all the goods that are shipped out each day. You alter the invoices by omitting a certain number of items. A box here, a box there, nothing too obvious to raise any red flags, but it can be substantial over the course of a month or a year. Now, Carl here loads all the goods into Frank's eighteen-wheeler, but he separates the omitted items. Frank delivers those items to your contacts and collects the money, which he hands over to you at the end of his shift. The actual recipients are never aware that they are missing any items because what is on the invoices is what is being delivered to them. If there is anything not on the invoice that they had requested, they would call you, Sandra, and you would tell them the item was out of stock or give them some other excuse, and that you will make sure they get it in the next delivery. Have I understood how it works, or am I completely off base?"

Sandra and Carl stayed silent.

"I also know that a Sandra Wolkoff and a Carl Wolkoff are wanted in Michigan for fraud and theft," Callaway added. "I'm certain your employer was not aware of this when they hired you both."

The blood had drained from Sandra's and Carl's faces. "What... what do you want?" Carl asked.

"First, tell me what the deal is with Frank Henderson," Callaway said.

Carl bit his lip and then exhaled. He knew the jig was up. "When we came up with the plan, we knew we could not do it without a driver on our side. We approached a couple of drivers, but we knew right away they were either straight and would rat us out, or they were crooked and would screw us. Sandra happened to talk to Frank and found out his wife had an accident."

Callaway remembered Betty mentioning her accident.

"Frank was drowning in debt from the medical bills. We decided to help him out."

"How much?" Callaway asked.

"Close to twelve thousand dollars."

Callaway grimaced. *No wonder Frank looked defeated,* Callaway thought. *It was a lot of money.*

Callaway said, "And now he works for you until his debt is repaid."

"Yes," Carl replied.

"It's repaid as of now," Callaway said firmly.

"What do you mean?" Sandra shot back.

"I mean, you are done with your operation, and Frank doesn't owe you a penny." Callaway could see they were not too happy, but he wanted a commitment out of them. "Listen, I have to file a report to your employer regarding my investigation. If you don't want me to include what I've uncovered, then you'll do what I say. Do you understand?"

Carl looked at his wife and then nodded. "Yes, we understand."

***

Callaway walked back to the Impala.
"How'd it go?" Jimmy asked.
"They had no choice."

106

Jimmy smiled. "That's what I'm talking about. This calls for a drink."

"I like the sound of that."

Callaway started the engine.

They had driven around the block when Jimmy said, "Hold up."

Callaway braked. "What's going on?"

"I just remembered I gotta do something first," Jimmy replied. "Why don't you go ahead and I'll meet you later at the bar."

Callaway frowned. "Are you sure? I'll drive you if you want."

"Listen, kid," Jimmy said, getting out of the Impala, "I don't need a chaperone, okay?"

Callaway watched as he disappeared from view.

Callaway sighed and drove off.

FORTY-ONE

Fisher was in a brightly lit room inside the Milton Forensic Center. The room was painted white from top to bottom. The lights bounced off the white walls. She had to blink a few times to let her eyes adjust.

Two tables were in the middle of the room. On top of each were dummy heads made from synthetic latex material. Red liquid was splattered all around the heads.

Wakefield stood between the tables. She had on a white lab coat, which was now stained with red. She was also wearing gloves and protective goggles.

"Thank you for coming, Detective Fisher," Wakefield said. "The victim, Dillon Scott, showed signs of blunt force trauma, likely caused by a heavy object. With your help, we concluded it may have been inflicted using the bookend in the house. This led me to conduct several tests in order to recreate what may have happened. The angle of Mr. Scott's wound is in the middle of the head." She pointed to the dummy head on her right. "Mr. Scott is five feet, ten inches in height." She pressed a button on the side of the table, and the platform rose to the required height. She then held up what looked like a hammer. "I am around five feet, three inches, and when I swung the hammer down onto this head, the splatter of the blood on the wall does not match the trajectory of the blood found at the crime scene."

Fisher squinted, confused. "There was hardly any blood."

"Exactly!" Wakefield agreed. "I then conducted a detailed examination of Mr. Scott's wound. The angle and the depth of the wound makes me conclude that the attacker was not my height." She pointed to the dummy head on her left. "I raised myself up on a stool, which elevated me up to a height of over six feet. I then conducted the same experiment. Again, the blood splatter was not useful in this test, but the angle and the depth of the wound was a match." She turned to Fisher. "I am confident Mr. Scott's attacker was taller than him."

Fisher mulled this over. "So, we are looking for a man over six feet in height?"

Wakefield frowned. "I'm not certain."

"But you just said the wound matched up when you elevated yourself."

"It does, but the wound is not deep enough to have caused Mr. Scott's demise."

Fisher blinked. "So it's not death by blunt force trauma?"

Wakefield shook her head. "The wound is superficial. The force of the impact did not penetrate or crack the cranium. There was no damage whatsoever to the brain or any vital nerves."

"What are you saying?"

"I am now leaning toward the conclusion that the head wound only rendered Mr. Scott unconscious, but it was not the cause of his death."

"So what was?"

"At the moment, I'm not sure. By all observations, Mr. Scott looks healthy and in good shape. But I will conduct further testing before I can give you a definitive answer as to the cause of death."

Fisher could tell Wakefield was perplexed by her findings. Determining how someone died without all the necessary information was like solving a puzzle without all the pieces. Wakefield would not stop until she satisfied both her curiosity and her duty as a medical examiner.

Fisher thought of something. "When I asked if we should be looking for a man over six feet in height, you looked uncertain."

"A man of that size would have caused more damage," Wakefield replied.

Fisher's brow furrowed. "So, should we be looking for a woman instead?"

"I'm not certain of that either, but if you were looking for a woman, it would surely narrow your search."

She's right, Fisher thought. *There aren't a large number of women in Milton who are six feet tall.*

But until Wakefield gave her more to work with, Fisher was no closer to finding who had killed Dillon Scott.

FORTY-TWO

Callaway was already on his second drink. He was at a bar not far from his office. Next to him was an empty stool and a glass of whiskey for Jimmy on the counter. They were supposed to celebrate the conclusion of a case.

Callaway was confident that Sandra and Carl Wolkoff would honor their agreement. They would stop selling stolen goods, and they would forgive all of Frank's debts. If they didn't, Callaway would make a phone call to the police department in Michigan, and another phone call to the department store's main office. Not only would Sandra and Carl be charged for crimes in their home state, there would be additional charges in Milton as well.

While he was waiting for Jimmy, he had called Betty Henderson. He omitted certain details, like how Frank was selling stolen property. He would leave it to Frank to break that to her. He did tell her Frank was involved in a complicated situation, but that it was all behind him now. He would be back to being a devoted husband and a wonderful father.

The excitement in her voice made all the hard work worth it for him. In his line of work, he mostly chased adulterers, and when he completed the job, the clients were too heartbroken to be grateful for his findings. But every once in a while, he would get a case that had a happy ending.

Betty and Frank seemed like good people. The end of their marriage would have been a tragedy. For the kids, it would have been worse. Callaway was glad he was able to help.

He finished his glass and frowned. He had a feeling Jimmy was not going to show up. The man was known to disappear for days, weeks, months, or years.

He wasn't even sure what Jimmy was doing in Milton. He had a feeling Jimmy needed money, but so far, he had not asked him for anything. Maybe after he saw his office and the Impala, he realized Callaway was in a worse financial situation than him. On top of that, the job for Betty Henderson only paid five hundred dollars, and most of it was already spent.

Callaway sighed. He was looking forward to spending time with the man who had taught him so much about the profession.

As he ordered another drink, the door opened and Jimmy sauntered in. He had a wide smile on his face. He came over and took a seat next to him.

"Is that for me?" he said, grabbing the glass of whiskey.

"I've been waiting for almost an hour," Callaway said, sounding like a kid whose parent had forgotten to pick him up from school.

"Don't look at me like that," Jimmy said. "I had a good reason, okay?"

He pulled out an envelope and dropped it on the counter.

"What's that?" Callaway asked.

"Take a look."

Callaway held the envelope. It was thick and heavy. When he looked inside, his eyes widened.

"How much is it?" he asked.

Jimmy grinned. "Three grand."

"Where did it come from?"

"It's courtesy of Mr. and Mrs. Wolkoff."

Callaway blinked.

"After you dropped me off at the corner, I went back to the house, and with my badge in hand, I told them someone had reported them to the authorities. They probably figured it was you. They were sweating bullets. They begged me to take it easy, that it was a mistake and they would never do it again. I then offered them a solution."

Callaway looked at the envelope. "You took a bribe?" he asked, disgusted at the thought.

Jimmy grimaced. "Bribe is too harsh a word," he replied. "Let's call it restitution for their crimes."

Callaway shook his head. "I don't know, Jimmy. This is not right."

"What's not right is that they committed a crime and you let them off the hook."

"They forgave Frank's debt," Callaway corrected Jimmy.

"Sure, but how many times have you seen someone rob a bank, and when the police catch them, they just hand the money back and nothing happens to them? *Never*. The police retrieve the stolen cash, and they charge the robber with the crime."

"You're not even a real cop!" Callaway said.

"They don't know that."

Callaway knew arguing with Jimmy would do no good. He looked away.

"Okay," Jimmy said. "If you don't want the money, I'll take it."

"I never said that," Callaway replied, still gripping the envelope. He knew the Wolkoffs were felons and they deserved more than a slap on the wrist. He could also use the money. The five hundred was nowhere near enough for the work he had done for the Hendersons.

Callaway exhaled. "So we split it fifty-fifty like the old times?"

"Why don't you keep the whole thing?" Jimmy said.

Callaway's jaw nearly hit the counter. When it came to money, Jimmy was not very charitable. There were even instances where they had split the money fifty-fifty, only for Callaway to later find out that Jimmy had taken his cut prior to the split. "What's the catch?" he asked.

"No catch whatsoever," Jimmy replied. "It was your case, and you did most of the heavy lifting. I just piggybacked on your hard work."

Callaway nodded. He quickly put the money in his pocket before Jimmy changed his mind.

Jimmy raised his glass and said, "So, is this my drink, or were you waiting for someone else?"

FORTY-THREE

Fisher walked into the restaurant and looked around. She spotted the woman at one of the tables in the back. She walked up to her and they embraced.

Laura Meskin was tall, slender, and she had golden hair that reached down to her waist. Laura was Fisher's best friend, and she had seen men swoon over her like she was the only woman on earth. They had met in high school when they both tried out for the volleyball team. Fisher was shorter than the other players, and she was a little heavier as well, so she played the back middle. She was the team's middle blocker. Laura was always tall and lanky, so she played the outside hitter. She could spike the ball with so much ferocity that the opposing team's players were afraid of getting hit by one of her spiked balls.

After high school, Laura went to Columbia and then wrote her bar exam. She now practiced civil law for one of the oldest law firms in Milton. She even managed to settle down and marry a trial lawyer, and together they had two boys, aged four and six.

Whenever Fisher compared her life to Laura's, she couldn't help but feel like she had fallen behind. She was not the least bit jealous of Laura's success. She was happy for her. Laura was not the type of person to flaunt her accomplishments to anyone. She was well grounded, and she deeply cared about her family and friends.

"Sorry I'm late," Fisher said, taking a seat across from her.

"It's okay," Laura said. "While I was waiting for you, I could have been working for my clients and billing them for the hours."

Fisher stared at her.

Laura broke into a smile. "I'm just kidding, Dana. I'm so happy I finally got to have lunch with you."

"I really feel bad about the last time," Fisher said. A few months back, she had taken the day off. She had hoped to catch up on some reading, and she was also scheduled to meet Laura for lunch. When Holt's nephew was found brutally murdered, Fisher had to cancel all her plans and focus on the investigation.

"Don't worry about it," Laura said, waving off her apology. "I can't imagine doing what you do. The pressure must be intense."

Laura was the one person Fisher could be truly honest with. She never judged her, and she always had something encouraging to say about a situation. Laura became the sort of sister Fisher never had.

Fisher exhaled. "There are days when I don't know why I'm doing it."

Laura reached over and put her hand over hers. "You are doing it because it makes a difference. We all have a role to play in life, and yours is to find out who committed these horrible crimes."

"You should be a life coach, you know that?" Fisher said.

Laura smiled. "Sometimes I feel I am doing exactly that at my job."

"What do you mean?"

"I got tired of doing employment law, so now I focus on immigration law. It breaks my heart to see people living in this country who have not seen their wives, husbands, or children in years because they can't get US residency or they keep getting rejected when they try to sponsor them from their country of origin."

"You're one of the hardest working lawyers I know," Fisher said. "You will do everything to help your clients."

Laura laughed. "Okay, let's stop complimenting each other like we're strangers." She waved the waiter over and they ordered their meals. When the waiter was gone, Laura asked, "How's the Dillon Scott murder investigation going?"

Fisher's shoulders slumped. "I'm not making much progress, I'm afraid."

"Your partner is still on vacation?"

"He's back in a few days, and he can't wait to start working on the case."

"I know you were a big fan of Scott when we were younger," Laura said. "You had one of his movie posters on your bedroom wall."

"I did," Fisher said. "But if I remember correctly, you hated him."

Laura frowned. "Hate is such a strong word, but yeah, I didn't like him."

"Why not?"

"There was something in his eyes that I couldn't put my finger on," Laura replied. "It was like he was hiding a deep, dark secret."

Fisher giggled. "Of course he was hiding something. He's an actor. It's his job to become a different person for each role."

Their meals arrived and they dug in.

"So, tell me more about this Officer Lance McConnell," Laura said.

FORTY-FOUR

Becky had a textbook open on her bed. Next to the book was her binder and calculator. Becky hated doing accounting. She could not wrap her head around income statements, balance sheets, journal entries, trial balances—they all looked the same to her.

Her mom wanted her to do something practical. Her mom's sociology diploma had not gotten her anywhere in life. Her dad was not educated, so he had spent his entire life performing manual labor.

Whenever Becky complained about school, her mom scolded her. She would remind her that had her father gone further in school, he would probably be sitting behind a desk.

Becky knew what she was trying to say. The wall would not have collapsed on him, and he would still be alive.

Becky had thought the same thing a million times, but that still did not make learning how to adjust entries easy.

She heard the front door open and close. Her mom was home. She heard footsteps race up the stairs, followed by a knock at the door.

"Becky?" her mom said.

"Yes?"

"Can I come in, dear?"

"Sure, Mom."

Her mom rushed in. She still had her coat on, and her purse was still slung on her shoulder.

Becky's back arched. She sat up straight. "Is everything okay, Mom?" she asked, concerned.

Her mom sat at the foot of the bed. "Something strange happened today."

Becky felt a sharp pain in the pit of her stomach. "What?"

"I had some bills to pay, so I logged on to my bank account, and I saw that someone had deposited close to eighty thousand dollars into our account. After work, I went to our local branch and I told them they had made a mistake. They checked, and they said it wasn't a mistake."

"It's not, Mom," Becky said.

"What do you mean?" her mom asked, confused.

"After the insurance company and the construction company refused to take responsibility for Dad's death, I set up an online fundraising campaign."

"You did what?" her mom asked.

"I told people how they had screwed us and how tough it is for us. People started sharing their own stories of how their employers or their insurance companies screwed them. They then started donating to help us out. It was small at first, but then it started to grow, and at the end, it was a lot of money."

Her mom took this in. "Why didn't you tell me, baby?" she asked.

"I thought you would be mad."

"Why would I be?"

Becky shrugged. "I don't know."

Her mom leaned over and hugged her. "I can never be mad at you," she said.

Becky shut her eyes and thought, *I wish I could tell you the truth about the money and about everything else that is going on with me, but you would hate me if I did.*

"So, the money is ours?" her mom asked.

"Yes."

"We can keep it?" Her mom was still unsure.

"Yes, we can do whatever we want with it," Becky replied.

"I think we should buy a nice headstone for your dad's grave."

"That's a great idea!" Becky said. "I know exactly what to put on it."

FORTY-FIVE

Osman stood in an alley across from the crack house. He had been there for almost an hour. He was anxious and jittery. He had a joint in his hand. He never liked putting drugs into his body, but he needed something to calm him down. He took a slow toke and let the drug work its magic. He could feel the hit course through him, almost giving him renewed energy.

After his visit inside the house, he was left considering all his options. Tamara Davis was a loose end that needed to be closed. She knew too much, and she could expose him at the drop of a hat.

No matter what he did for her, she could not clean herself up. He rented her a nice place. He bought her nice clothes. He paid for her groceries. Still, the woman could not stay away from drugs.

Once a crackhead, always a crackhead, he thought.

There was a reason for taking care of her. She was the golden ticket to make all his problems go away.

She was not lying when she said she was his ATM. He was going to use her to squeeze as much money out of his target as possible. But that was before two days ago. Now everything had changed, and Tamara was of no use to him.

She was a time bomb waiting to explode. She would blurt out their secret just to get her next hit. And if she spoke to the wrong people, Osman and his partner were looking at spending the rest of their lives in prison.

You should have never trusted an addict, he thought.

But he had no choice. He needed her in case his target got any wild ideas or decided to go to the police, which Osman was certain he would never do. The blowback would be devastating for him.

With him out of the picture, it was time to make Tamara disappear.

He took a final toke, dropped the joint, and stubbed it out with the sole of his boot. He placed a ski mask over his face. He pulled on latex gloves and then raced through the side of the tattoo parlor and up the narrow stairs. He didn't even bother knocking. He could tell from his last visit that the locks on the door were weak. He put his weight into his shoulder and rammed it into the door. The wooden panel next to the door snapped into pieces.

He entered.

The same young man who had answered the door previously rushed at him. Osman hit him with his fist and knocked him out. The other addicts were too high to react. One or two glanced his way, but they said nothing.

He moved through the apartment and found Tamara where he had left her. She was slumped on the floor next to the bathtub. Her eyes were glazed, and there was drool coming out from the side of her mouth.

A syringe was stuck in her arm. Osman saw blood in it.

He knelt down beside her and waved his hand over her face. Her eyes did not react, but from the movement of her chest, he knew she was still alive.

He composed himself and then placed a gloved hand over her mouth and pinched her nose with the other. He was going to constrict airflow to her body. She didn't put up a fight. She was too high to know what was happening.

Suddenly her body began to spasm as it fought for air. She moaned, but he kept both his hands firmly in place.

He was not sure how much time passed, but eventually her chest stopped moving and her body went limp.

He removed his hands and waited. When he was certain she was dead, he got up and left the bathroom. On his way out, he saw the young man he had punched. He was still on the floor, unconscious.

Whenever the authorities arrived, they would think the young man was attacked by another addict, and when they checked up on Tamara, they would think she had died from an overdose.

She would become another homeless person who had died from her addiction.

FORTY-SIX

After celebrating with a couple of drinks for helping Frank Henderson, and also for earning three thousand as a bonus, Jimmy told Callaway the reason he was in Milton.

After making the call, they drove to the restaurant where Joely worked and waited for Fisher at a table in the far corner.

Jimmy rubbed his hands nervously as he stared out the window.

"Don't worry," Callaway assured him. "Dana will hear you out."

An SUV pulled into a parking spot and Fisher got out. She then entered the restaurant, spotted them, and came over.

Callaway stood up. "Detective Dana Fisher, this is Jimmy Keith."

Jimmy shook her hand. "Lee speaks highly of you," he said.

"Unfortunately, he never mentioned you," she said.

"I don't blame him. I'm sort of like an absent parent."

"I guess you two have something in common," Fisher said. She knew Callaway rarely saw his daughter, and she had scolded him about it numerous times. Fisher and Callaway had dated once, and Fisher always believed Callaway still held feelings for his ex-wife, even if he chose to bury them deep inside.

"Ouch, Dana," Callaway said. "You don't have to speak the truth."

"So what did you want to tell me?" she asked, getting to the point.

"Take a seat, please," Callaway replied. She sat on one side of the table; Callaway and Jimmy sat on the other. Callaway turned to Jimmy. "Okay, tell her what you told me."

Jimmy took a deep breath and said, "I was hired by Gail Roberts's family to investigate what happened to her."

Fisher's brow furrowed. "Why does that name sound familiar?"

"She died after falling from her apartment balcony."

"Oh, yes, I remember. They said it was suicide."

"Her family doesn't believe it was."

"Okay," Fisher said.

"Gail was also Dillon Scott's personal assistant at the time of her death."

Fisher paused. "And you think he had something to do with what happened to her?"

"I'm not sure," Jimmy replied. "But he does have an alibi for the night of her death. He was shooting a movie in Vermont."

"Okay, so?"

"A few days before her death, Gail had confessed to her father that something was bothering her. She was torn about what to do. He pressed her for details, but she wouldn't say. She did mention it had to do with Dillon Scott. Like any father, he told her to follow her conscience."

"I still don't understand what this has to do with Scott if he had an alibi."

"Gail then told her father that she was going to make an announcement. She died the night before she was going to do this."

Fisher opened her mouth but then shut it. "So what are you doing in Milton now that Scott is dead?" she asked a few moments later.

"I want to know if you found anything that might link Gail's death to Scott's death," Jimmy replied.

"What would that prove?"

"It would prove Gail didn't commit suicide."

"And that she was murdered?" Fisher added.

Jimmy was about to say something but then decided against it.

Fisher said, "Listen, I understand you have a responsibility to Gail Roberts's family. They don't want to believe their daughter would take her own life. But if the investigators have concluded it was a suicide, then what good would it do to drag another person's name through the mud?"

Callaway sensed Fisher's defensiveness. He said, "We are not insinuating anything about Scott. We just want answers."

"So do I," Fisher shot back. "I have a beloved actor who was murdered in my city. Everyone is expecting me to find out who did it. I don't have the time to look into how this links to Gail Roberts's death."

"That's why we want to help you in your investigation," Callaway said.

"What?"

"We should work together. With Holt away, I'm sure you could use an extra pair of eyes and hands."

"I don't know," she said, shaking her head. "Let me think about it."

She got up and walked to the door.

Callaway caught up to her. "Dana…"

"Do you trust him?" she asked.

"Jimmy?"

"Yes."

"I do," he replied firmly. "If it wasn't for him, I wouldn't have become a private investigator."

Fisher gave him a look. "So he's the reason you quit being a deputy sheriff?"

"No, wait, I was going to leave anyway," he quickly backtracked. "What I'm saying is that Jimmy is one of the best PIs out there. He's actually one of the good ones."

"Coming from you, isn't that a biased opinion?"

"Don't take my word for it," he said. "Do your own research and find out."

"I looked him up the moment you mentioned his name," she replied, "and he's legit."

"I told you," Callaway said with a smile. "Come on, you've got nothing to lose."

She sighed. "Holt would be furious if he found out I was sharing information on an active investigation."

"Holt's head would explode if he found out you were discussing it with *me*," Callaway said.

"You're not helping."

"Sorry."

They went back to the table and sat down. Fisher said, "What I tell you should not leave this table."

"Understood," Jimmy said.

"Absolutely," Callaway added.

She spent twenty minutes filling them in on what she had found so far. At the end, Callaway said, "And you believe Scott went to Yonge Avenue to meet someone?"

"Yes," Fisher replied.

"And you don't know why?"

"I don't, but I intend to go back to Yonge Avenue and find out."

"In the meantime," Callaway said, "we'll see what we can uncover on Gail's death and if it links to Scott's. We'll let you know what we find."

FORTY-SEVEN

After Fisher left, Jimmy asked, "What do you want to do first?"

"There was something I wanted to do the moment you gave me the money," Callaway replied.

"Like what?"

"I'll show you."

They got in the Impala and drove straight to Julio's shop. They found Julio working underneath a red Corvette. He stood up, wiped his greasy hands on a piece of cloth, and said, "Lee, I have no jobs for you today."

"I'm actually here for the Charger," Callaway said.

Julio paused. "You know I can't let you take it without settling the bill, right?"

Callaway pulled out the envelope, removed a stack of hundreds, and handed it to Julio. "That should cover it."

Julio counted the money. A smile broke across his face. He escorted them to the corner of the shop. "I even polished and waxed it just for you," he said.

The car glistened under the fluorescent lights. Callaway had to admit, the Charger looked far better now than it did before it was damaged. Julio had taken extra care of it, just like he promised.

"This is Jimmy Keith," Callaway said, introducing the two.

"Nice place you got here," Jimmy said. He then pulled out his business card. "If you ever need information on your competition, you give me a call."

Julio took the card and said, "Lee said the same thing to me the last time he was here."

Jimmy smiled. "Great minds think alike."

Callaway got in the driver's seat. He placed his hands on the steering wheel. He inhaled. Even the interior smelled like new.

While he was learning the ropes with Jimmy, a case came through that Jimmy thought Callaway should take on alone. It was a simple case. A client wanted dirt on her cheating husband. They were in the process of a messy divorce, and she wanted a leg up on him. Callaway spent weeks tailing the husband. He found that the husband was not with one but three mistresses. He also caught the husband removing furniture and valuables from a property the court had frozen until all assets were accounted for. The information Callaway provided enabled the client to get a generous divorce settlement. The client's husband was a collector of cars. His garage was filled with some of the rarest automobiles on the planet. The wife despised the collection. Her husband was known to spend more time with them than with her. For a job well done, she offered Callaway his choice of any car. Callaway could have taken a Lamborghini, a Maserati, or even a McLaren, but he selected a car that was relegated to the back of the garage.

The Dodge Charger spoke to him, like it was made for him. Jimmy was livid when he heard Callaway had opted to choose the Charger over the likes of a Maserati, but Callaway didn't care. He knew he would end up selling a fancy car, but the Charger he would keep for life.

He turned the ignition. The Charger roared to life. He revved it a few times, and he could feel the power.

"You like the sound?" Julio asked over the noise.

"I love it. Thanks, Julio."

Jimmy got in the passenger seat and they drove out of the shop. When they were on the road, Jimmy asked, "You got any money left over?"

"Yeah, sure, about a grand."

Jimmy smiled. "We did something for you. Now why don't we do something for me?"

"What do you have in mind?"

FORTY-EIGHT

Fisher walked down the street and frowned. She was at Yonge Avenue, and she had already knocked on a dozen doors. She showed a photo of Dillon Scott to the owners and employees of each establishment. They all knew who Scott was. They just didn't remember seeing him on the night of his death.

She had considered requesting that patrol officers canvas the area, but she wasn't sure what Scott's visit to Yonge Avenue had to do with his murder.

What if he was here to shop? she thought. The street had a nice collection of businesses, and tourists were known to visit here.

She felt a headache coming on. She was hoping someone had seen him and could help fill in the blanks for her—the biggest blank being the time he left his home and the time he returned.

Why did he leave in the first place? Who was he meeting? Did this person ultimately murder Scott?

She made her way back to her SUV. She passed a bar she had parked in front of the last time she was here, but she remembered it was closed at the time.

She decided to go inside. She found the bartender behind the counter. He was a short man with wrinkles all over his hands and face. His eyes were dull and gray. "What can I get you, little lady?" he asked.

She flashed her badge. "I'm on duty, but I got a question for you."

"I hope I got the right answer for you," he said with a smile.

She held up Scott's photo. "Did you by any chance see this man in your bar?"

"I sure did."

Fisher arched an eyebrow. "You did?"

"Yeah, he came in wearing these large sunglasses, but the moment he ordered a drink, I knew who he was."

"What did he order?" Fisher asked, curious.

"Gin and tonic."

"And how long was he here?"

"Twenty minutes, I guess. He sat at the end of the bar, all the way in the corner. He spoke to a woman. He then got up and left."

Was this woman the person Scott was here to meet? she thought.

"You have security cameras?" she asked.

"Of course I do. I'd be stupid not to. You gotta take security seriously these days. And I even have a shotgun under the counter. And before you ask, I've got my firearm license over there." He pointed to a photo frame on the wall behind him. "I thought I'd put it up so that people would know I'm armed and ready to defend what's mine."

"Okay," Fisher said. "Can you show me the footage?"

He took her to a small windowless room. Bankers Boxes lined the walls. They likely contained invoices and documents. In the middle of the room was a table with a keyboard and monitor on it. "The system is easy to use," the bar owner said. "You punch in the time and date, and it will show you what you want to see. It's all saved on the cloud, so you can go back at least a month."

"You're not staying?" she asked.

"I'm the only one in today. One of my employees is sick, so I had to get someone else to come in at the last minute. They're on their way, but until then, someone's gotta serve the customers. Don't worry, if you get stuck, come to the front and let me know."

"Thanks," she said, taking a seat.

She played with the controls. The owner was right; the system was easy to navigate. The taxi receipt had said 7:20 PM. It was reasonable to assume that upon arriving at Yonge Avenue, Scott may have gone straight to the bar to meet whoever he was here to meet. She hoped it was the woman the owner had mentioned.

She punched in the time and date and watched the image on the screen instantly change. The camera was placed behind the counter with a panoramic view of the entire establishment. The image was black and white with no audio, but it was sharp and high-quality.

The owner was behind the counter. Two people were seated by the bar with drinks in front of them. A girl wearing an apron was taking drinks to a couple at a table by the windows.

She must be the employee the owner was talking about, Fisher thought.

Fisher waited eagerly for Scott to enter. As the clock ticked to seven forty-five, she got the feeling Scott had not come directly to the bar as she had initially thought.

She fast-forwarded the footage. People zoomed past the camera at high speeds. At precisely eight thirty-four, Scott appeared on the screen.

She played the footage at normal speed.

Scott made his way to the bar, spoke to the owner, and then moved to the far end.

Even though he was farther away, she could see he still had on his sunglasses, just as the owner said. His drink arrived and he gulped it down in one breath. His chin dropped to his chest, and he moved his hand through his hair. The movement reminded Fisher of someone who was under a lot of stress.

She squinted at the screen. On the taxi CCTV camera, she had clearly seen Scott carrying a backpack, but now it was not with him.

"What did you do with it?" she muttered to herself.

A woman approached Scott. They exchanged a few words. She then sat next to him on a stool and they began to talk. Their conversation lasted not even five minutes before he abruptly got up, said something to her, and stormed out of the bar.

Fisher wished she knew what was said, but it didn't matter.

She knew who the woman was, and she knew where to find her.

FORTY-NINE

Callaway and Jimmy were at a table at the Woodbine Racetrack. Callaway had his head buried in his drink. Jimmy, on the other hand, had a smile on his face.

"I can't believe we lost over a grand," Callaway said.

Jimmy slapped him on the back. "Come on, kid. Don't tell me you've lost your nerve? We used to lose more than that on a single horse."

"Yeah, sure, but it's still a lot of money."

"We'll find a way to get it back, Lee," Jimmy said.

Callaway took a deep breath and then exhaled.

"We always bounce back, don't we?" Jimmy added.

"I'm not so sure anymore."

"We're survivors, kid. We'll be fine."

Callaway took a sip from his glass. "I'm thinking of quitting, Jimmy."

"I don't blame you. The last across-the-board wager was a terrible choice. Our horse was dead last."

"I don't mean the race."

Jimmy stared at him. "Then what?"

"I'm thinking of shutting down the PI business."

"Why would you do that?"

"Things have been really slow, and I'm tired of always hustling for new cases. People no longer value the service we provide."

"Let me tell you something, Lee," Jimmy said. "They've *never* valued it, ever. You know why? Because they don't know what we can do for them. They think just because we don't have a badge, we can't solve a mystery. We can and we do. This gig is like any business. It has its ups and downs. When things go well, you have a great time. When they don't, it's not much fun."

"That's what I'm talking about. I'm not sure how long I can keep looking forward to the good times. Even when they do come, they don't last for long. I mean, until I got the Frank Henderson job, I had not had a case in almost a month. That's a long time to be without work."

Jimmy nodded. "If you quit, then what would you do?" he asked.

"I have no idea," Callaway admitted. "My last long-term job was as a deputy sheriff, and that was years ago."

Jimmy leaned closer and put his hand on Callaway's shoulder. "If you've already made up your mind, then I'm not going to try to convince you to change it. What I will say is that *you* are made for this business, kid. You have a knack for it that most people don't. Believe me, I've met quite a few people who think this gig is about sitting in your car, taking photos, and getting paid. It's more than that. It requires a ton of patience, knowing where to be and when, and also knowing when to show your cards and when to fold them."

Callaway understood what he meant by the last statement. He had the discretion to withhold information if he felt it necessary. He did that when it involved a woman named Elle Pearson.

They sipped their drinks in silence.

Jimmy stuck his hand in his pocket and pulled out a crumpled piece of paper. When he smoothed it out, he said, "Hey, look what I found."

"Is that a hundred-dollar bill?" Callaway asked, surprised.

Jimmy grinned. "You feeling lucky, kid?"

"Um... I think maybe we should call it a night."

"Don't be a wimp," Jimmy said, getting up from his chair. "This is a sign from Heaven. It's telling us we can win back all that we lost tonight."

Callaway wasn't sure, but Jimmy's enthusiasm was infectious. "All right, one last wager, okay?"

Jimmy laughed. "That's the Lee Callaway I know!"

FIFTY

Becky got off the bus and walked the two blocks to her house. When she opened the door, she said, "Mom, I'm home!"

She could tell from the lights inside the house that her mom had returned from work. She found her at the dining table.

"How was the clinic?" her mom asked.

Becky worked at the veterinary clinic. It had started off as a volunteer position, but after her dad died, the veterinarian turned it into a paying position. It was only part-time, but it helped cover a bit of the mortgage.

Becky headed straight for the fridge and scanned for something to eat. "I'm starving," she said.

Her mom pointed to a pot on the counter. "There's beef stew for dinner. You can warm up however much you like."

Becky filled her bowl to the top and then nuked it in the microwave. She said, "A Good Samaritan brought in a stray dog. The poor thing was malnourished, and it looked like someone had abused it."

"Oh my god," her mom said.

"We took it in, of course, and we put it on IV fluids so that it could regain its strength." The microwave beeped. Becky grabbed a spoon and dove into the bowl. She then went over to the dining table and sat next to her mom. "What're you looking at?" she asked with a mouthful of stew.

"It's just some brochures."

Becky made a face. "What kind of brochures?"

"I was thinking, now that we've had this good luck, why don't we think about what school you want to go to when you graduate high school?"

"Mom, I still have another year to go."

"But your dad—"

Becky put her hand up. "I know, Mom. Dad never got the chance to go to college because Grandma came down with leukemia…"

"…and your grandfather had abandoned them when your dad was still a baby. Don't forget that," her mom said.

Becky was quiet.

"Honey," her mom said in a soothing voice, "your grandmother raised your father on her own. When she fell ill, your father dropped out of school to take care of her and run the house."

Becky exhaled. "You've told me this story a dozen times. I know it by heart now."

"What you don't know is that these brochures were ordered by your dad *before* you even went to high school."

Becky looked away.

"I know you have your heart set on becoming a vet," her mom said, "but you should also look at other professions."

"But I like animals," she said.

"Just think about it." Her mom held up a brochure. "You can go to Harvard, Yale, or Stanford. We have the money to pay for a better education."

"I'm going to my room. Good night, Mom."

She stormed upstairs, taking the bowl of stew with her.

FIFTY-ONE

The tower rose five hundred feet into the sky. The exterior was covered in bronze glass consisting of more than twelve thousand windows. Each pane had cost over a hundred dollars at the time of the building's construction. From a distance, it looked like a gold bar that was specifically brought over from Fort Knox.

The lobby had twenty-five-foot-high ceilings, brown stone marble floors, and light strategically placed to give it a regal feel.

Fisher sat in the waiting area. There were two sofas and one chair. Across from her was a young man dressed in a suit with a folder on his lap. He looked anxious and excited. He was likely here for a job interview.

Her theory turned out to be right when a woman appeared from the elevator a minute later. She was wearing a blouse, skirt, and high heels. She approached the man, shook his hand, and then escorted him to the elevator. They then disappeared from view.

Fisher checked her watch but made no comment. She was here on short notice.

The elevator doors opened. A woman came out and approached her. "I'm so sorry to keep you waiting, Detective Fisher," she said.

She was young, attractive, and wearing a white top and blue jeans. Her name was Cameron Kilgane, and she was a reporter for the *Milton Morning* newspaper.

"I had an important call to take," Cameron said, "and it went longer than I had hoped."

"That's all right," Fisher said.

"So, why does someone from the Milton PD want to speak to me?" Cameron asked.

"It's about Dillon Scott."

Cameron's face narrowed. "Okay."

"The night before Mr. Scott was found dead, he had gone to a bar on Yonge Avenue, and he had spoken to you there."

"How did you find that out?" Cameron asked, surprised.

"The bar has CCTV cameras, so there is footage of you together."

"Oh, right, of course." She rubbed her forehead. "Yes, we did speak, but it was brief."

"Why didn't you come forward with this information?" Fisher asked.

"I didn't see the need to."

"Mr. Scott was found dead only a few hours later."

"If you think I had something to do with it, then you're wrong."

"How can I be sure?"

"If you saw the footage, you'll see that after Dillon Scott had left the bar, I was still there for another hour."

"Was he there to meet you?" Fisher asked.

Cameron looked confused. "Was that the reason he was at Yonge Avenue?"

Like any good reporter, Cameron was now prodding *Fisher* for information. Fisher said, "I was hoping you would tell me."

"I was surprised to see him at the bar. It's not every day you bump into movie stars in Milton."

"If you don't mind me asking, what were you doing at the bar?"

"I was at Yonge Avenue covering the premier of a new film. Afterwards, I decided to go to the bar to type up my story for the morning edition. It was then that I saw Dillon Scott, and I decided to approach him."

"What did you talk about?" Fisher asked.

"I'm not at liberty to say."

"Is that why Mr. Scott stormed off?"

Cameron looked away. "I asked him a few questions, and he didn't want to answer them."

"What kind of questions?"

"Again, I can't say."

"You *can't* say, or you *won't*?"

FIFTY-TWO

Cameron gave Fisher a hard look. She then relaxed and said, "Listen, I'm working on a major story, and I don't want it to leak, okay?"

"If it has something to do with Mr. Scott, then I doubt you have a major story."

"What do you mean?"

"I mean, if you did, it would already be on the front pages of today's newspaper. Dillon Scott is dead, and there is no better time to write something explosive about him than now."

"Fair enough," Cameron said. She crossed her arms over her chest. "How about this? I tell you what I know, and the moment you break this case, I will be the first one to know about it."

Fisher considered Cameron's proposal. "Okay, agreed."

Cameron said, "I have a popular online celebrity column that is read by over half a million people daily. It's not your typical gossip column. Instead of focusing on the glitz and glamour, I like to focus on the dirty aspects of Hollywood. Actors behaving badly. Directors fighting with studio heads. Production crews being mistreated."

"I've read your column," Fisher said. "That's how I recognized you."

Cameron was surprised that a homicide detective was interested in her stories. She then said, "About a year ago, I received a call. The caller ID was blocked and the voice was muffled, so I couldn't tell if it was a man or a woman, but the caller said they had information on Dillon Scott that was potentially damaging to him."

"What kind of information?"

"Before I could ask, the caller hung up," Cameron replied. "I waited for another call, but I never got one. After that, I began looking deeper into him."

"And what did you find?" Fisher asked.

Cameron fell silent.

"If you expect me to tell you about a major break in the case, then I expect something in return."

"Okay, sure. In my investigation of Scott, I found out that someone might have been blackmailing him."

"Blackmailing him?" Fisher repeated to make sure she heard correctly.

"Yes."

"How do you know this?"

"I had a source."

"You have to give me more than that."

"All right. About six months ago, during the shooting of another movie, Scott had his driver take him to a dozen ATM machines. The driver believes Scott withdrew a lot of money."

"How can the driver be sure?"

"Scott was carrying a duffel bag with him. The driver could tell it was heavy. Scott then had the driver take him to a location where the driver swears he saw Scott leave the bag under a park bench. He then asked the driver to drive away."

Fisher mulled this over. Scott was seen with a backpack when he had taken the taxi to Yonge Avenue. At the bar an hour later, he no longer had the bag.

Did the bag contain money Scott had withdrawn from his bank account? And was Scott meeting his blackmailer on the night of his death?

Fisher was hoping for answers when she came here. She got some, but now she had even more questions.

She suddenly realized Scott's murder could be more complicated than she first thought.

FIFTY-THREE

Osman walked back to his apartment building, feeling less jittery than before. After running out of the crack house, he hid in a dark strip club. He was shaking when he had ordered his first drink, but after his fourth, his hand became steadier.

He had never taken another person's life. He was not a murderer. He even hated being a drug dealer.

Tamara had to go. She had become a liability. Her death was not a tragedy, though. The woman was killing herself by injecting poison into her veins. Osman had tried to put her on the right path. He paid for all her basic needs. But her needs were darker. They were not going to be satisfied until she got her next hit.

I put her out of her misery, he told himself. *If I had not done what I did, she would have died a slow and debilitating death.*

Addicts were lucky if they overdosed. What awaited them after years of abuse was a life where they had no idea who they were, where they were, or what they were supposed to be doing with themselves. They wandered the streets aimlessly, like zombies. Or worse yet, they were confined to a bed in a vegetative state, their mental faculties forever destroyed by their drug of choice.

Even so, he would have to live with the fact that he killed someone.

Just because he worked at the fringes of society, it didn't mean he was a bad person. There was a demand for drugs, and he merely provided the supply. It was economics 101.

He was raised by a single mother who had her first child when she was sixteen. By the time she was twenty, she'd had four kids by four different men.

Osman was the youngest, which meant he had to fight his older siblings for scraps. All his clothes were hand-me-downs, and *if* there was food on the table, he would be lucky if he got enough to eat. His mother would try to make sure he was taken care of, but she had a lot on her plate. He never blamed his mother for what he didn't have. She herself was raised by a single mother, and she had a dozen siblings.

Osman had hoped to break the cycle. He was going to make something of himself. He was going to get an education. But society saw that he never lived up to his potential. He was marginalized and discriminated against because of his skin color. When his older brother was shot and killed by a police officer for refusing to obey his commands, Osman decided he was not going to live a straight life. There were different rules for different people, and he was not going to follow those rules.

He took the elevator up to his one-bedroom apartment. He entered his place and walked straight to the bathroom. He got on top of the toilet and pushed aside a panel in the ceiling.

He slowly and carefully pulled out a backpack. He put the bag on the bathroom sink and unzipped it. Inside were stacks of hundred-dollar bills. He lifted a bundle and sniffed it. The smell of money was the greatest thing in the world. It was his drug of choice—his aphrodisiac. With money, anything was possible.

He had counted the money the moment he brought it to his apartment, and now he would count it again. After doing so, he split the money in two. He placed his share back in the backpack and put it back inside the ceiling panel.

He then wrapped the other half in cellophane. When he was finished, the stack was thick and bulky, but it was watertight.

He pulled out a disposable phone and speed-dialed a number. He let it ring a few times and then hung up. The recipient on the other end would call him back. He always did.

Osman needed to speak to him. He had to tell him where to pick up the money, and also to inform him that their golden ticket had to be silenced.

FIFTY-FOUR

Callaway was working away on his laptop when Jimmy stirred on the bed. The night before, after their trip to the racetrack, Callaway had to carry Jimmy up to his hotel room. Jimmy had one too many drinks. He was drunk to the point of passing out.

I am in bad shape, Callaway kept thinking as he took each step. Jimmy was heavy, and he reeked of alcohol. Callaway had been around drunks before, so he was used to the smell, but it didn't help that Jimmy burped in his face every so often.

Jimmy was also muttering incoherently. He was apologizing for something—Callaway was not sure what. Then he was crying. He would suddenly show a spark of anger, but it was quickly overtaken by more crying.

Jimmy was a sad drunk. Behind his bravado and life-is-about-having-fun attitude lay a mountain of guilt and remorse. These feelings simmered underneath the surface, appearing during moments of weakness, which usually happened when he drank.

Callaway felt sorry for him, but he would never let Jimmy know. The old man would be furious with him. Jimmy was old school, and he did not want anyone's pity.

Callaway had somehow managed to make it to the room. Jimmy was snoring the moment his head hit the pillow. Callaway had grabbed a bottle of water from the fridge and sat down on the chair, feeling exhausted. He was soaked in sweat, and he quenched his thirst. He shut his eyes, and within minutes he was passed out.

When he awoke, he was still wearing his clothes from the night before, and Jimmy was still snoring on the bed. He had decided to use the quiet time to catch up on some reading.

He was scrolling through his laptop when Jimmy suddenly sat up. His eyes were wide as he took in his surroundings.

"Where am I?" he yelled. "And why am I still dressed?"

"You're not in some woman's bed," Callaway said. "You're in my hotel room."

"Oh," Jimmy said. "How did I get here?"

"I hired some guys to carry you."

"You did?"

"Of course not. I brought you here myself. You have to lose a few pounds, man. Better yet, lose a few hundred pounds while you're at it."

Jimmy rubbed his belly. "I would gladly, but the ladies love it."

"I'm sure they do," Callaway said with a small chuckle.

Jimmy shut his eyes as a sharp pain shot through his head. "At the racetrack, did we win that last bet?" he asked as he opened his eyes.

"No, we lost."

Jimmy frowned. "I was certain Churchill Down was a winner."

"It didn't even finish the race," Callaway noted.

"What're you working on?" Jimmy asked.

"I was reading up on your case. The night Gail Roberts died, there was a witness at the scene. He said he saw a woman run out of the apartment building Gail had fallen from."

"I looked into it, but I couldn't find this woman. It was like she disappeared into thin air."

Jimmy got up and stretched. He winced. "I used to be able to spend the entire night partying and still be ready for work the next morning."

"I know, I've seen you do it. By the way, when we were driving back, your phone was ringing off the hook."

"Was it?" Jimmy asked, surprised.

"Yeah, I didn't answer it, but it looked like someone was looking for you."

Jimmy grinned. "It could have been a woman. You know they can't live without me."

"They can't live *with* you, either," Callaway shot back.

"Funny guy." He shoved his hand in his pants pocket and pulled out his cell phone. "I'll take it in the bathroom," he said as he shut the bathroom door behind him.

FIFTY-FIVE

Fisher's conversation with Cameron Kilgane had left her with another puzzle to solve.

Cameron's sources believed someone was blackmailing Scott. While filming his last movie, he had withdrawn money from several ATMs and then left a duffel bag under a park bench.

Fisher had done an online search, and she found there was a small park next to Yonge Avenue. A narrow path cut through the street and into the park, which was built by a property developer as a green space for the residents of a nearby condo.

Could Scott have been meeting his blackmailer at that park? She had a strong inclination he was. She then had to confirm if Scott had withdrawn any money on that day.

It took her several calls to various banks. She could have driven to their main locations, but it would have taken time. She needed the information right away.

One bank gave her a hard time, while the others were more than willing to accommodate her request. She was eventually able to persuade the reluctant bank that it would be in their best interest to comply. It would be bad publicity for a detective to show up at their main office demanding information.

As she went through Scott's bank statements, she saw no large withdrawals on the day he was murdered, or any preceding days.

Then how did he get the money? she thought.

She did notice something while going through the statements, though. Scott's finances were a mess. He had no savings, and his checking account was close to nil. It looked like he was living off a large overdraft and a line of credit.

Scott once commanded a hefty salary, but those years were behind him. His last hit movie was over five years ago. Even then, it seemed like he was maintaining a lifestyle that did not reflect this change of stature. He was spending more than he was taking in. A lot more.

His monthly credit card bill was more than half a year's salary. There were amounts for expensive clothes, luxury trips, fine dining, liquor—the list went on. Then there were the extravagant purchases he made over the years. A brand-new Ferrari, a house in the Hamptons, an ultra-modern speed boat, not to mention a Picasso from an art auction.

Fisher could not help but think Scott was trying to give off the impression of success, while in reality, he was drowning in debt.

Her phone buzzed. When she saw the number, she decided to let it go to voicemail. It was the third call from the same number, even though it was still early in the morning.

She waited a minute before checking her voicemail. The first two messages were short. "It's Holt. Call me." The last one was interesting. "Hey Fisher, you have to get me out of here. I'm bored out of my mind. I can't listen to another person tell me how much they love this job. I love it too, don't get me wrong, but you don't hear me talk like some angel came down from the sky and chose me to be a detective."

Fisher chuckled. Holt was not known for his sense of humor, so she knew he was genuinely frustrated at the conference.

He said, "You got any leads on the Dillon Scott case? I've been reading up on it in my spare time. I've got some theories I think might help you solve it. If I catch the red-eye, I can be there later tonight. Call me, okay?"

She smiled and pressed Delete."

FIFTY-SIX

They were seated at the back of the restaurant. Jimmy wore dark sunglasses, but even then, the light bothered his eyes. He took a sip of coffee and made a face. "Damn, it's bitter."

"I asked Joely to brew it fresh," Callaway said.

"It's strong."

"Stop acting like a baby and drink it up. It's the best remedy for your hangover."

"I don't get hangovers," Jimmy corrected him. "I can hold my liquor, okay?"

"The only thing holding you up last night was *me*."

Jimmy brushed the quip off. "We had a great time, did we not?"

"We did," Callaway agreed.

They had blown through most of the money Jimmy had gotten from the Wolkoffs, but there was still some left over for a good breakfast. Callaway munched on waffles, eggs, and hash browns.

"You ever think about slowing down?" Callaway asked, concerned.

"Why? I'm still young."

"If you say so. But do you remember what happened to Walter MacTavish?"

Walter and Jimmy had entered the PI business at the same time. They even shared an office together and helped each other on cases. Walter fully embodied the spirit of live-fast-and-die-young. He was forty-two when they found his body in his home. It was the dead of winter, and he had forgotten to turn on the heating. One day, after having way too much to drink, he passed out on the floor. He eventually died from hypothermia.

"Walter was a good guy," Jimmy slowly said.

"He was," Callaway agreed.

Joely came over and refilled their cups with coffee. "Let me know if you guys need anything," she said.

When she walked away, Jimmy asked, "You make a move on her?"

"I did, but she turned me down," Callaway replied.

"You think I should give it a try?"

Callaway scoffed. "She's young enough to be your daughter."

"Never stopped me before," Jimmy said with a grin.

"She's a good girl. She's got a young kid. Leave her alone."

"Okay, okay, take it easy." Jimmy took another sip of coffee, grimaced, and said, "You ever think about having your own family?"

"You know I had a family once. I realized I'm not marriage material."

"Sure, but you can always be father material."

Callaway stared at him. "Is it the alcohol that's making you talk this way?"

"I mean, as you get older, you kind of start looking at your life differently."

"It sounds like you're getting soft in old age."

"What I'm trying to say is that you can't live your whole life alone."

"I thought you always said that in our line of work, family was extra baggage?"

"I did, but our work can't be all we have in our lives."

Callaway blinked. "Now you're scaring me, Jimmy. You sure you didn't hit your head somewhere? You've done it before."

Jimmy smiled. "You're right. I'm talking nonsense."

Callaway went back to his meal for a moment. "I spoke to Dana," he said.

"Detective Fisher?"

"When you were in the bathroom, she called me. She believes someone was blackmailing Dillon Scott."

"They were?" Jimmy asked, surprised.

"You didn't know?"

"No, I had no idea. It never came up in my investigation." Jimmy paused for a moment. "Did she say why they were blackmailing him?"

"She has no clue," Callaway replied, "and that's why I think we should look into it."

Jimmy shook his head. "It might be better if we focus on Gail."

144

"What if everything is linked somehow?"

"What do you mean?"

"I mean, what if Gail Roberts's death is tied to the person who was blackmailing Scott?"

Jimmy thought for a moment. "The blackmail will only distract us from our goal, and that is to find out how Gail died. If we solve that, we just might be able to solve the remaining mysteries."

FIFTY-SEVEN

Fisher watched the CCTV footage from the taxi again. Scott was clutching the backpack like it contained something precious to him. She believed it was a large sum of money—something Scott's bank statements indicated he had very little of.

So where did he get the money? She had made a call to David Gill, the limo driver, and was waiting to hear back.

In the meantime, the taxi footage answered a lingering question: Why didn't Scott just have Gill take him to Yonge Avenue instead of taking a taxi?

The answer was simple: Scott did not want his actions leaking to the press. He was likely aware of what had happened during the last movie shoot, where the driver was suspicious of him leaving a duffel bag under a park bench. Scott figured by taking the taxi, he would leave no traces of where he was going and why.

The blackmail may be the motive she was searching for. What if Scott was not able to meet all the blackmailer's demands? What if the blackmailer later decided to teach Scott a lesson?

There were so many what-ifs, but they were all she had to go on at the moment.

Her cell phone buzzed. It was David Gill.

"Mr. Gill, I know you're busy, but I have a few questions to ask you," she said.

"Um... okay, sure," Gill replied.

"You said you had picked up Mr. Scott from the airport."

"I did."

"And when you did, do you remember what luggage he brought with him?"

Gill paused for a moment. "He had two large pieces of luggage."

Fisher remembered seeing them in the bedroom.

"He was holding a hand-carry and..."

Fisher's back arched.

"I think he also had a backpack with him."

"A backpack?" she repeated in case she didn't hear correctly.

146

"Yes. It was blue. I put the two pieces of luggage and the hand-carry in the trunk, but Mr. Scott wanted to keep the backpack with him."

"Was he holding it tightly?"

Gill paused again. "I'm not sure, but I can tell you that he did not let me touch it once, even when I unloaded the rest of the luggage and carried it into the house."

Fisher mulled this over. "Okay, one more question."

"Sure."

"Mr. Scott arrived in Milton two days ago. During this time, did he ask you to take him to a bank or an ATM machine?"

"No, never," Gill quickly replied. "For the past two days, I've taken Mr. Scott straight to the studio from his home, and then back. He never asked me to take him anywhere else."

"Thank you."

Fisher hung up and leaned back in her chair. She now had a better idea of why Scott was at Yonge Avenue, but she still didn't know who he was meeting.

FIFTY-EIGHT

"Tell me more about Gail Roberts," Callaway said. They were still at the restaurant. Callaway was done with breakfast. Jimmy had ordered a boiled egg and more coffee.

"What would you like to know?" Jimmy asked.

"How did she get involved with Dillon Scott?"

"His previous assistant had abruptly quit, and Scott's agent had hired Gail to replace her."

"Why did the previous assistant quit?"

"I spoke to her on the phone, and she said she wanted to go back to school and finish her degree in communications."

"What did she have to say about Scott? I mean, what kind of a boss was he?"

"She found him pleasant, albeit a little demanding. But he was a big star when she worked for him, so he was under a lot of stress."

Callaway mulled this over. "What was Gail like?"

"I spoke to her friends and family, and they all said she was caring, pleasant, and outgoing."

"Was she suicidal?" Callaway asked.

"Absolutely not," Jimmy replied. "On the day she died, she had gone out with her friends, and not one of them is convinced she committed suicide. She was stressed about something, but she was not depressed."

"What was she stressed about?"

"They don't know, but they said she was thinking about doing something else with her life. She had aspirations to be a writer."

Callaway raised his eyebrows. "Writer?"

Jimmy nodded. "She had started work on a novel when she was in college, but she didn't finish it. She figured she needed more life experience before she could write the great American novel. After leaving her job, she was hoping to pick up the novel from where she had left off."

Callaway looked down at the table. He then looked up. "The authorities believe her death could also have been an accident. Why are you so sure it was not?"

"I checked her apartment."

"You broke in?" Callaway asked. Jimmy was never good with rules, but being a private investigator, he did not have to follow procedures like he had to as a cop—or so his superiors kept telling him.

Jimmy smiled. "I gained access to it, okay? The balcony railing in the apartment building is at least four feet in height. Gail was five-two, and she was a little on the heavier side. It just doesn't seem logical for someone like her to—" Jimmy made air quotations with his fingers, "—accidentally slip or fall over."

"Was she drinking?"

Jimmy shook his head. "I checked the police report, and the police found no open bottles of alcohol in her apartment. I went further and queried her friends, and they said she did not have a single drink while she was with them that night."

"Out of curiosity, how did you manage to get your hands on the police report?" Callaway asked.

"You have Detective Fisher at the Milton PD, I have someone at the Bayview PD."

"Fair enough."

"I also read the autopsy report—again, courtesy of my connection at the police department—and according to it, Gail had very low traces of alcohol in her blood stream. She must have likely had wine or some other alcoholic beverage the day before."

"What about drugs, prescription or otherwise?"

"She was clean. She didn't even smoke."

Callaway was quiet. He had thrown every imaginable question at Jimmy, trying to see if there were any holes in the police's theory.

By all accounts, Gail was a fully functioning person who was not inebriated, depressed, or under the influence of narcotics.

Then how did she fall fourteen floors to her death? he wondered.

FIFTY-NINE

At the veterinary clinic, Becky's duties were to feed the animals, assist the veterinarian during clinical and medical procedures, restrain the animals when needed, and also keep the clinic clean by vacuuming and mopping the floor, sterilizing the lab, and doing laundry.

The clinic had a full-time receptionist, but when she was off or away from her desk, Becky would answer phone calls, schedule appointments, bill clients, and sell products. This was on top of restocking animal food, which required her to lift heavy boxes.

It was a lot of work, but Becky loved every minute of it. She couldn't wait to come to work, and if need be, she would stay late, even though she was not getting paid for the overtime. Whenever she did that, the veterinarian would thank her in other ways. She would give Becky gift cards, movie passes, and dinner vouchers to various restaurants. She didn't have to, but Becky was appreciative.

Becky fed a labradoodle who had been abandoned by its owner. She was thinking of adopting the dog. She used to have a Jack Russell terrier, but it had so many health issues that Becky and her parents were always bringing it to the vet. Perhaps that was why she wanted to be a vet. The terrier died several years earlier, and Becky didn't have the heart to get another dog.

Maybe now's the time, she thought as she scratched the labradoodle behind the ears. A new dog would fill the empty space in the house left by her dad's death. A dog would also give her mom company when Becky was at school or at the clinic.

"Do you want to come home with me?" Becky said to the labradoodle. She had named the terrier Calvin, and she was thinking of naming the labradoodle Hobbes. Her dad loved reading *Calvin and Hobbes,* so it would be a nice way to remember him.

The vet came over. She was short, slim, and she wore thick prescription glasses. "I just received a call from animal services. The police raided a house and they found a dozen cats inside. They're asking if we can take some in. I said yes."

"Oh," Becky said. "Is anything wrong with them?"

"There is a chance they are malnourished and unhygienic. We'll need to wash them and have a place for them to sleep."

"How many are we getting?" Becky asked, excited to help.

"Let's prepare for half a dozen. It could be less or it could be more. I'll find out once I visit the house. Can you work late tonight if we need extra help?"

"Of course," Becky said. It broke her heart whenever she heard of animals being abused. *These creatures hurt like us, but they can't complain like us, so why torture them?* she always thought.

"Make sure you let your mom know," the vet said.

"I'll do that right now," Becky said as she pulled out her cell phone and dialed her mom's number.

SIXTY

Fisher was at her desk when an officer came over and informed her that someone was looking for her in the police station's main lobby.

Fisher took the elevator down and found Rachel Scott seated in the waiting area. She was wearing a long brown dress that went down to her ankles, a light jacket, and she had on overly large sunglasses. She also had on a lot of makeup, just like last time.

"Mrs. Scott," Fisher said.

Rachel did not remove her shades. She said, "I apologize for dropping in unannounced."

It was not uncommon for the grieving to show up unexpectedly at the police department. They were anxious for answers as to who could have harmed their loved one. Fisher was always courteous to them. She couldn't imagine what they were going through.

"It's absolutely fine," Fisher said. "Why don't we sit down?"

They sat on hard plastic chairs. Rachel finally removed the sunglasses. Fisher could see stress on her face. There were heavy bags under her eyes. Even with the foundation, it was easy to see her skin had started to break out. Her lipstick was caked on her dry lips.

Rachel said, "I wanted to know when I can take Dillon's body back to Bayview. His family wants to see him, and we still haven't decided if it'll be a private or public funeral."

"I'm sorry, but we need to conduct more tests." Fisher couldn't tell her the medical examiner no longer believed the cause of death was blunt force trauma.

"What kind of tests?" Rachel asked.

"I'm not at liberty to say."

Rachel nodded in understanding.

"Mrs. Scott, can I ask you a few questions?" Fisher said.

"Okay."

"Does your husband have any foreign bank accounts?"

Rachel frowned. "I'm not sure. If he did, he never mentioned them to me."

"Do you have a separate bank account?"

"Of course I do. It was Dillon's idea. After we got married, he wanted me to have financial independence. I think it had more to do with the fact that he didn't want me knowing how much money he was spending on a regular basis."

"So you are aware of his financial situation?"

"He didn't tell me much, but I could sense that we were living beyond our means."

"The reason I ask is... did your husband ask you to withdraw a large sum from your bank account?"

She shook her head. "No, he did not."

"Nothing in the last couple of days?"

"No. If he did, I would have asked him why."

Fisher nodded. "Do you and your husband have a prenuptial agreement?" she asked.

"No, we don't," Rachel replied, surprised. "However, I can tell you that Dillon has more debts than assets. His lawyer is currently looking into it and will let me know how bad it is."

"But he must have life insurance," Fisher said.

"He does."

"And are you the beneficiary?"

"As his wife, I am." Her lips suddenly quivered. "Are you saying I had something to do with what happened to Dillon?"

"I didn't mean it like that..."

"I was in Bayview when he... he..." Rachel suddenly choked up. "I flew in the moment I found out what had happened."

"I know," Fisher said. "I just wanted to make sure I've covered all bases."

Rachel stood up. "Call me when I can bring my husband home."

"I will."

When Rachel Scott turned to leave, Fisher thought of something. "One more question. Do you know anyone who could have lent your husband money?"

Rachel pondered the question. "You can talk to Brad Kirkman. He and Dillon were business partners. They owned a production company together."

SIXTY-ONE

Callaway hung up the phone and turned to Jimmy. "Fisher is on her way to Bayview."

"Bayview, why?" Jimmy asked, surprised.

"She is going to speak to Dillon Scott's business partner. She will let us know if she finds anything on Gail's death."

"I already spoke to him, and he has an alibi at the time of her death."

"Okay, but someone was blackmailing Scott, and Fisher wants to know where he got the money to pay his blackmailer. We should go to Yonge Avenue and check it out."

"Wasn't Fisher already there?"

"She was, and she found out that Scott had met a reporter at a bar. This reporter confirmed that Scott was not carrying a backpack, which Fisher believes contained money for the blackmailer."

"He may have dropped off the backpack before going to the bar."

"Exactly, and we need to see the drop-off for ourselves."

Jimmy made a face. "How do we even know where it is?"

"Fisher thinks it's at a park next to Yonge Avenue. Scott's previous drop was at a park as well."

Jimmy shook his head. "I don't know. The blackmailer is long gone. What will we learn by going there?"

"Right now we have nothing that helps us find out what happened to Gail. You've looked into her case and gotten nowhere. Isn't that why you're in Milton? You think Dillon Scott had something to do—"

"Yes, but he's dead as well," Jimmy interrupted. "I was hoping to find out who killed him, but so far, Detective Fisher has made no progress on her case."

"That's why we should go to Yonge Avenue and see if we can dig up something."

Jimmy did not look convinced.

"Why are you so against going there, anyway?" Callaway asked.

"I'm not," Jimmy replied. "I just think we could be wasting time."

"Listen, I asked Fisher to trust *us*. She is keeping us updated on her investigation, which is against all procedures. The least we can do is knock on some doors, ask a few questions, and maybe, if we're lucky, catch a break."

Jimmy stared at him and then smiled. "Hey man, this is your city, and she's your friend. We'll do whatever you want."

It was a twenty-minute drive during rush hour, and they even managed to find a parking spot without any trouble.

There was a narrow path that led them from Yonge Avenue to a small park adjacent to a condo building.

Three park benches were on one side, and a tiny children's playground was across from them. Callaway spotted a garbage bin next to one of the benches.

"He must have dropped off the backpack next to the garbage can," Callaway said.

"What makes you so sure?" Jimmy asked.

"It's more obscured than the other benches."

"What if he dumped the backpack in the garbage can instead?"

This was something Callaway had been thinking too. The benches were exposed. A person at the playground could easily spot the backpack.

"It's a perfect drop-off location, though," Callaway said, looking around. "There are no cameras, and look over there." He pointed to a stairwell in the distance with a sign above it. "That's an entrance to the subway. The blackmailer was likely standing there, watching Scott as he made the drop. The moment Scott left, the blackmailer raced over, grabbed the backpack, and disappeared underground."

"The subway must have cameras," Jimmy said.

"Sure, but Yonge Avenue is a busy street. It would be impossible to spot someone even if they are carrying a backpack. And what if the blackmailer was wearing a disguise? Fisher wouldn't even know who she was looking for."

"I told you it was a waste of time coming down here," Jimmy said.

"Fisher thinks the blackmailer could have killed Scott because he may not have met all the demands," Callaway said.

"Oh, that's interesting," Jimmy said. "But how does this link up to Gail?"

Callaway thought for a moment.

His eyes widened. "Didn't you say that a few days before her death, Gail had told her father that something was bothering her and it had to do with Scott?"

"She did."

"What if she was thinking of going to the authorities and telling them about the blackmail?"

Jimmy's mouth dropped. "And to silence her, the blackmailer killed her."

"It makes sense," Callaway said. "Scott was famous. He would rather pay than let bad publicity ruin his career, and the blackmailer knew this. He had already extracted money from Scott before, and here comes Scott's assistant who could end this perfect scheme, so she had to go."

They mulled this over.

Callaway said, "We now have to find out what the blackmailer had on Scott that made him come down here to pay him off."

SIXTY-TWO

Brad Kirkman was tall with broad shoulders and dark, curly hair. His grip was strong, which told Fisher he worked out. He had emerald green eyes and an easy smile.

Kirkman's spacious and tidy office was on the fourteenth floor of a glass tower. His mahogany desk was near windows that took up an entire wall. Behind him, Fisher could see an aerial view of Bayview. All along the other walls were posters of movies Kirkman and Scott's company had produced. On the left was a shelf full of awards the production company had won. On the right were framed photos of film crews on movie sets.

"At the beginning of each production," Kirkman said, catching her gaze, "we get everyone who is involved in the movie and we take a group photo. At the end of the shoot, we ask all the stars of the film to sign copies for the crew members. This way the crew can show their family and friends that they got to hang around with movie stars."

Fisher smiled at the nice gesture.

"Can I get you something to drink? Coffee or tea?" Kirkman asked.

"No, thank you. I'm good."

"May I ask if you've made any progress on Dillon's murder?"

"We have some leads, which is why I have driven all the way here to speak to you."

Kirkman's eyebrows shot up. "Oh, really? Maybe *I* could use a drink then." He walked over to a small cart and filled his glass with water. He took a sip and sat behind his desk. "You can ask me whatever you like. I have nothing to hide."

Fisher dove right in. "Were you aware that someone was blackmailing Mr. Scott?"   "I was."

Fisher was surprised by the quick reply. "And you didn't think to mention this to anyone?"

"What good would it have done? Dillon is dead, and the blackmailer can't squeeze another penny out of him."

"But this person could be responsible for what happened to Mr. Scott. Isn't that important?"

"I understand your concern, and I see where you're coming from."

Fisher got the impression that Kirkman was used to putting out fires on a movie set. If it wasn't the stars fighting with the director, then it was the director fighting with the producers, who in turn were fighting with the studios or independent investors.

"But you have to realize," he said, "that Dillon was not just an actor, he was a movie star. He could get a movie greenlit with just his name on it, so the reason I didn't come forward with this information was because Dillon's last movie was scheduled to be released in two months, and he was also a producer on an upcoming TV series."

"The blackmail would have been bad publicity," Fisher said.

Kirkman nodded. "Dillon is gone, and there is nothing I can do to bring him back, but I still have a production company to think about. We have a lot of employees, and they have worked tirelessly on projects for us. I didn't want Dillon's death to mar their good work."

"But it wouldn't have impacted your company," Fisher said. "It was Mr. Scott who was being blackmailed, not the other way around. In fact, people would have sympathized with his plight."

"Would they?" Kirkman asked. "Do you know why Dillon was being blackmailed?"

"Do you?" she asked in return.

"No, but I wish I did. What I can say, though, is there must have been a reason why Dillon was paying off this person. I don't know what it is, but I can only imagine it must not be good. Why else would he go through all this trouble to keep silent?"

He has a point, she thought.

"Can I ask you about Gail Roberts?" Fisher said.

SIXTY-THREE

Kirkman's shoulders sank. "That was a big loss for all of us. I know Dillon was haunted by Gail's death. I was even more so."

"You?" Fisher asked.

He looked at her with a pained expression. "I was the one who hired Gail. She was smart, hardworking, and above all, honest. She had what you would call a moral compass. It's something you don't see much in Hollywood. I've seen people do just about anything to get ahead in this business. There is big money to be made, and morality plays a very little role in it. You wouldn't believe how many girls show up each day wanting to be big stars, and some of the things they are forced to do in order to get a role..."

Fisher knew he was referring to the infamous "casting couch."

"Our office used to be in Los Angeles, but then Dillon wanted to get out of the limelight, so he decided to move his family to Bayview, and we figured it might be better if we set up an office here as well." He lowered his voice and said, "I still can't believe how she died."

"The police dubbed it a suicide, but her family thinks otherwise."

"I am aware of that," he said. "Her family even hired a private investigator to look into her death."

"Jimmy Keith," Fisher said.

His eyebrows shot up. "You've spoken to him?"

"I have."

"Then he must have told you Dillon had nothing to do with her death. He was shooting a movie in Vermont."

"I am aware of that," Fisher replied. "And what about you?"

Kirkman opened a desk drawer and pulled out a boarding pass. He placed the pass on the table before her. "On the night in question, I was on a flight out of Bayview. I was scouting a location for another project."

Fisher picked up the pass and scanned it. Kirkman was telling the truth. "You keep it conveniently nearby?"

"I do, especially when the police show up, and a private investigator, all asking questions about my whereabouts. Listen, I don't know why Gail fell from her apartment. I don't believe it was a suicide either."

"Then what was it?" Fisher asked.

"Likely an accident. How else do you explain it?" Kirkman replied.

Fisher waited a moment before she said, "When Mr. Scott arrived in Milton, he brought a backpack which I now believe contained a large sum of money. I have traced his movements in Milton and never once did he withdraw any money from any bank or ATM. This was further confirmed when I accessed his bank statements. Mr. Scott then took this backpack to a busy intersection in Milton, where he left it for the blackmailer. Were you aware of what Mr. Scott was up to?"

"I was, and I approved it," Kirkman replied.

"What do you mean?"

"I mean, *I* gave him that money."

Fisher's mouth nearly dropped. *No wonder I couldn't find the money's origin*, she thought. "How much was it?"

"Fifty thousand dollars."

"Why did you give it to him?"

"He asked me to."

"And you thought it was better to pay such a large amount than go to the police?"

Kirkman smiled. "Detective Fisher, for Dillon, it was a drop in the bucket."

"His finances would say otherwise."

Kirkman frowned. "I had no idea he was underwater until *after* his death."

"But even so, didn't you think the blackmailer would have continued to demand money after you'd paid him or her?"

"Of course it crossed our minds," Kirkman said. "Dillon and I had long discussions about it, but Dillon was going to start shooting a new movie in Milton in a few days. There was also the matter of his previous movie that was soon to be released. Dillon had not had a hit in some time, and we figured we would agree to the blackmailer's terms until we could get Dillon's career back on track. Later, we would get the FBI involved and let them handle this mess. Also, you have to understand that people in Dillon's position would rather pay up than deal with the public fallout. It's quite common in the business."

"I don't understand."

"Haven't you heard of settlements?" Kirkman asked.

"Are you saying Mr. Scott paid other people to stay silent?" Fisher replied.

"Yes."

"Why?"

"I am not at liberty to say. Both parties sign confidentiality agreements, which are sealed by the courts. You will have to speak to a judge to break the agreement."

Fisher knew that was never going to happen. No court would permit it.

"Plus, Dillon is dead, and it's better that the public remember him as an all-American hero who upheld the value of truth, justice, and the American way of life."

The phone on the desk rang. Kirkman looked at the number and sighed. "I have to take this. A lot of projects are now in limbo after Dillon's untimely death."

Fisher stood up to leave. "One last thing. Did you give the money to Mr. Scott from your personal bank account?"

"No. It was from the production company's business account."

SIXTY-FOUR

Callaway walked back to the Charger and pulled a camera from the trunk.

"What're you doing?" Jimmy asked.

"We know where Scott dropped off the money," Callaway replied. "I want to make sure I get evidence for Fisher to build her case."

Jimmy nodded. "If the blackmailer killed Scott, then you want to be able to recreate Scott's movements on that night."

"Exactly."

Callaway put a wide zoom lens on the camera. He was checking the focus when a man approached them. He was dressed in a long-sleeve shirt, and he had earrings in both ears and a stud on his tongue.

"You guys tourists?" he asked.

Callaway shook his head. "No."

Jimmy said, "We got no money."

Street kids loved to panhandle on Yonge Avenue.

The man laughed. "I'm not begging, man. I got a job."

"Then what do you want?" Jimmy asked, annoyed.

"I work at the ice cream shop." He pointed to a store behind them. "On my break, I usually cut through the park and go to the vape store on the other side."

"Vape store?" Jimmy asked.

"You never heard of e-cigarettes?" the man replied, surprised. "You gotta try it. It's better than actual cigarettes that have nicotine and carcinogens and—"

"We know what it is," Callaway said. He didn't want to get into a long discussion about why vaping is better than smoking.

"Okay, sure," the man said. "So, when I was crossing the park, I saw you guys walking around checking every inch of it. If you're not tourists, then are you guys like reporters?"

"Not quite," Callaway said.

"We're actually private investigators," Jimmy said with pride.

"You guys are *real*?" the man excitedly asked.

Jimmy frowned. "Why wouldn't we be?"

"I thought you guys were only in the movies."

Callaway and Jimmy rolled their eyes.

"Nice talking to you," Callaway said as he moved away from the man.

"You guys investigating Dillon Scott's murder?" the man asked.

Callaway's ears perked up. "Do you know him?"

The man scoffed. "Who doesn't? I'm a huge fan. I've seen all his movies. My favorite is the one where he plays a father who goes after a gang who killed his daughter. That scene where he beats up six people all by himself... I mean the way he punches, kicks, and..." The man began to reenact Scott's moves.

"Get to the point," Callaway said.

"Oh, right." The man straightened up. He pointed at the bar where Scott had spoken to a reporter. "At first I didn't recognize him when I saw him come out. He was wearing these dark shades, but when I looked carefully, I knew it was him. I had heard he was in town shooting a movie. Like I said, I am a huge fan, and I knew it was my only chance to meet him. I ran back inside the ice cream shop to get my cell phone. I had put it on to charge. The battery drains so fast, you know. I'm thinking of getting a new one, but I'm waiting for my contract to expire so—"

"Dillon Scott," Callaway said, trying to bring the man back on topic.

"Right, right," the man said. "When I came out of the shop with my phone, he was gone. I had seen him go in the other direction, so I rushed over. I went down the block and turned the corner, and I saw him. He was talking to a girl."

"A girl?" Callaway asked.

"Yeah, they looked like they were having a conversation. They were both smiling. I think she might have been a fan too. They were standing next to a taxi. By the time I got to them, they were inside the taxi as it pulled away." The man shook his head. "I missed my chance to meet my hero. And then I heard he was dead. I cried all night, and I—"

"Did the girl go with him?" Callaway asked.

"I thought I said they both got in the taxi, didn't I?"

"What did this girl look like?"

He shrugged. "She was short, kind of skinny, I guess, and her hair was maybe brownish."

"What was she wearing?"

"I dunno… clothes."

"What kind of clothes?" Callaway said, feeling exasperated.

"I dunno… girl clothes."

Callaway exhaled. "Did you get the taxi's license plate number?"

The man smiled. "That I got."

"You did?" Callaway was shocked and relieved.

"Yeah, man. I was like five feet away when the taxi drove off."

"Give me the license plate number."

SIXTY-FIVE

Detective Armen Woodley was five-ten with a medium build, and his head was shaved clean. His eyes were black and haunting, as if he could see into people's souls.

Before returning to Milton, Fisher decided to visit the Bayview Police Department. She was now seated before Woodley's desk as he went over Gail Roberts's case with her. Woodley was the lead detective on her death.

Woodley had a wedding ring on his left hand, and there were photos of young children on his desk. These eased her comfort as his eyes bore into her.

"It's not a murder, I'm afraid," he said. "I've looked into it from all angles."

"Gail's family thinks otherwise."

"They do, of course," he agreed with a nod. "They want to make sense of what happened. They just don't want to face the truth that her death was perhaps an accident, or even worse, a suicide."

"Do you believe it was a suicide?"

He shook his head. "I don't think she was depressed. I think she was of clear mind on the night she died."

"Then what happened?" Fisher asked.

"It's something that still baffles me," Woodley replied. "I've spoken to her neighbors, and they don't remember seeing anyone in her apartment. They are certain they heard no voices from inside. If there was an argument, then we would know she was not alone, and that someone may have pushed her over the balcony. But again, we have nothing."

"What about security cameras in the apartment?"

"They are located in the main lobby of the building, right by the elevators. I checked them myself, and there was no one suspicious entering or exiting the building at the time of her death. In fact, the cameras caught Gail Roberts taking the elevator up to her apartment, but no one racing out after she had fallen, which would be the normal course of action for someone fleeing the scene."

Fisher absorbed this information.

Woodley said, "We do have a witness who was walking his dog at the time of the incident. He remembered hearing a scream, followed by a noise. When he went to check, he saw Gail Roberts's body on the ground. He then saw a woman run out the back of the building."

Fisher sat up straight. "Did you speak to this woman?"

"We tried to locate her, but it was not possible. The residents of the building told me they had seen her sleeping in the stairwell on a number of occasions. She was homeless, and an addict. On a number of occasions, police were called to remove her from the property. She was harmless from what I've been told."

"Why was she running away when Gail died?" Fisher asked.

"I don't know. Like I said, I never interviewed her, but if I can take a guess, I'll say that she must have heard the commotion outside and thought it might be the police looking for her, so she ran."

"Why couldn't you find her?"

"I looked everywhere. It was like she just disappeared. I even had a name."

"What was it?"

"Tamara Davis."

Fisher quickly pulled out her pocket-size notepad to jot the name down.

"It won't do you any good now," Woodley said.

"Why not?"

"Tamara Davis was found dead in a crack house from an overdose."

"Oh."

Woodley put his hands together. "Why are you so interested in Gail Roberts? I know you are investigating Dillon Scott's murder, but I don't see how it is linked to hers."

"Gail's family hired someone to look into her—"

"Jimmy Keith," Woodley said with a smile.

"You know him?" she asked.

"I do, and I've worked with him." He paused and said, "I know this may come as a surprise to you, but a police detective normally doesn't share information with a private investigator."

"I'm not surprised, I assure you," she said, thinking of Callaway.

"Jimmy is a good PI," Woodley said. "I've had to seek his help on a number of cases. He doesn't care for the recognition, he just cares about doing his job and getting paid. This suits me nicely because I don't have to explain to my superiors how I came to know certain information."

"Were you aware that someone was blackmailing Dillon Scott?" Fisher asked. Woodley shook his head. "That's the first time I've heard of this."

Fisher thanked him and left.

SIXTY-SIX

Callaway was excited. He and Jimmy were driving back from Yonge Avenue when he said, "This could be the break we've been looking for."

"How can you be so sure?" Jimmy asked.

"Come on, you don't see it?"

Jimmy shrugged.

Callaway continued. "We have a witness who saw Dillon Scott leave in a taxi with a girl. This means there was someone else other than the reporter who saw Scott before his death."

"You're forgetting the blackmailer. He may have also seen Scott. In fact, there is a possibility Scott could have died at the hands of this person. What if the blackmailer picked up the backpack from the park, realized Scott did not bring all the money that he demanded—we know Scott was having financial troubles—and then went to his house to get the rest of the money?"

Callaway shook his head. "It sounds plausible, but I don't think that's what happened."

"Why not?"

"If the blackmailer already knew where Scott lived, then why not just go there and pick up the money himself? Also, I don't think the blackmailer would expose himself to Scott out of fear that Scott would turn him in to the police."

"What if the blackmailer had something on Scott that would prevent him from going to the police in the first place?" Jimmy asked.

"True, but then why go through the trouble of driving to Yonge Avenue, dropping the backpack under a park bench, and then leaving?" Callaway replied.

Jimmy thought for a moment. "You've got a point there."

"Also," Callaway added, "we don't know who this blackmailer is, and so we have no idea where to find him, but we do know something about this girl. She got in the same taxi with Scott. We find this girl, and she might tell us more about what happened that night."

"How do we do that?"

"Simple. We have the license plate number. We contact the taxi driver and we get access to his CCTV footage."

"Okay, but how does the footage from the taxi help us identify this girl?" Jimmy asked.

Callaway pondered this. "The witness said the girl looked like a fan. Let's assume that Scott had offered to share the taxi with her. If he did, then the taxi driver must have dropped her off somewhere, presumably at her house."

"What if he dropped her off at the bus stop or subway station?"

"Even if the taxi driver dropped her off somewhere other than her house, the footage from the taxi will still be useful. Fisher can release it to the press in order for someone to identify her."

They were silent for a moment.

Jimmy broke into a smile. "Good job, kid. I knew you still had it in you. That whole bit with Frank Henderson had me worried. I thought you had lost your touch and were now scraping the bottom of the barrel for any case that came through your door."

"I was desperate and still am," Callaway corrected him. "The five hundred dollars Betty Henderson gave me was a lifesaver at the time."

"I'm sure it was. Don't get me wrong, but you have it in you to do greater things. The way you see the forest for the trees. Even I can't do that at times," Jimmy said. "I get obsessed about minor details. But you, you see the bigger picture. Nice work."

Callaway didn't know why, but his chest swelled with pride. Jimmy rarely showered praise, and to have Jimmy compliment him like that meant a lot to him. Callaway felt like a boy who had shown his father that he can be a man too.

"We have to go tell Fisher," Callaway said. "I think it might be better if we do it in person."

Jimmy pulled out his cell phone. After reading a message, he frowned.

"Everything okay?" Callaway asked.

"Yeah, yeah, everything is fine. Why don't you go meet Fisher and I'll see you later."

Callaway stopped the Charger by the side of the road. Jimmy got out, waved goodbye, and walked away.

It was typical of Jimmy to disappear unexpectedly. Callaway could have queried Jimmy as to where he was going, but the old man would have quipped, *There's a reason I didn't get married. I didn't want my wife asking me too many questions, so don't start asking me questions, either.*

Callaway shook his head and drove away.

SIXTY-SEVEN

Osman had just gotten off the phone with his contact. As agreed, Osman had dropped off his contact's share of the money in the bathroom at the Bayview Central train station. The cellophane-wrapped bundle of cash was placed inside the toilet bowl of stall number three. His contact would know where to find it.

Osman had considered skipping down with *all* the money, but his contact knew his identity. Osman doubted his contact would expose him if he did that. It was his contact's plan to blackmail Dillon Scott, after all. But his contact owed money to the wrong people, which made him a desperate man. There was no telling what he would do—even go to the police and squeal on him if Osman tried to swindle him.

The police would believe his contact over a low-level drug dealer, but Osman had taken precautions. Even though he used a prepaid phone as his contact had instructed him, Osman had recorded all their telephone conversations.

In his line of work, you only watched *your* back and no one else's. Backstabbers were all too common. This made him suspicious of those around him. It was also how he survived on the streets this long.

His contact had told him to destroy the prepaid phone, but Osman would do no such thing. He would keep it, along with everything else he had on his contact.

His contact had set up the entire blackmail scheme, and Osman followed it to perfection. Osman had called Dillon Scott and told him to bring the money to a park in Milton. Osman would have preferred to have him deliver the money in Bayview, but his contact believed a change of venue was for the best. It would keep Scott on his toes.

Also, if Scott decided to involve the police or the FBI, the new location would require extra time to mobilize a new plan. By then, Osman would have picked up the money or, at the very least, known something was up and aborted the mission.

Osman walked out of the train station and straight to a bus stop. He knew the station had cameras at every corner. They would capture his license plate number if he drove here.

When his contact had instructed him to wrap the money in cellophane and leave it in the bathroom, Osman rolled his eyes. It was too over the top, akin to something he had seen in the movies.

But now he realized why all the extra steps were necessary. His contact was protecting himself, but in a different way, he was also protecting Osman. If someone caught them together, they would be guilty by association. By separating their actions, nothing would lead back to either of them.

Osman cared little for what happened to his contact, but he cared immensely about what happened to him. If his contact was being careful, so would Osman.

His contact was pleased, though, when Osman had told him Tamara was out of the picture. After Scott's death, she was no longer useful in their plans. She had to be taken care of before she became a bigger problem for either of them.

Osman had initially offered to get rid of her for a fee, but it was his contact who had devised a plan to get money out of Scott. It was a risky move, one even Osman would have hesitated making. Tamara knew too much, and what she knew would send his contact to prison for life.

Tamara's death had not appeared in the newspapers, which told him the police did not suspect foul play.

The bus approached the stop. Osman lined up to get inside. He smiled.

The job was done, and he was glad to leave it behind him. He could now take his share of the money and do whatever he wanted with his life.

SIXTY-EIGHT

Callaway returned to his office and sat down behind his desk. He was fortunate to catch Fisher at the Milton PD. She had just returned from Bayview. She was unable to get much information on Gail Roberts's death. Callaway could see her disappointment. Fisher took her job seriously. She wanted to help him and, in the process, also help Jimmy with his case.

Callaway had asked if she found anything on Scott's blackmail. She told him she had discovered that the money had come from Scott's business partner, Brad Kirkman. This solved the mystery as to how Scott got his hands on the cash, but it still did not solve who the blackmailer was.

Callaway then told Fisher about the girl who was last seen getting in a taxi with Scott. He also gave her the taxi cab's license plate number. The moment Fisher heard this, she was out the door. She didn't even wave goodbye.

Callaway smiled. The excitement on her face was worth telling her in person. Sometimes detective work or PI work required a heavy dose of luck. If that man on Yonge Avenue had not approached Callaway and Jimmy, they would not have caught a break.

The girl in the taxi was the key to this whole investigation. Callaway had no doubt Fisher would find her, and quick.

He turned on his laptop to check his messages.

He heard footsteps coming up the stairs.

His smile widened. *Jimmy's back so soon*, he thought.

His smile dropped when he saw it was his landlady. Ms. Chen was short, slim, and she had her hair tied into a ponytail. She wore a loose dress, heels, and around her neck was a string necklace which had a small marble animal. According to the Chinese calendar, Ms. Chen was born in the year of the dog.

Per Ms. Chen, people born in the year of the dog were cautious, and they did not trust very easily, but when they did, they were loyal to a fault.

Callaway never gave her much reason to trust him. He was always feeding her lies about when he would have the rent money, or when he would do something he agreed to do. Ms. Chen owned the noodle restaurant below his office. He once offered to help her clean out the restaurant's freezer. He was way behind on rent, and it was his way to repay her. Instead of doing the work, however, he avoided her like the Black Plague.

"What can I do for you, Ms. Chen?" he asked.

"Someone wants to see you. They are in the restaurant," she replied.

"Who?"

"I don't know, but they bring their whole family and they eat a lot of food. You bring more people like that, and I'll think about giving you a discount on your rent."

His eyebrows shot up. "Really?"

She laughed. "Of course not. Your rent is already too cheap. You want to pay *no* rent?"

"That would be nice."

"In your dreams, buddy."

She turned around and disappeared down the stairs.

He frowned. He was not expecting anyone. The frown quickly turned into a smile. *If these people ordered a lot of food, then that means they have money*, he thought.

He rushed downstairs. When he entered the restaurant, he found Frank and Betty Henderson seated at a table with their four children. Frank stood up the moment he saw him. He came over and shook his hand.

"I'm not sure what you did, Mr. Callaway," he said, smiling, "but Sandra and Carl quit the company, and they even forgave my loan before they left."

"Hey, that's great news," Callaway said. "I'm so happy for you."

Betty came over with tears in her eyes. She gave him a big hug. "Thank you for giving me back my husband and for not letting my family fall apart."

Callaway's eyes moistened too. The Hendersons were good people who never wanted to harm anyone. They were just pushed into a difficult situation where they had no choice but to work with bad people.

Frank stuck his hand in his pocket and pulled out an envelope. "This is for you, Mr. Callaway."

Callaway stared at it. "What is it?"

"Betty gave you five hundred, which I know was not nearly enough for the service you provided. It's not a lot, but we managed to come up with another five hundred as our appreciation for what you did for us."

Callaway opened his mouth but no words came out. He choked up. He had done work for the rich and wealthy. What he dug up for them in the course of his investigations enabled them to get a significant divorce settlement. Even then, some of those people would try to cheat him out of his fees. The Hendersons had very little, but they were willing to give whatever they had.

"Thank you," he said, taking the envelope.

SIXTY-NINE

Callaway went back up to his office in a euphoric daze. Not only was he able to help nice people, he was also compensated for it. The additional five hundred was nothing to crow about, but it was money he desperately needed.

Normally he would go to a bar and celebrate, but he didn't want to burn through a significant chunk on alcohol. Now he could meet his obligations and still have some left over until his next case.

The laptop was fully booted, and he decided to quickly check his emails. Luck had struck him twice already. First there was the girl in the taxi with Dillon Scott, and now the Hendersons appearing out of nowhere to give him money. He wanted to see if he could ride this luck out.

He quickly went through the messages and sighed. People were asking about his services, but none of the prospects sounded promising. While the Hendersons' case turned out well for everyone involved, he did not want another case where the financial reward was minimal.

He heard footsteps coming up the stairs.

Did my landlady see Frank give me the money? Callaway suddenly thought. *Does she want her rent now?*

To his relief, it was Jimmy. He was out of breath as he came over and sat on the sofa next to him.

"You need to exercise," Callaway said.

"I need to retire," Jimmy said.

"I don't know how you can." Like him, Jimmy did not have a pension plan. Callaway doubted if he even had any savings. "You can start by slowing down."

Jimmy nodded. "I saw your landlady on my way over. She seemed pleasant."

"Only today," Callaway said.

"Was that Frank I saw in the restaurant?" Jimmy asked.

"Yep, and he gave me another five hundred for all the hard work I did."

"You mean *we* did," Jimmy said.

Callaway paused. "You want half, like we used to?"

Jimmy laughed. "I'm only busting your balls. It's all yours, kid. But you wanna go down to the bar and celebrate?"

Great minds think alike, Callaway thought. "I think I'm going to hold on to this money," he said. "I've had enough fun to last me a while."

"Fair enough," Jimmy said, wiping sweat from his forehead.

Callaway's phone buzzed. He answered. He listened, spoke, and then after five minutes, he hung up with a frown."

"What's wrong?" Jimmy asked, concerned.

"It was Fisher."

"And?"

"She was able to track down the driver from the license plate number, but the driver said he had already provided his taxi's CCTV footage to another detective."

Jimmy shot up from the sofa. "Which detective?"

"The driver's not sure, but he said the detective took the entire data storage unit as evidence."

"How's that even possible?"

"The driver is a new immigrant. He barely spoke English, so he had no idea who Dillon Scott was or that he was with a girl. Fisher pushed him, but he kept saying he gets a lot of passengers during his shift and he doesn't pay too much attention to them," Callaway replied. "Maybe that's why this *detective* was able to convince the driver to hand over the footage without much protest."

Jimmy's mouth was open. "So what are you saying? We don't have anything on who this girl might be?"

Callaway didn't want the old man to have a heart attack. He smiled and said, "Fortunately, the vehicle is affiliated with a taxi corporation. All footage is transmitted wirelessly to their main office. The backup is stored for thirty days. It is wiped clean after that period. Fisher will visit the main office first thing in the morning. She assured me she will have the footage soon enough."

Jimmy exhaled. "Well, that's good to hear. I still say we go and celebrate."

"Jimmy…" Callaway began to protest. He could feel the envelope with the money burning a hole in his pocket.

"Relax, kid," Jimmy said as he pulled a fifty-dollar bill from his sock. "I keep this for emergencies, and for times when I need to reward myself. If you're interested, drinks on me."

Callaway smiled. "In that case, count me in."

SEVENTY

Callaway groaned as an unpleasant sound pounded in his ears. He grumbled and then blinked a few times to clear the fog from his eyes.

The sound did not cease, getting louder by the minute.

How's that even possible? he thought.

He squinted and looked around. He was on the bed in his hotel room. He tried to get up, but a sharp pain pierced his skull. The noise stopped, and he shut his eyes to let his mind adjust.

He had a splitting headache. He knew why. The night before, after leaving the office, he and Jimmy had gone to the bar around the corner. They were only supposed to have one drink, but they were having so much fun that they ended up having one too many.

I can't do this every time I go out, he thought.

When he saw he was wearing no shoes, he jumped off the bed. He felt dizzy. He placed his hand on the wall for support and then searched for his boots. He found them next to the front door.

There were a few times when he had lost his shoes while out drinking. Once, it was during a blizzard. It was still a mystery as to how he made it to his house without them. He was glad he didn't lose any toes to frostbite.

He sat on the edge of the bed and rubbed his eyes. He remembered leaving the bar with Jimmy. He also remembered walking with Jimmy to his hotel room.

A thought hit him like a thunderbolt. He instinctively reached for his jacket. He let out a long sigh of relief. The envelope with the money was still in the inside pocket. It wasn't that he didn't trust Jimmy. Callaway was worried *he* might have spent all the money at the bar.

Callaway was a happy drunk, and he was known to give generous tips. There were times when he would return to the bar the next day and beg the owner or bartender to return the tips. This would not go over too well, and the people who received the tips would downright refuse. They had earned the money, after all. Some, however, would pity his situation and agree. They must have thought he was a no-good drunk who was used to throwing all his money away on booze.

He went into the bathroom, washed up, and returned to the bed. He searched his jacket pocket again and found the culprit that broke his sleep: his cell phone.

There were several missed calls, and they were all from Fisher.

Maybe she found something on the taxi cab's CCTV, he thought. He then checked the time and realized it was still early in the morning. *Man, this lady is dedicated. She must have spent the entire night hounding the taxi company to provide her with the footage.*

He pressed Redial. Before he could say a word, Fisher's voice came on. "Where have you been? I've been calling you for over an hour."

"Sorry, I was sleeping," he said. "Which, by the way, you should do more of as well."

"Lee," her voice was hard. "You have to come to the station."

"Okay, I'll drop by later."

"No! Right now!"

He was startled by her response. His back tensed. "Why? What's going on?"

"I'll tell you when you get here."

The line went dead.

SEVENTY-ONE

Callaway arrived at the Milton PD. He found Fisher waiting for him by the elevators. "What's going on?" he asked.

"It's about Jimmy," she replied.

"What happened? Is he okay?" he asked, concerned.

"He's fine… but…"

"But what?"

"Lee," she said slowly. "Jimmy just confessed to killing Dillon Scott."

Callaway stared at her. He burst out laughing.

Fisher scowled. "What's so funny?"

"Jimmy's probably drunk. Last night we were out at a bar and we had way too much to drink. I don't even remember how I got home."

"Listen," she said sternly. "He confessed to the crime. He even agreed to it being recorded, and on the video, he stated that he is of sound mind and that he is under no duress and/or under the influence of alcohol or narcotics."

Callaway was still smiling. "I don't believe it. I know the man. He's a lot of things—a dirtbag, a cheat, a swindler—but he is *no* murderer. That I can assure you."

"He told me exactly how the crime was committed. He had information no one knew except for *me*. The press was never provided the details, and I never told you or anyone else either. Not even Holt."

Callaway turned pale. "What did he tell you?"

Fisher was silent.

"Please, Dana. He's my friend. What did he tell you about the murder?"

Fisher exhaled. "The press was told Scott's death was caused by blunt force trauma. They didn't know he was hit on the head with a heavy object—specifically, an ivory bookend."

Callaway blinked. "He told you that?"

"He described the bookend in detail."

"Maybe he accessed the crime scene. He's done it before on other cases. Jimmy doesn't go by the book, you know."

"We have an officer stationed twenty-four seven outside the property. It's a high-profile case, so we're not taking any chances. Also, there were *two* ivory bookends in the house. One was taken by Scott's attacker, and the other we removed as evidence. There is no way for a person to go into the house now and know they were even there."

Callaway swallowed.

"He also knew there was a stain on the carpet. When the police got there, it had been cleaned. He said it was vomit. After he killed Scott, he threw up from the shock of what he had done. He also removed two glasses from the scene. He said the glasses contained his and Scott's fingerprints. They apparently had a drink before the altercation. Jimmy had bourbon, and Scott had wine."

Callaway felt like someone had placed a giant boulder on his chest. He could barely breathe. "It doesn't make sense," he slowly said. "Why have a drink with someone and then kill them?"

"I asked him the same question," Fisher replied. "He said he showed up at Scott's house unannounced. He had introduced himself as a local producer. He was desperate, and he wanted information out of Scott regarding Gail's death. When the truth came out about who he was, Scott ordered him out of the house. Things got out of hand, and Jimmy took the bookend and hit him on the head. The medical examiner believes the attacker was over six feet. Jimmy is the same height."

"But why would he confess now?"

"He said the guilt was eating away at him. He couldn't take it, and he decided to save you and me the trouble of investigating this further. He has asked for leniency. The murder was not premeditated, although he *did* try to cover up the crime, but his confession and remorse will go a long way to convince the prosecutor to accept a plea bargain. I will push for it."

Callaway's knees buckled under him. He quickly sat on the nearest chair.

He covered his face with his hands.

Fisher came over and sat next to him. "I'm so sorry, Lee."

His head was spinning, and the first thing he thought of was reaching for a drink. This was a nightmare he never thought possible.

Jimmy… a killer?

He lifted his head up. "Can I see him?" he asked.

"I don't see why not," Fisher replied. "He's been read his rights, but he hasn't been charged of any crime yet. I have seventy-two hours to charge him, though, so it's not something I need to do right at this moment."

"Thanks, Dana."

"One more thing," Fisher said. "He has refused counsel. Maybe you can convince him to change his mind. This is a serious crime he's confessed to, and he's going to need all the help he can get."

SEVENTY-TWO

Jimmy was seated in a windowless room. A metal table was in the middle, with chairs on either side of it. The room's walls were painted white but had started to turn yellowish.

Jimmy looked drained. He smiled when he saw Callaway. "Hey, kid," he said. "Thanks for coming."

Jimmy wasn't cuffed, but he didn't offer his hand for Callaway to shake. Callaway stared at him for a good minute before he took the chair across from him and sat down. "Jimmy, tell me this is some kind of a sick joke."

"I'm afraid not," Jimmy replied.

"What are you doing?" Callaway's voice quivered. "This doesn't make any sense."

"I know it doesn't, but I couldn't hide it anymore."

"How could you hide it from *me*?"

"I didn't know how to tell you, kid."

"You could have said you made a mistake, that it was an accident. I would have tried to help you."

"Like how?" Jimmy asked. "You would have hired me the best lawyer money could buy? You and I both know people like us are not good with money. The only lawyer I'll get is the one appointed by the court. And most of them are either straight out of law school and inexperienced, or too overworked and jaded to give a damn about what happens to an old man like me."

"Is that why you didn't want a lawyer?" Callaway asked.

"What would be the point? I said I did it, and I am willing to pay for my crime."

Callaway sighed and rubbed his temples. He could feel a migraine coming on. "I'm confused, Jimmy. Help me understand what's going on."

"There is nothing to explain, kid. I killed Dillon Scott."

"But why?"

"He knew what happened to Gail and he wouldn't tell me."

"He knew nothing!" Callaway said, raising his voice. "He wasn't even in Bayview at the time of her death. He was miles away, shooting a movie in Vermont. Isn't that what you told me? So what made you go to his house and confront him? Tell me!"

Jimmy was quiet for a moment. "Gail didn't die because of an accident," he said. "She didn't commit suicide."

"What proof do you have?" Callaway demanded, pounding the table. "No one saw anyone in her apartment at the time of her fall, so what proof do you have?"

"I don't have any proof, and that's what frustrates me!" Jimmy yelled back. "I promised her family I would get to the bottom of this. I've spent a year looking into her death from every angle imaginable, and I've come up empty."

"You know why you haven't found anything?" Callaway leaned closer. "Because there is nothing to find. No one is responsible for Gail's death. But you are now responsible for Dillon Scott's death." Callaway got up and paced the room. "How could you, Jimmy? How could you play me like a fool?"

Jimmy stared at him in silence.

Callaway balled his fists. "You didn't come to me for help with finding Gail's killer, you came to me so you could get information on Fisher's investigation. You knew she and I were friends."

"I had no idea," Jimmy protested.

"Stop it!" Callaway spat. "Your lies end here. You said you kept an eye on what I'd been up to. You knew about the cases I'd worked on. I know for a fact you never jump into anything without doing your homework. It's something I learned from you. What was that phrase you used to say when you were training me?" Callaway searched his mind. "Yes, I remember. 'Whenever you go into a situation, make sure you know all the exits. You never know when you're going to have to make a run for it.'"

Jimmy shrugged. "I don't remember saying it…"

"I do! Because I've always wanted to be like *you*."

Jimmy winced and looked away. Callaway's words had stung him like a hot poker.

Callaway was still fuming. "When you showed up at my office, I was over the moon with joy. When we worked together on the Henderson case, it felt like the good old times. I never thought for a minute you were only spending time with me to save yourself."

Jimmy's shoulders sagged. He nodded. "You're right. I'm sorry. I never meant to use you. When something like this happens, your survival instincts kick in. I just wanted to find a way out of it."

"You murdered someone, Jimmy!" Callaway roared. "And you wanted my help to cover it up!"

Jimmy opened his mouth but then shut it.

"You are nothing but a selfish prick, you now that?" Callaway said. "I hope they hang you for what you did."

Callaway left the room.

SEVENTY-THREE

Fisher watched as Callaway stormed past her. "Lee," she said. He didn't stop, nor did he turn to her. He wiped his eyes and disappeared down the hall.

She thought about going after him, but she knew he needed space. Jimmy meant a lot to him. She couldn't imagine what he was going through.

When Jimmy walked into the Milton PD and specifically asked for her, she was not surprised. She figured he wanted to know what she had found during her trip to Bayview. She wasn't sure how much to divulge to him, though. Jimmy was Callaway's friend, not hers. Plus, she had already crossed a line by telling Jimmy and Callaway certain details about her investigation. She was prepared to fill Jimmy in on whatever she had on Gail Roberts's death, but she would go no further.

Before she could speak, he told her he had a confession to make. Her response—which she now regretted—was "Go confess to a priest." But the look on his face told her he was serious.

She took him to an interview room, and he had laid it all out for her. Her shock matched Callaway's. His confession had come out of left field. She never realized all along that the real killer was right in front of her. Her initial instinct was to arrest him on the spot, but she didn't want to jump the gun.

Even though he told her he was there on his own volition, she had to make sure she did it by the book. She asked him a series of questions, and he answered them without a stutter. She asked if he would agree to confess on tape. He agreed without hesitation. He even offered to sign a written confession on top of the video. He wanted her to have an ironclad statement.

She remembered his words vividly: "Detective Fisher, I don't want you wasting your time investigating this case any further. You have your killer, and he is sitting before you."

In other circumstances, Fisher would have been elated. But she was not. This was too much too fast. Even though Jimmy's reasoning was that he could no longer take the guilt, she had to be sure she had the right man. If she did not, Jimmy's confession could blow up in her face.

She took Jimmy's confession, but she told him she would confirm certain details of his story. Jimmy was a person of interest in Dillon Scott's death. After she had all the facts, he would be formally charged. Jimmy sounded displeased, but he accepted her decision.

She got the impression he wanted this behind him as soon as possible, but there were procedures she had to follow, and they required time. She also wanted the opportunity to speak to Callaway. He had a right to know what his friend was up to.

Fisher sighed. She knew her emotions were overtaking her judgment. If her superiors found out they had a full confession, they would be irate as to why charges had not already been laid.

She suddenly regretted not taking Holt up on his offer to return to Milton and help her. He would be able to see this more objectively.

Or would he? she thought.

Holt had no appreciation for PIs There was nothing they could do that a police officer could not. He believed PIs skirted the law in order to "solve" their cases. A police officer's objective was to provide justice, but a PI's objective was to make money, regardless of how they completed their duties.

Fisher did not hold the same sentiment. She knew the value of having an extra pair of eyes. Plus, Callaway was a good investigator. He was as determined as her to solve a case.

Then there was Holt's personal opinion of Callaway. To say Holt didn't like him would be an understatement. Holt would relish the chance to poke him in his time of weakness.

She shook her head. She would have to handle this on her own. She still had seventy-two hours to build her case, enough time before Holt returned.

She pulled Cameron Kilgane's card from her pocket. Cameron had told her about Scott's blackmail, and in return, Fisher had given her word she would let Cameron know the moment they had caught a break in the case.

This was more than a break. This was a full confession.

Fisher didn't want to make the call, but she knew someone in the police department would eventually leak Jimmy's confession to the press. Might as well be her.

She dialed Cameron's number.

SEVENTY-FOUR

Becky waved goodbye to Ester and walked out of school. She normally had lunch with Ester in the school cafeteria, but Ester had choir practice. Becky didn't want to eat alone, so she decided to go home for lunch.

Becky went around to the back of the school. She cut through the football field and made her way up a side path that led to another street. Her house was seven blocks away, but by taking this shortcut, she could cut two blocks from her journey.

She was carrying her backpack, and she had her headphones on. They were blaring pop songs. She loved listening to them at full volume. They made her feel empowered on her walk to school and back. She knew she was damaging her eardrums, but it was a ten-minute walk, so she figured it was okay for such a short time.

She sensed movement behind her. She turned and saw Daniel Bailey running toward her. He mouthed something, but she couldn't hear him because of the music.

She pulled the headphones off. "I've been calling out your name since the moment I saw you on the football field," he said.

"Sorry, I didn't hear you," she replied.

He caught up to her. He was out of breath. "Man, you walk fast."

Becky had always been a brisk walker. Whenever she daydreamed, people had to jog to keep up with her.

"Do you mind if I walk with you?" he asked.

Becky blushed. She had a crush on Daniel. He always smiled at her when he saw her. Only Ester knew her secret. *Did she tell on me?* Becky instinctively thought. *I'll kill her if she did.*

"Sure," Becky replied, turning away. She didn't want Daniel to see her face burning.

Daniel got next to her. They walked in silence for a couple of minutes before Daniel asked, "You live nearby?"

"I'm only a couple of blocks away. And you?"

"I'm actually on the other side of the school."

Is he walking this way just for me?

"One of my friends lives on Strathmore," he added. She knew it was a few streets away from her house. "I have to pick up my laptop from him, and when I saw you, I thought I'd tag along."

They walked a few more minutes before she asked, "What's wrong with your laptop?"

"My friend is going to install a new operating system. I've had the laptop for years, and I've never bothered to upgrade it. It's been freezing up on me the past few weeks. I've lost a couple of projects I've been working on for class."

"I'm sorry to hear that," she said, genuinely sad for his plight.

"I've been meaning to talk to you for a while now," he said.

Her mouth went dry. "You have?" She barely got the words out.

"Yeah, right after I heard what happened to your dad last year."

Is that why he always smiled at me? she thought. *He was feeling sorry for me?*

"I lost my dad in a car accident," he said. "I know how it is to lose someone so quickly."

"Oh."

"I wanted you to know that if you wanted to talk, or hang around, or whatever, I'm cool with that."

She smiled. "I would like that."

"Cool, cool, cool," he said, stammering.

She could tell he felt the same way about her. It must have taken a lot of courage for him to approach her.

They walked half a block. His phone dinged. He pulled it out and scrolled through the screen with his finger. "Wow."

"What's wrong?" she asked.

"My friend just messaged me. The police caught someone in Dillon Scott's murder."

Becky turned pale. "They have? Are you sure?"

"If you don't believe me, you can check on your phone yourself."

"My phone battery is low," she said sheepishly. The truth was that Becky was avoiding all forms of news. She preferred being in the dark over knowing what was happening with the case.

"Okay," he said, and he kept staring at the screen.

She hesitated, but she wanted to know. "Who did they catch? Does your friend know?"

"Some private investigator… his name is… Jimmy Keith."

Her knees suddenly buckled. She grabbed Daniel's arm for support.

"You all right?" he asked.

After she got her bearings, she said, "I'm fine. I just feel a little lightheaded. I have to go."

She hurried ahead.

"Hey, wait, I can walk you home," he said.

"I'll be fine. I'll talk to you later."

She didn't wait for his response. She was already running toward her house.

SEVENTY-FIVE

Callaway was at a bar, drowning his sorrows in a glass of scotch. He was in tears as he took one sip after another.

He was devastated. He could not believe what was happening. Jimmy was not just a mentor to him, he was more like a father.

Callaway came from a long line of law enforcement officers. His grandfather and uncle were state troopers. His father was a prison warden, while his older brother was a captain for a local county police department.

Callaway continued the family tradition, but he soon realized he was not cut out for it. To the dismay of his brother, he quit, but it was only after his father had passed away. He couldn't bear to see disappointment in his old man's eyes. Once he was gone, Callaway was free to do whatever he wanted with his life.

The only problem was that he didn't know what to do with himself. He was lost when he walked away from the sheriff's department. This was also around the time he left his wife and infant daughter.

He never regretted leaving the sheriff's department, but what he did to his family at a time when they needed him most was unforgivable.

Jimmy is not the only selfish prick around here, Callaway thought. *I am just like him.*

Maybe that's why Callaway was drawn to a man like Jimmy Keith. Jimmy epitomized a life of self-indulgence, danger, and recklessness. Jimmy lived for the day, and he lived for himself. He *did* care about what happened to those around him, just as long as it did not interfere with his life of fun and excitement.

It now dawned on Callaway that Jimmy lived a life bereft of responsibility. Jimmy disappeared if things got too personal, which explained why he didn't return Callaway's calls these past few years.

Callaway wanted to work with Jimmy forever. He had even suggested they open up their own agency together. Jimmy was not too keen on the idea. He liked working alone. He also thought it was better for Callaway to strike out on his own. Callaway figured Jimmy was teaching him to be more independent. What he did not realize was that Jimmy was pushing him away.

For a man who ran away from his problems, why did he confess now? Maybe murder was something he could not just walk away from.

Jimmy had a lot of faults, but the man also had a lot of good in him. Callaway had seen it with his own eyes, or else he would have left Jimmy a long time ago. Jimmy was kind to the less fortunate. If he had a dollar in his pocket and someone was begging on the street, Jimmy would give him that dollar. Callaway would ask him why he would do that when it was his last penny, and Jimmy's response would be, "The guy needs it more than me."

Jimmy also took on cases where he knew the money did not compensate the amount of work required to complete the job. If there was a wrong that needed to be righted, Jimmy would go out of his way to make it happen.

Perhaps Jimmy knew he was wrong to hide Scott's murder, and he saw no other option except to come clean. How else could one explain what he did? Fisher had nothing that linked him to Scott's death. There was even the possibility she might have never solved the case.

Callaway shook his head and downed the remainder of his scotch. He waved the bartender over.

"You sure you should be drinking this early in the day?" the bartender asked.

Callaway dropped another large bill on the counter. "Keep bringing them, okay?"

"Sure," the bartender said, and he returned with another glass.

Tears streamed down Callaway's face as he took another long gulp. The scotch burned the back of his throat, and he winced. If he had to go through the five hundred dollars the Hendersons had given him, he would. The alcohol helped numb the pain.

His mind was swirling with all sorts of emotions. One second he would be angry, the next he was sad, and then it would quickly turn to regret. Emotions were coming at him full-force.

Someone entered the bar. He felt a shadow behind him. He turned and saw it was his ex-wife, Patti.

"Lee," she said. "I just saw the news about Jimmy."

There was genuine concern in her eyes. His lips quivered, and then he broke down crying.

Patti came over and hugged him.

Callaway let her. He didn't want to be alone.

SEVENTY-SIX

Rain pelted the windshield in a rhythmic motion. The rain had started light, then it turned hard in a matter of minutes.

Inclement weather was not forecast when Fisher decided to drive twenty miles to a location outside the city.

She was parked at the edge of a cliff. A sign on the way over warned drivers to be careful. The cliff itself was not steep, but the turn was sharp. There were reports of cars skidding off the cliff.

Fisher was familiar with the location because she had been here once before, on the night of her high school prom.

Barry Kessel was the football team's star defenseman. He was built like an ox. When he asked her to be his date, her friends told her not to accept. Barry was not the most handsome man. He looked more like a Neanderthal. He even had a bushy unibrow.

Fisher felt sorry for him, so she agreed. But there was another reason why. The boy she had a crush on had asked another girl to be his prom date. Fisher was heartbroken. She even considered not going to the prom.

The night was awkward. They hardly spoke, and the one dance they had together made them the center of attention for all the wrong reasons. She looked like a princess, and he looked like an ogre.

Afterwards, she couldn't wait to go home, but then he asked her to go on a drive with him. She hesitated, but when she saw the eagerness in his eyes, she agreed.

The moment they arrived at the spot on the cliff, she immediately regretted her decision. If he chose to have his way with her and then dump her body over the cliff, she would be helpless to stop him. She only wished the students at the prom remembered her leaving with him. They could identify him as her killer.

To her surprise, unlike the other boys in her class, who were prepared to make a move on their dates, he was a complete gentleman. He had brought her to this spot because it overlooked Milton. He had been here countless times. He would sit and think about his future as he looked at the city.

They talked for hours. She found that behind the rough exterior, he was a kind soul. He disliked football, but he only played it because it stopped other kids from making fun of him. He was thoughtful, intellectual, and he had a wry sense of humor. At the end of the night, she even gave him a kiss. That made him feel special.

The last she heard of Barry Kessel, he was a professor at Columbia, and he was married with three children. Fisher knew if he could make her feel special for one night, he must make his family feel special every day.

The rain slowed when she got out of the SUV. She went over to the edge of the cliff and peered down.

I should call for backup, she thought. *I shouldn't be doing this alone.*

The dirt on the side of the cliff had turned into mud. Scaling down could result in her slipping and falling hundreds of feet to her death.

She could always come back on a nicer day, but she didn't want to waste time. She had seventy-two hours to complete her investigation, and she had to confirm or deny that something vital lay at the bottom of the cliff.

She went back to the SUV, removed a nylon rope from the trunk, and tied one end to the SUV. She tied the other around her waist.

She slowly and carefully began to scale down the side of the cliff. Her feet dug into the dirt and mud, causing her legs to work extra hard. Her thighs burned, but she made it to the landing twenty feet below. She pulled out a flashlight and shined the light around.

She spotted what she had come to find. The white kitchen towel had turned dull and brown.

She reached over and grabbed the towel, pulling it closer until she was holding it. She unwrapped the towel and found an ivory bookend shaped like a Roman column.

The bookend had been cleaned of fingerprints, but that didn't matter. The bookend was an obvious match for the other found at the scene of the crime.

Fisher had found the bookend exactly where Jimmy had told her it would be.

Jimmy was telling the truth.

He had murdered Dillon Scott.

SEVENTY-SEVEN

Becky entered the house. She spotted her mom in the living room. Becky had forgotten her mom started work late that day.

"I didn't know you were coming home for lunch," her mom said with a smile.

Without replying, Becky raced up the stairs and went straight to her room. She shut the door and fell on the bed. She covered her face with a pillow and began to sob uncontrollably.

It was not supposed to be like this. He had assured her everything would be okay. He told her he would take care of things, so how did this happen?

A part of her wanted to scream at the top of her lungs, telling the world the truth as she did, but she could not. Her mom had been through so much already. She didn't deserve to be in the middle of her daughter's mess.

She pushed the pillow aside. She couldn't breathe. It felt like someone had gripped her throat and was squeezing tight. Hot tears streamed down her cheeks.

She sat upright. Her chest tightened as if she was deep underwater and the pressure was crushing her like a can. The walls were caving in on her. She wanted to get out, but where could she go? Who could she turn to now?

He made her promise him she would let him handle the matter. She would *not* get involved. She had kept her end of the bargain, but how could she keep her mouth shut now? She couldn't hide the truth forever. It was bound to come out.

What if it doesn't? she thought. *What if no one ever knows that I was responsible for what happened?*

She hugged herself and began to cry again. She was scared, even more so than the time she heard her dad was gone. She feared for the future without him. He was the foundation that kept her and her mom steady.

Somehow they had managed to get through the year. Her mom grieved in silence, but Becky had a shoulder to cry on.

Now even that was gone.

There was a knock at the door. "Honey, are you okay?"

Becky wiped her eyes. "I'm… I'm fine, Mom."

"Can I come in?"

"Mom… I just need…"

"Becky, *please*…"

She hesitated for a moment, but she relented. "Okay, Mom."

Her mom entered. The moment she saw her, she said, "Baby, what's wrong?"

Becky covered her face with a pillow. She could not face her mom. Not like this.

Her mom came over and sat next to her. "You can talk to me, you know that, right?"

"I know, but I can't."

Her mom waited a moment before she asked, "Do you want me to cook you something special?"

"I'm not hungry."

"Okay, so you're not hungry, and you don't want to talk. I'm certain you're upset about a boy? Is it Daniel Bailey?"

Becky pushed the pillow aside and asked, "How do you know about Daniel?"

"I've heard you mention his name on the phone."

Becky scowled. "Have you been eavesdropping on my conversations?"

Her mom smiled. "When you and Ester talk on the phone, you don't realize there are other people in the house. These walls are made of drywall, not concrete."

Becky placed the pillow back over her head. "This is not about Daniel."

"Then what is it about?"

"Please leave me alone, Mom."

Silence hung between them.

Her mom sighed. "After your dad died, the only thing I wanted to do was stay inside my room and cry. I did that for many days. I'm sure you heard me."

Becky did, but she never told her.

"Your father was not only my husband, he was also my best friend. I couldn't see myself going forward alone. I thought about swallowing a bottle of pills to end my misery."

Becky whipped the pillow off her face and looked at her mom. "You did?" she asked, shocked.

Her mom nodded. "But then I thought of you. With both of us gone, who would take care of you? Your father never chose to end his life, and I couldn't choose to end mine either. I flushed the pills down the toilet."

"I didn't know this, Mom."

"And I never wanted you to know it, either."

"Why wouldn't you tell me? I'm your daughter."

"That's right, baby. You and I are the only family we have left. If you don't talk to me now, I will never know what you're going through. Like you never knew what I was going through."

Becky stared at her mom. She knew her mom would never judge her.

Tears brimmed in Becky's eyes.

"Mom, I did something very bad, and I don't know what to do."

SEVENTY-EIGHT

Callaway sat on the sofa. His shoulders were slumped, and his face was a mask of agony. Patricia "Patti" Callaway sat across from him with a cup in her hand. She had dark hair that used to be short but was now shoulder-length. Her brown eyes could spot a lie a mile away, which was why Callaway had stopped bullshitting her. He respected her too much to pull a fast one on her.

She always had a smile on her face, even when things were going bad. Unlike Callaway, she had the internal strength to not let the world get to her. She managed to raise a child on her own when Callaway abruptly left her.

Any other spouse would have been bitter, angry, and would have done everything to make his life miserable. Patti took the high road. She let him walk away without many repercussions. She knew he was unhappy, though not with the marriage—this was something he was adamant about—but with life in general. He wanted more out of his existence. Unfortunately, he was not mature enough to realize how much he mattered to his family.

He did, however, leave everything behind: the house, the car, whatever savings he had in their joint bank account. Enough for her to start all over again.

Callaway knew why she never retaliated for his cruel actions. Patti had grown up in a broken home. Her parents divorced when she was very young. She saw how one parent used their children against the other. She saw how the pettiness and vitriol impacted her and her siblings. She vowed she would not let that affect her little girl.

Sabrina "Nina" Callaway was nine years old, and she was as smart and grounded as her mother. There were even times when Callaway would ask Nina for advice. He knew it should be the other way around, but he was such a screwup that Nina was sometimes the parent. Nina had her mother's dark hair, but she also had his green eyes. She looked more like Patti than him, which was perfectly fine by Callaway. If he had a boy, he would have wanted his son to be more like his mother as well.

Even after all these years, Callaway still found Patti attractive. He had imagined them getting back together and becoming a family again, but he wasn't sure Patti would be up for it. Callaway never once cheated on her during their marriage, but he was so miserable while they were married that Patti was perhaps relieved to let him go.

He doubted she would let him back in.

She took a sip from her cup but said nothing. His empty cup was on the coffee table. After he had cried his eyes out, he asked for a glass of water. Patti then made him a fresh brew of coffee to help him sober up.

"I'm sorry about Jimmy," she said.

He shrugged.

"I didn't know he was in town," she then said.

"He showed up unannounced."

"That's typical of Jimmy."

After walking out on his marriage, Callaway landed at Jimmy's doorstep. Patti could have blamed Jimmy for how things had turned out with her and Callaway. Callaway was going through an early midlife crisis, and he may have returned to his family once he saw what he was missing being a parent and a husband. But Jimmy exposed him to a life where he could do whatever he wanted whenever he wanted. To say Jimmy corrupted Callaway would be a lie. Callaway was corruptible to begin with, and Jimmy only showed him the way. Patti also believed that if it wasn't Jimmy, it would have been someone else who pulled Callaway away from her and Nina.

If Callaway was in her place, he would have held a grudge, but not Patti. Another reason he kicked himself for letting this amazing woman get away.

"When's Nina coming home?" he asked.

"I have to pick her up after school. Do you want to do it?" she asked. Whenever he was over, which was rare, he cherished the opportunity to spend time with her.

He shook his head. "I don't want her to see me like this," he said.

"She'll understand," Patti said.

"I'm crying like a bubbling fool."

"What happened is devastating. Nina knows how much Jimmy meant to you."

He scowled. "He used me." He told her what had happened. She had opened her arms and her home to him, even though he deserved nothing but a cold shoulder. He would not take her kindness for granted, and he would not shy away from the truth.

"Even then, he is your friend," she said when he was done.

Friend... that stings, Callaway thought. "Friends are supposed to be honest with each other," he said.

"What did you want him to say? 'I killed a man, and I want you to help me get away with it?'"

He opened his mouth, but he had no reply. She had a point. She always did.

"Jimmy was in a tough position. He did what anyone would do when faced with a difficult situation. You said yourself that it was an accident, that Jimmy never went to the house to hurt him."

"I would have helped him if he'd asked."

"How?" Patti asked.

Again, Callaway had no reply.

"If you had helped him, that would have made you accessory to murder. By hiding the truth from you, he was also protecting you."

Callaway wasn't ready to hear that. He was angry, and he was using it as fuel to despise Jimmy. He didn't want her words to take that away from him.

He stood up. "I have to go."

"Where are you going?"

"I don't know, but I can't stay here."

"You can have dinner with us tonight," she offered. "I know Nina would be so happy to see you."

He shrugged as he moved to the front door. He turned to her. "You didn't have to do this, but thank you."

She smiled. "If you change your mind, you're welcome to drop by."

EIGHTY

Fisher was not surprised to see a throng of reporters gathered outside the Milton P.D. After Cameron Kilgane broke the news of Jimmy's arrest, other news outlets quickly picked up on the story. Fisher's cell phone had been ringing nonstop. The press wanted a quote or a short sound bite. Her friends wanted to know the details of how it had gone down. Even Holt had left her several messages.

Fisher didn't answer any of the calls, nor did she reply to her messages. She was not prepared to say anything about the case.

She parked her SUV in the back of the police station and took the elevator up to the squad room.

Jimmy had confessed to killing Dillon Scott, but he never confessed to blackmailing him. Fisher had pressed him on it, but he was adamant he had no idea.

Scott had gone to Yonge Avenue with a backpack full of cash. He could not have done this without specific instructions. *So who was this person blackmailing him?* she thought. *And what did he have on Scott that made him agree to pull out fifty thousand from his production company's bank account and hand it over?*

She shook her head. She should forget about the blackmail. Scott was dead, and his killer was in custody. That was all that mattered. Who cared if there was another layer to this mystery? She should just close the case and move on to a dozen other cases that required her attention.

On her way to the Milton PD, she had stopped over at Scott's house. The crowd at the front gates had quadrupled since her previous visit. The press was obviously there for a story, but Scott's fans and even curious spectators wanted one last chance to be at the spot where Scott was found dead. With a suspect in custody, they could sense the end was near.

Once Jimmy was charged and convicted, the entire case would be relegated to the back pages of many newspapers. In a year, Scott's murder would be a distant memory. Something else would occupy the public's conscience. Scott would forever be remembered as a great actor who met an unfortunate end.

There was a reason for Fisher's visit to Scott's house, though. She wanted a section of the carpet where Jimmy had allegedly thrown up after realizing he had killed Scott. The carpet had already been cleaned with bleach, which would make it difficult to get a DNA match, but it would prove Jimmy had tried to dispose of the evidence. The wine glasses were not recoverable. Jimmy had tossed them over the cliff too. The glasses had also been wiped clean of fingerprints, and they too were wrapped in a towel, but unlike the bookend, they had not survived the fall.

It was her job to build a case against him whether she liked it or not. The prosecutor would then weigh the evidence and determine a reasonable sentence to put before a judge. She would request leniency, but she feared the public outcry would be too much to ignore. They would argue that a famous star was brutally taken away in his prime—even though, truth be told, Scott's career was on a downward trajectory. Regardless, optics mattered in a high-profile case like this, and Fisher worried that the state attorney might not consider her opinions.

Fisher hoped Callaway was able to convince Jimmy to seek out counsel. Without legal help, Jimmy was looking at spending the rest of his life behind bars.

EIGHTY-ONE

After leaving Patti's house, Callaway had driven to his office, but the mere thought of being stuck inside a windowless room suffocated him. He wanted to be outside, another reason why he didn't stay at Patti's. He felt like he couldn't breathe.

He figured a quick stroll around the block would cheer him up. It did not. Instead, he walked aimlessly down the streets for almost an hour. Where was he going? He didn't know, and he didn't care.

He had passed several bars, but he never once considered going in. Patti had pulled him out of one. Had she not shown up, he would have drunk himself into oblivion. When he got going with the booze, he didn't know when to stop. While he was married, there were times when Patti had to literally carry him home from the bar. It wasn't that Callaway was an alcoholic, he just didn't have much self-control. This trait was what got him in trouble. With booze, with money, with women, he just couldn't help himself.

It would be so easy to fall back into the trap of just one drink, but he owed it to Patti not to. When he thought about it, he owed her a lot. She gave him the freedom he so coveted. Others would have hung it around his neck like a leash. But not her.

He still didn't know what she saw in him that made her marry him. It wasn't Nina. She came a year after they tied the knot.

The two happiest days of his life were when he got married and when Nina was born. But that happiness didn't last long, and it had nothing to do with either Patti or Nina. It had everything to do with him. His restlessness took over.

He was feeling restless right then. He couldn't sit at Patti's, and he couldn't sit in his office. The bar was out of the question, so where should he go? Maybe to his hotel room, but then do what? Watch TV? Sleep?

He had to do something to keep him busy. His mind was all over the place, and each time he tried to focus, his mind came back to Jimmy.

Callaway had always wanted to follow in the man's footsteps. He wanted to be him. Now he loathed him.

Jimmy was a criminal!

Patti may have been right when she said Jimmy kept Callaway in the dark because he didn't want him implicated in the murder. But then why show up at his office in the first place? Jimmy ought to have known Callaway would help him and end up becoming part of the narrative.

Callaway was grateful that Fisher didn't question him as to how much he knew of Scott's murder. Jimmy was Callaway's friend, and he had introduced him to Fisher. She would be right to be suspicious of him. But she was not. She could see the shock and pain in his eyes.

Jimmy had betrayed him!

He stopped in the middle of the sidewalk and took a deep breath. He could not fall apart here. There were too many people on the street, and a public meltdown would only draw attention to him.

He slowly exhaled. He could feel a strong sensation surge through him—resentment mixed with sadness. He resented the fact that Jimmy had used him. He was sad that his relationship with Jimmy had now come to an end.

After Jimmy was locked away, Callaway didn't know if he would ever see him again. He hoped in time his anger toward Jimmy would fade, and that he would want to visit him in prison. But what if Jimmy didn't want to see *him*? What if Jimmy was angry at him for abandoning him in a time of need?

Why do I feel like the guilty one? he thought. *It was Jimmy who weaved a web of lies.*

He turned around and headed back the way he came. He walked past the noodle shop and entered the alley next to it. He made his way to the back of the property and suddenly stopped in his tracks.

Standing at the bottom of the metal stairs was a girl. She looked like a teenager, and next to her was an older woman who looked a lot like her. *Probably her mother*, Callaway figured.

He hardly ever received any visitors, so he was surprised to see them. Even if someone did show up unexpectedly, they would see the telephone number taped to the door and call him.

"Lee Callaway?" the girl asked.

"I'm sorry, we're closed," he said. He was in no mood to take on a case, even if the money was good. "Call tomorrow… or better yet, call next week."

He walked past them and went up the metal stairs.

"Mr. Callaway, I need to speak to you," the girl said.

He kept going.

"It's about Jimmy Keith."

He stopped mid-step. He turned to look at her. "What did you say?"

"I need to speak to you about Jimmy Keith."

Callaway's eyes narrowed. "How do you know him?"

"I'm his granddaughter."

EIGHTY-TWO

The girl and her mother were seated on the worn-out sofa. Callaway sat on a chair across from them.

The mother and daughter eyed the interior of his office, and Callaway immediately felt self-conscious. The office was a reflection of his success—or lack thereof—as a private investigator. Some of his contemporaries had offices in skyscrapers with views of the entire city. Callaway, on the other hand, was holed up in a cramped space with no sunlight.

He thought about offering them something to drink, but he had nothing, not even water.

He coughed to clear his throat and said, "I'm sorry, but Jimmy doesn't have a grandchild. I mean, if he did, he would have mentioned it to me."

"Jimmy didn't know until a year ago," the girl said.

Callaway almost laughed. "It's a little hard to believe, you know."

"Jimmy had a son, whose name was—"

The realization hit him like a thunderbolt. "James Keith, Jr.," he said. Jimmy had mentioned it to him once when he was drunk. Callaway thought it was the alcohol talking.

"Yes," the girl said. "That was the name on the birth certificate, but Jimmy wasn't there for the birth. My grandmother always told us my grandfather was a decorated police officer who had died in the line of duty."

This was partially true, Callaway knew. Jimmy was an officer for the Miami Police Department, and he was shot in the arm when a perpetrator made a run for it during a routine traffic stop. But he didn't die, nor was he highly decorated. He quit after getting in a fight with his superiors.

"Didn't you realize the story about Jimmy was a lie?" Callaway asked. "I mean, if you just went online and did a search, you'd have seen that he hadn't died."

"I know that sounds simple now," she said. "You see, right after my dad was born, my grandmother married Jacob Miller, and he immediately adopted my dad and gave him his name, so he became James Miller."

"And you are…?" Callaway asked.

"Becky Miller, and this is my mom, Sara Miller."

He smiled at Sara, and she smiled back.

Becky said, "Until recently, I didn't even know my grandfather was not really related to my dad by blood. I think even my dad didn't know this. My grandfather died from lung cancer when my dad was four. My grandmother raised him on her own, but then she got sick with leukemia when my dad was sixteen."

"I'm sorry," Callaway said. He could not imagine a family being hit with so many tragedies.

He thought of something. *Did Jimmy know what was happening to his son?*

"Where is your dad now?" he asked.

Becky took a deep breath. Her eyes turned moist. "My dad died last year in a construction accident."

Callaway's heart ached for the girl.

Becky said, "I met Jimmy at my dad's funeral. He introduced himself as a colleague from the construction company. I could tell he wasn't telling the truth. My dad had never once mentioned him before, but I had seen him crying next to my dad's casket. When I looked carefully, I could see a strong resemblance between him and my dad. Before I could press him on it, he disappeared." She paused to collect her thoughts. "A month later, I caught him standing outside our house. I was coming back from work. He tried to run away, but I cornered him. I asked him how he knew my dad. He eventually confessed to me. He always knew he had a son, but he never wanted to be a father—he didn't want the responsibility."

Callaway suddenly felt guilty. *I never wanted to be a father either, but I have Nina.*

"Over the years, my grandmother had made several attempts to contact Jimmy. She wanted him to look after my dad when she was gone. She knew her time was coming to an end, but Jimmy never responded. More time went by, my dad got older, he got married, he had me, and then Jimmy had a heart attack."

Callaway nodded. He had heard about that.

"I think it was then that Jimmy began to search out my dad. He tried to approach him a few times, but he wasn't sure how my dad would react. He always thought he had time to build a relationship with my dad until he found out about the accident. He was really torn up about it. I had to console him, even though it was my dad that was gone. After that, we kept in touch on a daily basis. Jimmy even sold his condo and boat when he found out we needed money."

"How much money was it?" Callaway asked, curious.

"Around eighty thousand dollars."

Callaway's mouth nearly hit the floor. Jimmy was not known to be charitable when it came to money. That was his entire life savings.

Sara Miller said, "I thought the money came from a fundraiser, until Becky told me the truth just now."

Becky said, "Jimmy told me that if I ever needed help, I should come to you."

Callaway was flattered, but he said, "I'm not sure how I can help you."

Becky turned to her mother, who gave her a reassuring smile. "It's okay, baby. You tell him the truth."

"Mr. Callaway," Becky said, tearing up. "Jimmy didn't kill Dillon Scott... I did."

EIGHTY-THREE

Callaway almost fell off his chair. "What?!"

Becky didn't reply.

Callaway stood up and began pacing the room. He turned to Becky. "How could you have killed Scott when Jimmy just confessed to the crime?"

"He confessed to it to protect me," she replied.

Callaway stared at her.

A light bulb went off in his head. "You're the girl in the taxi with Dillon Scott."

She looked away.

It's now making sense, Callaway thought. When Fisher had gone to see the taxi driver to retrieve the footage, the driver told her another detective had taken it. That other detective was *Jimmy*. He must have shown the driver his replica Miami PD badge. He took the footage so that nothing led back to his granddaughter.

Callaway walked back to the chair and sat down. "Tell me what happened the night Dillon Scott died."

Becky's hands shook. Her mom placed her hand over hers and gave her daughter another reassuring smile. "Tell him," she said.

Becky took a deep breath. "I work as an assistant at a veterinary clinic. It's only part-time, but whenever we have an emergency at the clinic, I stay later than usual. Anyway, I was leaving the clinic that night when I saw Dillon Scott coming my way..."

"The clinic is on Yonge Avenue?" Callaway asked.

"It's not on Yonge Avenue, but on the street next to it."

"Okay."

"Jimmy had told me about a case he was working on."

"Gail Roberts?"

"Yes. He would call me up and we would talk for hours. What he really wanted was to know more about my dad, but deep down it hurt him that he had missed all the major events in his life, so instead we would talk about the case. From Jimmy, I knew Dillon was in Milton shooting a movie."

"You call him Dillon?" Callaway asked.

"That's what he told me to call him when we met."

"Go on."

"When I saw Dillon, I don't know what I was thinking. Maybe I saw an opportunity to help Jimmy. I approached Dillon and told him I was one of his biggest fans. It was a lie. I've never seen any of his movies, but I knew of his work. I asked if I could take a photo with him. He was in a hurry to catch a taxi. He asked if I needed a ride. I told him yes. He offered to drop me off at my house." She shook her head. "I should have never gotten in the taxi with him, but I did. We started talking, and I asked him a lot of questions about being a famous movie star. I think he liked the attention because a minute before, when I'd seen him walking up the street, he looked stressed."

He was, Callaway thought. *He'd just stormed away from a reporter at a bar.* "How did you end up at his house?" Callaway asked.

She sighed. "He said he wanted to show me something, but it was at his house."

"What?"

"One of his acting awards."

"And you agreed?"

She nodded. "I figured I could get him to tell me something about Gail Roberts. I was so stupid and naïve."

"Then what happened?"

"We got to the house, and I was surprised when he sent the taxi away. I thought he'd show me the award and then I would go straight home. He said he would call another taxi. He seemed so nice, and I was never worried because he's Dillon Scott, you know? I've seen posters of him outside movie theaters. I was kind of flattered a famous movie star was giving me all this attention. He asked about my family. I told him about my dad, and he looked genuinely sad. But now that I think about it, maybe he was only acting, and he really didn't care about what I'd been through. We went inside the house, and he offered me a drink. I told him I was sixteen, but he smiled and said there's always a first time for everything, and that years later, I would tell my friends that I had my first drink with Dillon Scott. I think he had wine, because it was red, and I don't know what he brought me, but it was brown."

It was bourbon, Callaway thought.

"I took a sip and hated the taste. It burned the back of my throat. Dillon saw the look on my face, and he laughed. He encouraged me to drink some more. He said I'd get used to it very fast."

Callaway's jaw tightened. *He was trying to get you drunk.*

Becky said, "After a couple more sips, the burning got so intense that I threw up on the carpet."

That explains why the carpet was cleaned up later.

"He gave me water, but then suddenly he tried to kiss me. I told him I had a boyfriend. I was lying, but I didn't like what he was doing. He said he would teach me some things I could show my boyfriend later. He tried to get on top of me. I couldn't believe what was happening. He was old enough to be my father."

Callaway could feel anger rise up in him. He balled his fists.

"He kept saying I should feel lucky someone like him was interested in me. He was a big movie star, and if I let him do what he wanted, he could try to get me a part in one of his movies. I told him I didn't want to be an actress. He just laughed. I was on the sofa, and he was on top of me. I knew what was going to happen next. We were shown videos of situations like that in school. He had the wine glass in his hand, and when he turned to put it on the coffee table, I pushed him back with my knees. I then jumped up on the sofa, reached over and grabbed a bookend that was on a bookshelf. The wine glass fell from his hand and spilled on the carpet. He cursed and turned back to me." Becky took a deep breath. "I hit him on the head with the bookend. I don't think he had time to react, and then he dropped to the floor." Becky shook. Tears streamed down her cheeks. "I never meant to hurt him. I only wanted him off me so I could run out of the house."

Her mom put her arms around her and hugged her tight. Becky sobbed into her chest.

Callaway looked up at the ceiling in deep thought. More questions were answered. Fisher believed Scott's attacker was over six feet, which is what Jimmy was. But Becky, who was five-three at best, was on the sofa when she hit Scott from above, thus giving the impression that Scott's attacker was taller than him.

Callaway asked, "Afterwards, you called Jimmy, is that right?"

Becky nodded. "He drove straight over and asked me exactly what had happened. He told me not to worry about anything, and that he would take care of it."

Callaway knew what Jimmy did next. He had laid it out in his confession. He cleaned Becky's vomit off the carpet, took the wine glasses with her and Scott's fingerprints, and he also took the bookend with her prints on it.

Callaway realized Jimmy had taken the fall for Becky. He was not a murderer.

Jimmy is innocent!

"Mr. Callaway."

Becky's words broke his reverie.

"Jimmy is locked up because of me. He lied to protect me. What should I do?"

Callaway had no idea. His head was reeling.

EIGHTY-FOUR

Callaway told Becky to go home. He would call her later if he needed more information. At the moment, he needed to see Jimmy.

After speaking to Fisher, he was allowed back in the interview room. He found Jimmy seated behind the metal table. He had a smile on his face. "Hey, kid," he said. "I knew you couldn't stay angry at me for long."

"I met your granddaughter," Callaway said. "Becky Miller."

The smile evaporated from Jimmy's face. "Oh god, no. She didn't…?"

"She told me everything," Callaway said, taking a seat across from him.

Jimmy put his hands over his face and shook his head. "Don't listen to her. She's just a child."

"She's old enough to know what's right and what's wrong."

"How'd she find you?" Jimmy asked, looking up.

"Apparently, you told her to seek me out if she needed help."

"I meant if *she* got in trouble, not to involve you in this."

"Why didn't you tell me the truth?" Callaway asked.

"About Becky?"

Callaway leaned closer. "About Becky, about what happened at Scott's house, everything."

Jimmy sighed. "What was I gonna say?"

"You could have started off by telling me you had a grandkid."

"How would that look, huh?" Jimmy replied. "I spent my whole life telling you and everyone else that family means nothing and that they only bring you down. But you know what? It's all bullshit. You need people in your life. You need someone to remember you when you're gone."

"I would have remembered you," Callaway said.

Jimmy smiled. "I know you would have, kid, but you know what I mean."

Callaway said nothing.

Jimmy said, "After a while, you begin to realize you need something more in your life. I've always looked out for number one, but what I should have been looking out for was other people. That's what makes life worth it. It can't be all about you. You can't go from one thing to another, always looking for excitement and adventure."

"Are you dying, Jimmy?" Callaway asked.

Jimmy blinked. "What?"

"You sound like a man who has seen the end and wants to make amends for his sins."

"No, I'm not dying, and yes, I do want to make amends for what I've done." Jimmy reached over and placed his hand over his. The gesture surprised Callaway. "Lee, you got a precious little girl. Don't waste your life like I did. Go and make sure you're part of her life. Before you know it, she'll be all grown up. Right now she needs you, whether you see it or not.

Callaway's head began to spin. He pulled his hand away. "You fed me the I-should-be-a-lone-wolf crap, that I should be free to experience life and squeeze every drop out of it. What was that all about, Jimmy?"

"When I met you, I really believed that stuff. But now I don't."

"Was it the heart attack?"

"It was the catalyst, but it was so much more. When I had the heart attack, I was at home, drinking a beer and watching TV. That was my routine each night. And I loved that I didn't have to change it for anyone. But when I collapsed on the floor, clutching my chest, I kept thinking about Walter. I didn't want to die alone. Luckily, I had my cell phone in my front pocket. I was able to dial 9-1-1." He stared into Callaway's eyes. "When I was asking about Nina and Patti, there was a reason. I was hoping to steer your mind back to them."

Callaway looked away. "I was a terrible husband and a lousy father," he said.

"I can't give you any marriage advice because I never got married, but I can tell you, don't push Nina away like I pushed my son away."

"I don't know how to be a father," Callaway confessed.

"Then be her friend. Or better yet, just be there for her."

Callaway crossed his arms over his chest. He could not believe the man who had once told him having a family was akin to getting an incurable disease was now telling him the opposite. Maybe it wasn't Jimmy who was the fool all these years, maybe it was Callaway. He listened to Jimmy's words like they were gospel. Jimmy was nothing more than a male fantasy of booze, women, and danger. In reality, he was a sad old man.

Jimmy shook his head. "My son, James, he was not like me in many ways, but in other ways, he was. He didn't gamble, he didn't drink all that much, he loved his wife, Sara, and he adored his little girl, Becky. But like me, he was reckless…"

Callaway's eyes narrowed. "What do you mean?"

EIGHTY-FIVE

"After I heard about the accident at the construction site, I started looking into it," Jimmy replied. "I'm a private investigator, after all. I wanted justice for Sara and Becky. What I found out was that James was addicted to prescription medication. He'd hurt his back and was popping two dozen painkillers a day. On the morning of the accident, he had downed a handful right before he picked up the sledgehammer. The wall he was digging next to was safe. An engineer had evaluated it only a day before. James dug too close to the wall, and it caved in on him."

"How did you find this out?" Callaway asked.

"I tracked down one of his buddies from work. He was torn up about what happened. Apparently, he was helping James get the painkillers. No doctor would prescribe someone that many pills a day, but with his buddy's help, James got all the meds he wanted. The buddy had warned James to get help, but James was a sweet talker, like me. He convinced his buddy that it was only for a short period, until his back healed up. James's back had healed up months earlier. I saw the doctor's reports. He was just not strong enough to stop using painkillers."

"The Occupational Safety and Health Administration made no mention of the painkillers in their findings," Callaway said, aware of some of the details, thanks to Becky. "They did, however, mention the marijuana."

"Right after the accident, the buddy realized the investigators would start digging into the prescription medication and how James was able to get so many pills. The buddy was afraid he'd get in trouble for supplying him the drugs. He was able to remove the bottle of pills from his lunch pail. Also, James was not getting the painkillers under his name but under the buddy's, so it didn't raise any red flags. And as for the pot, like I said before, James was reckless. Some of the guys used to smoke it before their shift, including his buddy, and James would join them. When the government investigators questioned the buddy about it, he fessed up to the pot because it's a misdemeanor, but he never told them about the painkillers, which would have been a federal offense."

Callaway was silent.

Jimmy continued. "Becky and Sara have no idea. They think James was squeaky clean, and I don't have the heart to tell them otherwise. And why would I? I was never there to guide my son in the right direction. Heck, I might have made him worse, like I did with you."

"I wasn't good to begin with," Callaway said.

"You weren't bad, either. You were lost when you came to me, and I could have molded you right, but instead I gave you all my bad traits, and for that I'm really sorry, Lee."

Callaway just stared at him. "Don't beat yourself up about it. I wasn't some fresh-faced kid. I was married, and I had a kid of my own. I knew what I was doing when I knocked on your door."

"All I have to say is that our actions have consequences," Jimmy said.

"But that's not what happened with Becky," Callaway said. "She killed Dillon Scott, but you're not letting her actions have consequences."

Jimmy's face turned dark. "You can't tell anyone what she told you."

"It was self-defense," Callaway said. "They'll show her leniency once they know the details about what happened."

"She killed someone…"

"But it was—"

"She can't go to jail!" Jimmy roared. "She's still young. You know what happens to people with a murder conviction, don't you? It stays on their record for a long time. If they're lucky, maybe it can be expunged, but until then, you're known as a person who killed another human being. Becky can't be that person. She just can't. No employer will hire her. No one will want to work with her. No one will give her a loan or want to do business with her. Murder can't be ignored. Its stench follows you forever."

"She never meant to hurt Scott," Callaway insisted.

"Even then, I don't want her going through a trial, the scrutiny, all of it. Let me take the fall. I'm old. I've lived my life. She still has a future. Let me make it up for all the mistakes I've made in my life."

Callaway felt like someone was hammering nails in his head. He winced as pain shot through his brain.

"I'm begging you, kid," Jimmy pleaded. "If you care even a little bit about me, then forget what she told you. Prison is nothing for the damage I've caused. I ignored my only son. I let him grow up without a father. I deserve a fate far worse than this. He's not here to protect his daughter, so I will. Walk away and forget about me. I…"

Callaway's ears began to ring. He could no longer hear what Jimmy was saying. So many emotions were raging through him, he felt like his head was about to explode.

He wanted to scream and make the pain go away, but he couldn't.

He got up and left.

EIGHTY-SIX

Fisher sat on a bench that faced Milton Harbor. There were two other benches, and they were both occupied. It was midafternoon, and people were eating their lunches while enjoying the stillness of the water. A hot dog stand was not far from her, and the smell made her mouth water. But Fisher was not here to get a bite to eat or soak in the view.

At the Milton PD, she had received a call. The caller did not give her name, but she urged Fisher to meet at this location. She said she had information on Dillon Scott, and she wanted to share it with Fisher.

Fisher's inclination was to be suspicious. After Scott's death, the department had been inundated with tips regarding the murder. It seemed everyone and their uncle had a theory as to who had done it. But there was something in the caller's voice that told her she was not making the call to gain attention. She was calling because it was necessary.

Fisher agreed and drove straight over.

As she waited, she began to feel it might have been a mistake. There were people looking for a place to sit, and Fisher was tempted to let them take a spot on the bench.

A woman came over and sat next to her.

She had dirty blonde hair, pale skin, and mascara around her eyes. She was wearing jeans, boots, and a long coat. She wasn't carrying a purse, and her hands were shoved inside her coat pockets.

"Detective Fisher?" she said.

"You are?" Fisher asked.

"My name is not important, but I have information that might be useful to you."

Fisher didn't appreciate the clandestine way the woman spoke, but she was used to dealing with informants. She would give the woman some leeway before she decided to end the meeting.

"You said it was about Dillon Scott," Fisher said.

The mere mention of his name made the woman scowl. "He's not who everyone thinks he is."

"Then who is he?"

"He's a predator who preyed on young women."

Fisher didn't know how to respond.

"I worked as his publicist until last year, when…"

She paused and looked away.

"It's okay," Fisher said in a soothing voice. "Whatever you tell me will not leave this bench." Fisher had worked with sexual assault and domestic violence victims. She knew how hard it was for them to speak up. They feared no one would believe them, or worse, they would be ostracized for coming forward.

The woman nodded and said, "One day, Dillon called me into his office. He wanted to discuss a photo shoot he had done for an upcoming movie. Gail was also there…"

"Gail Roberts?" Fisher immediately asked.

"Yes, she was his assistant at the time." The woman shut her eyes and took a deep breath. "I can't believe what happened to Gail. She was such a wonderful person."

"When you went to the office, what happened?" Fisher asked.

"I went in when Dillon asked Gail to go home for the day. I didn't think it was odd. I figured she had something to do. After she was gone, we spent half an hour going through the photos, but I could sense something was different. I had been alone with Dillon before, and he was always professional, but that day he asked me personal questions."

"What kind of questions?"

"He asked if I had a boyfriend, how many guys I had been with, and if I found him attractive. Really inappropriate stuff, you know? I tried to focus on the task, but then he suddenly put his hand on my leg. He then told me he liked me. I don't remember what I had told him, but I knew I didn't like that he was touching me." The woman choked up. "Before I knew what happened, he was on top of me. It was all a blur after that. I remember being in shock. I didn't know why he would do such a thing. I admired him a lot."

"Did you go to the police?"

She shook her head. "He warned me not to. He said if I did, he would tell them I had seduced him. He was rich and famous, so it was common for women to want to sleep with him."

"Did you tell anyone what happened?" Fisher asked.

EIGHTY-EIGHT

"I told Gail the next day," the woman replied. "I had never seen her so angry. She told me to go to the police, but again, I remembered what he had told me, and I was worried it would be his word against mine. But Gail said she would go with me to the police. She would corroborate my story. She would even contact a reporter and have her dig into Dillon's past. If he had done this to me, he must have done it to other girls."

Fisher mulled this over. Cameron Kilgane had received an anonymous call regarding Scott. She always assumed it was about the blackmail, but it was really about the sexual assaults.

The woman said, "Before we could go to the police, Gail had her accident."

Fisher now had a feeling it was no accident. Someone wanted her gone.

"I then quit as Dillon's publicist, but before I left, I signed a non-disclosure agreement. I was paid a lot of money to keep my mouth shut about the incident."

"Who gave you the money?"

"Brad Kirkman, Dillon's business partner."

Fisher's brow furrowed. Both Scott and Kirkman had alibis for the time Gail died. She then said, "You shouldn't have signed the non-disclosure or taken the money. It was his way of silencing you."

"I know, and I'm ashamed for taking it, but it was more money than I had ever seen at the time. I just wanted this nightmare behind me."

After a moment of silence, Fisher asked, "Why are you coming forward now?"

"Once we heard you had a suspect in custody, we wanted the world to know who Dillon Scott really was."

"We?" Fisher asked. "There are other women?"

The woman nodded. "I thought I was the only one, but we found each other online. People would post on forums praising Dillon's work as a humanitarian, a fighter for women's rights, a kind and decent soul, but there would be others who would say he was a wolf in sheep's clothing. The messages were cryptic, but I knew what they were talking about. I reached out to them, and what they told me horrified me. They all had to sign non-disclosure agreements, so like me, they were prevented from speaking out. One was a writer. Dillon invited her to meet him at his cottage to discuss a script she was working on. He said he had ideas he wanted her to incorporate in the script. When she got there, she found he was alone. Like me, they went over the script, but then he attacked her. Fortunately, she was able to push him away and get to her car and drive off." The woman paused and then continued. "Another was an actress. She met him during a stage production they were both in. Right before they were to go on stage, he called her to his dressing room and he groped her. She later told the director what happened. He advised her to keep it to herself or else she could be fired from the production." The woman put her hand over her face. "There are so many other stories. I don't think I can go through each and every one of them."

"That's fine," Fisher said. She was already sick to her stomach.

Like millions of people, Fisher had no idea of the evil that lurked behind his handsome smile. Dillon Scott was the worst of the worst. He had used his power and privilege against the young and helpless. These women never imagined the danger they were in until it happened to them. It reminded Fisher of an old saying: "You should never meet your heroes. They will end up disappointing you."

Fisher said, "Did Gail know about the other women?"

"I don't think so. It was before her time. But I know that with Gail's help, had I gone forward with my story, more women would have had the courage to come forward with theirs."

Fisher had a strong feeling someone had prevented Gail from doing just that.

EIGHTY-EIGHT

Joely came over and placed a piece of pie and a cup of coffee on the table. "It's on the house," she said.

Callaway looked up and gave Joely a smile. He knew she was going against her boss's wishes giving him a free meal, so he appreciated the kind gesture. "Thanks, Joely," he said.

Joely didn't know how much Jimmy meant to him, only that he was a friend who was now in jail for murder. "Let me know if you need anything," she said before she walked away.

He slowly took a bite of pie. It was crunchy on the outside and soft in the middle. He washed the bite down with a gulp of coffee.

After speaking to Jimmy, Callaway had come straight to Joely's restaurant. He needed a place to clear his head. He was so torn up about what to do. A part of him wanted to tell the truth and hope the judicial system would do the right thing and not harshly penalize Becky. Scott had attacked her, and her actions were in self-defense. She was also a minor, which worked in her favor.

Jimmy, on the other hand, would never forgive him if he did that. Jimmy was right. Prison was no place for a girl like Becky. Even if she escaped a prison sentence, the stigma that she killed another person would follow her wherever she went.

He should just forget about it like Jimmy had told him. There was nothing he could do that could fix this tragedy.

It was a tragedy in every sense of the word.

Becky had gone with Scott to his house to help Jimmy in his investigation of Gail's death. When things turned horribly wrong, Jimmy saw no other alternative but to take the blame for what happened, even though he had nothing to do with the crime. Jimmy would live out his remaining years behind bars while Becky lived her life knowing Jimmy had sacrificed himself for her. The guilt would eat away at her—it had already started to. Why else would she show up at his door asking for help?

But how can I help them? Callaway thought. *What can I do to undo what has already been done?*

The restaurant's door chimed. He saw Fisher enter. She looked around, caught him at a table, and came over.

"I knew I'd find you here," she said.

"Yeah, well, it was either here or a bar."

"I'm glad you chose here," she said, taking a seat across from him.

Joely came over. "Can I get you anything?"

"Coffee. Black, please," Fisher replied.

When Joely left, Fisher asked, "How're you holding up?"

He shrugged.

Joely returned, placed the cup on the table, and left. Fisher leaned closer and said, "I've got a problem."

Callaway's eyebrows shot up. "You've got a problem? Get in line, sister."

Fisher scowled. "Listen, I just came back from speaking to a woman. I can't go into the sordid details, but Dillon Scott was not who the public thought he was."

Callaway made a face. "I always knew he was a lousy actor."

"No, not that. He was a predator who took advantage of young women. He then wielded his power by silencing them with money and threats of legal action if they didn't comply."

"He attacked them?" Callaway asked.

Fisher's face was hard. "Yes."

Callaway suddenly debated whether to tell Fisher the whole truth. Scott had attacked Becky like the other women before her. Becky, however, did what no other woman could do. She stopped Scott from hurting someone else. No jury would convict her for this. But Callaway didn't know which way the wind blew. The prosecutor could be someone out to make a mark, and they could use a high-profile case like Scott's to make an example of Becky. Murder was murder, no matter the reason, he would argue. And everyone should be held accountable for their actions, regardless of their age and stature. On top of that, the prosecutor might even throw the book at Jimmy as an accessory to murder. There were too many variables at play.

He slowly sipped his coffee.

Fisher said, "I don't believe Gail's death was an accident or a suicide."

"Okay."

"I think someone wanted her out of the way."

"Scott?" Callaway asked.

"No. He has an alibi, but maybe he hired someone to do it. Gail knew too much. She was prepared to expose the truth to the world. It can't be a coincidence that the day before she was going to make an announcement, she falls fifteen floors to her death."

"Scott's dead too," Callaway said with a shrug. "What good would it do to start digging into his past?"

Fisher gritted her teeth. "Death is not enough for what this monster did to these women. He damaged them, and in some cases, he destroyed who they were as people. They trusted him, and he abused this trust. I want his name destroyed forever."

Callaway stared at her. He admired her determination, but he wasn't sure how helpful he could be in his current mental state. "Why are you telling me this?"

"Gail's family had hired Jimmy to find out how their daughter died. Jimmy has been looking into this for some time. He must have a file with all the information he had dug up on her case."

"Jimmy was a great PI If there was anything linking Scott to Gail's death, Jimmy would have found it by now."

"Maybe the case needs a fresh pair of eyes. You wouldn't believe how many cold cases were solved after a new detective took over them."

"You want me to look at it?" he asked.

"Yes. I'm too tied up with Scott's murder to do it myself."

"Jimmy confessed. What more do you have to do?"

"I still need to build a case for the prosecutor to win," she replied. "It's my job. That's why I'm asking for your help, Lee."

"I don't know," he said.

"I know you're hurting, but remember why Jimmy is in a cell right now."

He looked at her, doing his best to mask his horror. *Does she know the truth?* he thought.

Fisher said, "Jimmy went to Scott's house to confront him about Gail's death. I know he didn't mean to kill him, but Scott is dead. There is nothing we can do to change that. What we can do is continue Jimmy's work and provide answers for Gail's family. If Jimmy meant something to you, you wouldn't let him rot in prison for nothing."

Callaway stared at her. Finally, a smile crossed his face. "You know, you should have been a lawyer. You make a very convincing argument."

Fisher smiled. "Well, I am friends with one. Maybe I learned it from her."

EIGHTY-NINE

The first thing Callaway did was drive straight to Alderson County. When Jimmy was booked at the Milton PD, he provided an address for the record. Callaway wasn't sure if it was correct, but he wasn't ready to go see Jimmy to confirm it.

Jimmy was known to not stay in one place for too long. He was always on the move. Callaway had a feeling he was trying to distance himself from people, relationships, and even the problems he found himself in. Jimmy was often unreliable if you needed him in an emergency.

Callaway couldn't wrap his head around the man sitting in a cell at the Milton PD. Jimmy had changed almost overnight, but Callaway knew it was not that sudden. Jimmy was likely reassessing his life for a long time. Callaway had seen him become contrite when he got drunk. Alcohol enabled him to be more reflective during those times.

The bravado he presented was just a façade to cover his inner turmoil. He sold all his possessions so he could give his granddaughter a better life. He then gave up his freedom so that she could have a future that did not involve being stuck inside a cell.

Alderson County was a small town in the middle of nowhere. Callaway wasn't even sure if the town had a police station. He was not about to find out. He drove at the speed limit and followed all laws.

He pulled onto a dirt road and drove up to a weathered house. The roof was missing shingles, the exterior paint was peeling, and the steps that led to the front porch were uneven.

He parked and got out. He walked up to the house and knocked.

The door swung open. Callaway was hit with thick smoke. A man squinted at him. He had a cigarette between his lips, and he was wearing a wife-beater, pants, and no socks. "What do you want?" he muttered.

"Jimmy Keith live here?" Callaway asked.

The man eyed him suspiciously. "Who wants to know?"

"I'm his friend."

"I didn't know Jimmy had any friends."

"So he does live here," Callaway said.

"I never said that."

"But you know Jimmy, don't you?"

"Hey, buddy, why don't you get off my property before I make you?" the man said with a scowl. He was bigger than Callaway, but Callaway knew he could take him down.

"Jimmy owe you rent money?" Callaway asked.

The man's brow furrowed. "How'd you know?"

Because Jimmy is always behind on his rent, Callaway thought. "He owes me money too," Callaway claimed. "I want to see if he's got any cash stashed in his place."

"I haven't seen Jimmy in weeks," the man said.

"He's renting a room from you?"

"Yeah, the one upstairs."

"Let me take a look," Callaway said.

"It's locked, and I don't have a key."

"Don't worry about it," Callaway said.

The man hesitated.

"You want your money or not?" Callaway asked.

The man bristled. "Is it legal?"

"If Jimmy fails to meet his obligations, then as his landlord, you can access *your* property." Callaway wasn't sure if this was true, but he didn't care. He had to know what Jimmy had found on Gail's death.

"Okay, follow me," the man said.

The house smelled even worse than it looked, a mixture of body odor and cigarettes. They went up a creaky set of stairs and stopped at a door. Callaway looked at the keyhole and pulled out a metal tool from his pocket to rake the lock. In less than thirty seconds, he was in.

"Do you mind waiting outside?" Callaway asked the man.

The man scowled at Callaway. "How do I know you're not going to keep all the cash for yourself?"

Callaway pulled his jacket back, revealing his holstered gun. "You're going to have to take my word for it," Callaway said.

The man swallowed and disappeared down the stairs.

The room was small, with a bed in the middle and a dresser next to it. There were three pieces of luggage stacked on top of each other. Callaway wasn't sure if they held all of Jimmy's belongings, but if they did, he wouldn't be surprised. Jimmy had a saying: "Always pack light. You never know when you're going to have to get on the next train out of town."

There was a framed photo on the dresser. Callaway walked over and picked it up. It showed Callaway and Jimmy outside a bar. Callaway remembered that the picture was taken right after they had completed their very first case together. They were celebrating like they had won the World Series.

Callaway bit his bottom lip to control his emotions. He couldn't believe it had come to this.

He placed the photo back and walked around the room. He didn't see anything that resembled a file or folder.

He was walking around the bed when his foot hit something underneath. He leaned down and pulled out a shoebox. He opened it and found notes, police reports, and photos. One of the photos was of Gail with her friends.

Jackpot! he thought

He grabbed the box and went downstairs.

The landlord hurried up to him. "You find any money?"

Callaway pulled out two hundred dollars. "It was tucked under his pillow," he said.

The landlord smiled. "I knew it." He took the bills.

Callaway hated having to spend the money Frank Henderson had given him, but he couldn't leave without greasing the landlord's palm.

Callaway got in his Charger and drove away.

NINETY

Fisher found the medical examiner in the morgue. She was dressed in green overalls, and there were specks of blood on the front of her shirt and her sleeves.

"I was in the middle of an autopsy," Wakefield said as a way of apologizing.

"I can wait until you're done," Fisher said.

"No, this is important."

Fisher was across the city when she received the call. She had dropped everything and rushed over.

They walked to another room. Wakefield stopped next to a gurney. A white cloth was covering a body. She slid the cloth down to reveal Scott's face.

Fisher no longer shared Wakefield's admiration for how handsome Scott was, even in death. Behind the good looks lurked a hideous human being. Instead of using his fame to help others, he used it to help himself.

"I believe my initial instincts were correct," Wakefield said.

"What do you mean?" Fisher asked.

"The victim did not die of blunt force trauma. The wound on the head is superficial and could not have caused significant damage that would lead to death."

"Okay, but how did he die?" Fisher asked.

"It was a puzzle that kept me up many nights."

I don't doubt it, Fisher thought.

"I couldn't pinpoint the basis of his demise. How could a man in relatively good health die from a bump on the head? There had to be a logical explanation for this."

Fisher could tell Wakefield was enjoying this. The big reveal would come after she had set up the mystery.

"If it wasn't blunt force trauma, then what? The victim showed no other signs of physical distress. There were no marks on the face, torso, arms, or legs. That means death was not caused by external factors, but internal."

"Internal?" Fisher repeated.

Wakefield nodded. "I had to go back and conduct a fresh autopsy. I had to ignore what I saw before—the wound on the head—and focus on what I knew about the victim. You mention in your report that you had seen an insulin injection in the victim's home."

"I did, in his bedroom."

"This reminded me of a study I had read a few years ago. It took some work, but I was able to dig it up."

Wakefield walked over to a table and returned with a document. "Scientists in the U.K. have demonstrated that having high sugar levels could affect blood vessels, which in turn could lead to heart attacks."

Fisher blinked. "So he died of a heart attack?"

Wakefield nodded. "The coronary artery provides blood to the heart muscle to give it oxygen and nutrients. When that artery is blocked, it can lead to heart attacks. The study showed that high glucose in the blood can change the behavior of the blood vessels, making them contract even more. What's more interesting, a significant portion of the population who suffers a heart attack will show high glucose in the blood stream because of the stress response from changes in the blood vessels. In order to further confirm my findings, I had to request the victim's medical records. They took some time to arrive, but when they did, they confirmed the victim was suffering from DHD."

"DHD?" Fisher asked.

"Diabetic Heart Disease. The victim had had this disease for over twenty years. Over time, high blood sugar levels can damage blood vessels and nerves that connect to the heart. For diabetics, the most common cause of death is from heart disease and stroke."

"So are you saying he was not taking his insulin shots?" Fisher asked.

"I think he was." Wakefield pulled up the white cloth, revealing Scott's stomach. "There are tiny puncture marks in the stomach where the victim was injecting insulin. Also, like you said, the victim had an insulin kit next to his bed, which indicates he was taking his daily required dose."

"Then how did his blood sugar level go dangerously high?" Fisher asked.

Wakefield pulled a magnifying glass from her coat pocket and held it over Scott's arm. "It took some sleuthing, but I found a puncture wound on the right arm. It's fresher than the marks on the stomach. The toxicology report showed no traces of drugs of any kind, which would eliminate recreational drug use. The mark could have appeared from giving blood or getting IV fluids, but I am inclined not to go with either of those scenarios."

"Then what are you saying?" Fisher asked.

"It seems someone may have injected the victim with enough glucose to induce him to have a severe heart attack."

NINETY-ONE

Callaway spent an hour going through the contents in Jimmy's shoebox. The police report concluded that Gail's death was either an accident or a suicide. They could not say which one with certainty, but they had ruled out murder.

The autopsy report explained Gail had suffered a ruptured spleen, cracked ribs, broken arms and legs, facial fractures, and brain hemorrhaging. The latter was the cause of her death.

Anyone who fell fifteen floors would suffer that, and much more, Callaway thought.

Scott's statement was verified by the lead detective on the case. Scott was indeed in Vermont shooting a movie at the time of Gail's death.

A statement by Brad Kirkman was also verified. He was on a flight out of Bayview on the night Gail died.

Then there was the witness at the crime scene, Douglas Hoyte. He said he had seen a woman run out of the building right after Gail's fall. The woman's name was Tamara Davis, and she was homeless and a drug addict.

According to Jimmy's notes, he had searched for Tamara throughout Bayview and had come up empty. Jimmy believed Tamara had either left the city, was dead, or perhaps someone was hiding her. He had no proof to confirm his theories, but Callaway could tell he was troubled by the fact he was unable to locate her.

Jimmy had a nose for trouble and for sniffing out clues. He was like a bloodhound who could follow a trail from one end of the city to the other, so it wasn't inconceivable for Jimmy to think someone was helping Tamara elude the authorities.

But why? Who would want her to stay quiet?

After an online search, Callaway found she had died of a drug overdose.

Callaway decided to start his investigation by speaking to Douglas Hoyte.

The apartment building was two blocks from where Gail lived. When Callaway knocked at Hoyte's fourth-floor unit, he didn't look displeased or annoyed by the unexpected visit. He smiled and invited Callaway in.

"I worked thirty-two years as an electrician," he said. "It got me out of the house every day. But after I got severe arthritis, I had to retire and stay home. Now all I do is take Goldie out for a walk or watch TV all day."

Goldie, Callaway assumed, was the Golden Retriever in Hoyte's one-bedroom apartment. "I don't get many visitors, you see," Hoyte said.

Callaway nodded.

"Can I get you a beer?" Hoyte asked. He had gray hair, taut skin, and droopy eyelids. When he smiled, he revealed yellow smoker's teeth.

"I'm good, thanks," Callaway replied.

"You said you wanted to know what happened to that girl who fell from her apartment, is that right?"

"Yes."

"I'm not sure what more I can tell you that I didn't already tell the police, or the private investigator that showed up at my door."

"I'm just trying to get a better idea of what might have happened, so whatever you tell me is greatly appreciated."

"Okay, sure. I guess I'll start by saying that every night after dinner, Goldie and I go out for a walk. I don't like smoking indoors, so while she gets her exercise, I can light up, you know? Anyway, we usually go a couple of blocks. When I first started, I could barely walk one block before I started wheezing. The smoking doesn't help. You smoke?"

Callaway shook his head.

"Don't ever start. It's worse than having a nagging wife. At least you can divorce the wife, but if you're not strong enough, the smoking will stick with you until you die."

"I'll keep that in mind."

"So, I was doing my usual walk when I heard a scream. I first thought it was screeching tires or something else, but a few seconds later, I heard what sounded like a wet bag hitting concrete. Goldie started going crazy. I had never seen her like that. She's very nurturing. She knows when I'm sick or if I'm feeling down, so when she started barking persistently, I had to check it out. I knew where I had heard the sound come from, and when I went over, I saw the girl on the ground. I thought maybe she had slipped and hurt herself, but then I saw the blood." Hoyte sighed. He shook his head. "There was so much blood, I knew something bad had happened. I then dialed 9-1-1."

"Did you see anyone on the balcony?" Callaway asked.

"Sure."

Callaway blinked. "You did?"

"Yeah. I think all the neighbors heard the scream like I did, and they all came out onto their balconies to see what it was."

Right.

"Did you notice anything suspicious?" Callaway asked.

"I saw a lady run out of the back of the building. She was black, and she wore dirty clothes. She looked homeless, but it was dark, so I can't be a hundred percent sure. I told the police about her, though. I don't know what they did with that information."

The police did search for her, Callaway thought. *But Tamara Davis was eventually found dead.*

"I feel bad for the girl," Hoyte said. "She was young, and I saw photos of her family in the newspaper. They looked like nice people. It was a real tragedy."

"It was," Callaway agreed.

There was a reason Jimmy's visit to Hoyte was fruitless. The man didn't know anything. He was merely the first person at the body.

"Thanks for your time," Callaway said.

"No problem," Hoyte replied.

Callaway was moving to the door when he stopped. There were two hand-carries in the hallway. "You're going somewhere?"

Hoyte smiled. "As a matter of fact, I am. You were lucky to catch me at home when you did."

"Lucky?"

"I was supposed to be on a flight to Minnesota to meet my grandson. He was born last night. There's a pilot strike, so my flight got delayed. I always call before I go. I hate waiting at the airport. And I'm glad I called. My plane doesn't leave for another couple of hours. You can tell Goldie is not talking to me."

The Golden Retriever had her head down. Callaway had to admit she did look sad.

"She wants to go with me, but I have to leave her with a neighbor until I get back," Hoyte said.

He knelt down and rubbed Goldie behind her ears.

Callaway thanked him and left.

NINETY-TWO

Fisher was in Sherman Grumbly's office.

"Thank you for having an officer bring the script to my office," Grumbly said. "It took years to get this project off the ground. When Dillon signed on, it was a bittersweet moment. I thought all the hard work and dedication had finally led us to this point. With Dillon, we knew we had a hit on our hands. Now I'm not so sure. The movie was financed through private investors and government grants. The investors started pulling out once they heard what happened, and unless we have money to start the production, we will lose the grants as well."

Grumbly looked like he was under immense stress. This was likely his last chance to show the industry he could release a successful movie. Fisher was aware that actors, directors, and producers lived and died by their last movie. If that failed, there was no guarantee they would get picked up for another project, or in the producer's case, have their next project greenlit.

"I will be flying to Los Angeles tomorrow," Grumbly said. "I will speak to agents, managers, and lead actors to try and drum up interest in the project."

She could tell from his face that it was going to be an uphill battle. If Grumbly could not sign another star, the project might never see the light of day.

Fisher was not here to discuss the movie business, but before she got to the main reasons for her visit, she wanted to ask something. "There were rumors that Mr. Scott had non-disclosure agreements with certain individuals. Were you aware of this?"

Grumbly looked taken aback. "What kind of agreements?"

Fisher wanted to see if Grumbly knew of Scott's sordid past. She also wanted to know how complicit he was in working with a man who preyed on innocent women.

"Dillon had a great reputation," he said. "It was what helped us raise the funds to get the project off the ground."

"Yes, of course," Fisher said. She then dove in. "Did you know about Mr. Scott's medical condition, specifically about his diabetes?"

"Sure. We had him do a physical to make sure he could complete the project. It's a requirement for insurance purposes. His diabetes was under control, and his overall health was excellent."

"Who else was aware of his condition?"

Grumbly frowned, thinking. "Um… I guess his doctors… his agent… and his wife for sure."

"Mrs. Scott?"

"Absolutely. Before you qualify for insurance, they look at the actor's family medical history. Mrs. Scott is also diabetic."

"She is?" Fisher asked, surprised.

"Yes. But it's standard procedure because of the amount of money invested in the project. It also lets the director know how far he can push the actor."

"What do you mean?"

"I mean, we knew Dillon was diabetic…"

"Did you also know he suffered from Diabetic Heart Disease?"

"Oh yes, but I was assured by medical professionals that if Dillon kept his sugar levels under control, it was not going to be a health issue. In fact, in his contract, it was outlined that he could not be forced to do any cardiovascular activities, so we had stunt people perform scenes that required a lot of running or jumping. We once had an actress who was allergic to a specific plant. When we shot a scene in a forest, we had to remove all traces of that particular plant. It was a costly thing, but a necessary one. The actors' union would have crucified us, not to mention the press if they found out we were negligent. So, yes, we took all precautions with Dillon."

NINETY-THREE

Brad Kirkman was in his office. He was seated behind his desk, and he had a cell phone cradled to his ear.

Callaway knocked on the door. Kirkman looked up. "Can I help you?" he said.

"I'm from the *Daily Times*," Callaway claimed. "I was hoping to ask you a few questions."

"Where's Louise?" Kirkman asked, annoyed.

"Who?"

"My secretary. You can book an appointment with her."

"There was no one at the desk," Callaway said.

Kirkman frowned. "She's probably out to lunch. Why don't you leave your name and telephone number and I'll have her schedule you in. I'm very busy at the moment."

"I'm sorry to bother you, but I drove all the way from Franklin."

That caught Kirkman's attention. "Did you say Franklin?"

"Yes, I did."

"And what was the name of the newspaper?"

"*The Daily Times.*"

"I've read it. You know their lead reporter, Hyder Ali?"

Callaway was familiar with the name, but he had never met Ali. "Of course I am," he claimed. "Hyder and I share desks."

"I'm a fan of his work," Kirkman said, putting the phone down. "Brad Kirkman."

He extended his hand. Callaway shook it.

"Gator Peckerwood."

Kirkman's eyes narrowed. "Is that a real name?"

"Unfortunately, it is." He pulled out a business card. "My parents are from Louisiana."

"That explains it." Kirkman looked at the card. "It doesn't have the name of your newspaper."

"I was in a rush. I left all my official business cards behind. If you call the number, you will get the *Daily Times'* main directory." Callaway doubted Kirkman would call.

"So, what can I do for you?" Kirkman asked.

"I'm writing an article on Gail Roberts, and I was hoping you'd give me a quote."

Kirkman frowned. "She died over a year ago, so why the sudden interest?"

"After Dillon Scott's murder, I wanted to focus on a different angle to her story."

"Angle?"

"I mean, don't you find it odd that an employee of this production company is found dead, and then a year later, the co-owner of the same company is found dead as well? Could the same person who killed Gail Roberts have also killed Dillon Scott?"

Kirkman's expression hardened. "Is this some kind of joke?"

"No joke at all."

Kirkman stared at him and sighed. "First of all, Gail's death was an accident. The police conducted a thorough investigation and came to that very conclusion. As for Dillon, didn't someone confess to his murder this very morning?"

"They did, yes. Did Gail Roberts have any enemies?"

"No, she did not. Gail was a wonderful person. She was a valued member of our company. Her death was a loss we were still mourning when we found out what happened to Dillon. Now, if you'll excuse me, I have an important call to make."

"Sure," Callaway said. "Just one more question. Where were you on the night—"

Without letting Callaway complete his sentence, Kirkman opened his desk drawer and held up a boarding pass. "I have shown this to everyone who has walked through the door asking if I had anything to do with Gail's suicide."

"I thought it was an accident," Callaway said.

"The police believe it could have been either."

"What do *you* believe?"

"I believe Gail was a talented person who could have done amazing things if she was still alive. She may have been suffering mentally, I don't know. If she was, I would have tried to get her professional help. Unfortunately, her life was abruptly cut short. That's my quote for your article."

Callaway examined the boarding pass, smiled, and said, "Thank you for your time."

NINETY-FOUR

Fisher was back at her desk. She had checked her voicemail, and there was another message from Holt. He was flying back from Las Vegas the next day, and he was eager to get to work. He was excited and even proud that Fisher was able to wrap up Dillon Scott's murder in less than a week. It was a great accomplishment for a detective to solve a case of this magnitude all alone.

Fisher didn't share his enthusiasm. She didn't find a suspect. The suspect came to her. She had nothing to do with it.

Which brought her back to Jimmy's confession. Something did not add up.

After her meeting with Wakefield, she was left with more questions than answers. Jimmy admitted to hitting Scott on the head with the bookend, but according to Wakefield, Scott did not die from the head wound. He died from a heart attack caused by alleviated sugar levels.

Jimmy never once mentioned injecting Scott with any substance. Fisher doubted that Jimmy was even aware that Scott suffered from diabetes.

She could feel the pressure building up. Time was running out. When Holt arrived the next day, the seventy-two hours would be up. She had that much time to charge Jimmy with the murder. Her superiors and the public were waiting on her to do just that.

By all accounts, Jimmy truly believed he was responsible for what happened to Scott, but the medical examiner's findings had shed a different light on his death. Maybe someone other than Jimmy had killed Scott, but in order to prove that, she had to find this person.

Whatever personal opinion she had of Scott, the fact was that he was murdered. Scott deserved a fate far worse than what he ultimately received. He died of a heart attack, induced or not. Millions of people die from one each day.

But millions of people did not use their power and privilege to hurt other people.

What Scott did was unforgivable. He destroyed and damaged who knew how many young women. Some would never be able to trust another man again.

This made her job difficult. Scott got what he deserved. But she had a duty to keep the public safe. The only way to do that was to find Scott's killer.

She just wished she knew where to look.

Her eyes caught an object next to her laptop. She leaned over and picked the object up. It was a toll pass. All detectives were given one. Their jobs required them to cross cities, states, and borders, so it was easier for the department to pay for a monthly pass than reimburse them for the cost of each toll. She had used her pass when she drove through the Norton Bridge on her way to Bayview.

She was turning the pass over in her hand when a thought occurred to her.

NINETY-FIVE

Callaway had gone to Kirkman's office for one reason: He wanted to see with his own eyes that Kirkman was indeed on a flight out of Bayview on the night Gail died. Kirkman was more than willing to wave a boarding pass for him and anyone else who showed up at his door with questions. He even said so himself.

His eagerness to provide this information was something even Jimmy noted in his diary. The boarding pass was genuine, no doubt about it, but why try to prove his innocence when he wasn't guilty? He had a rock-solid alibi.

Or did he?

The boarding time on the pass was 9:20 PM. Gail fell to her death at 10:38 PM. So, if Gail died *after* the plane had already taken off, then there was no way Kirkman could be on the plane and in her apartment at the same time.

Or could he?

Callaway was waiting when his phone buzzed. He checked, and a smile crossed his face.

Prior to going to Kirkman's office, he had called Echo Rose. Echo was a reporter in Fairview. She had helped him out on a case while he was there. In return, he had found the names of her birth parents.

He always hesitated about contacting her for help. He didn't want to burden her with his problems. But Echo relished the opportunity to get justice.

She had what you would call "exceptional skills." She was one of the best hackers he knew. She could break into anything— given time, of course.

The information he needed was urgent.

He had tried to get the information himself, but neither the people at the airline nor his online search were fruitful. The flight was a year ago, and such information was not readily available.

What Echo discovered answered the mystery that eluded the police, Jimmy, and—until now—even him. However, if the police had looked carefully at the time of Gail's death, they would have seen a glaring hole in Kirkman's story.

Echo was able to gain access to Bayview Airport's Flight Information Display System. According to the FIDS, Kirkman was indeed scheduled to be on the 9:45 PM flight out of Bayview, but that flight had been delayed two and a half hours due to bad weather on the East Coast. The flight eventually took off after midnight.

The drive from the airport to Gail's apartment was only twenty minutes. The delay gave Kirkman more than enough time to go to Gail's place and be back before the flight took off.

But if Kirkman did go to Gail's apartment, then why did her building security cameras not catch him?

Callaway was able to answer that quandary right after he spoke to Douglas Hoyte.

He went to Gail's apartment building. As he expected, there were CCTV cameras in the front lobby and near the elevators. Callaway then went to the back of the building, where Gail had fallen to her death. The exits were next to the building's stairs.

Lo and behold, there were no cameras at that spot.

Whoever had used that exit must have been familiar with the building. They had to have visited Gail before, and that's when Callaway's interest in Kirkman was piqued.

He now had to prove the theory formulating in his head.

NINETY-SIX

Osman was still pissed that his cash cow was gone. He was hoping to milk Dillon Scott out of money for a very long time.

Scott acted like a tough guy on film, but when push came to shove, the man was a coward. He used his money to make his problems go away.

Osman found out Scott had paid off a lot of women. He wasn't sure why. His contact never revealed this information to him, but this told Osman that Scott would be an easy target. He would have kept paying as long as it didn't affect his career.

Scott was all about being a movie star. He lived for the fame and adulation. He would have done anything to not jeopardize what he had, even if that meant delivering bags of cash to random locations.

Osman had to hand it to him; Scott knew how to follow orders. He never deviated from Osman's instructions. Maybe he learned that from being an actor. They were always doing what the directors wanted them to do.

Actors were not wolves. They were sheep. And Osman was a lion.

He smiled at the last bit. He always viewed life on the streets as a jungle, and for a while, he was food for other animals, until he met his contact and decided to take matters into his own hands.

His contact told him the plan, but it was Osman who executed it. Without him, there would be no cash for either of them.

His cell phone rang for the umpteenth time. He recognized the number. It was his contact. He had been calling nonstop for the last day and a half.

Per his contact's instructions, Osman should have dumped the prepaid phone a long time ago, but he didn't, and now his contact was desperately trying to reach him on that very phone. How ironic.

He felt the phone buzz in his hand. He grunted. He knew he should answer, even though he knew what his contact was calling him about.

He pressed a button and put the phone to his ear. "I thought you said no more calls on this phone?" he asked.

"You ripped me off!" the voice roared. "I picked up the money from the train station bathroom, and it was missing five grand."

"Listen, I could have kept it all and given you nothing, but I didn't, so consider yourself lucky."

"I need that money. I told you some dangerous people are looking for me."

"That's your problem."

"We had a deal," the voice said.

"Scott is dead, so we got no more deal, you got that?"

There was silence on the other end. Osman could hear breathing.

"Come on," the voice said, now calm. "You have to give me that money."

"I don't have to give you shit," Osman shot back.

"Osman…"

"Hey, no real names, okay?"

"Sorry, I… I…" the voice stammered. "It's just that, I'm in deep trouble, and if I don't pay these people back, they'll hurt me."

"Listen, man, we're already in deep trouble for what we did. If I were you, I would dump that phone and never talk about this ever again."

Osman ended the call.

He wasn't worried about his contact going to the police. Osman was a low-level drug dealer who had been in and out of jail many times, but his contact had not even driven past a prison.

His contact would keep his mouth shut, Osman knew. He had far more to lose than Osman did.

NINETY-SEVEN

Callaway sat outside Kirkman's office. He wasn't sure what his next step should be. He couldn't very well go into his office and accuse him of anything. He believed Kirkman knew more about Gail's death than he was letting on, but whatever Callaway had on him was circumstantial at best.

The flight Kirkman was on was delayed a couple of hours. This still did not prove he had actually left the airport and driven to Gail's apartment. It would require a ton of man hours to go through ample airport CCTV footage to see if he had done that. Only Fisher could compel the Bayview Airport to provide her this information, but even she would be hesitant to make such a request based on just a theory.

If someone had seen Kirkman at Gail's apartment prior to or after her death, that would have been different. That would have given the police a reason to trace Kirkman's steps on the night of her death.

A thought suddenly occurred to Callaway. What if someone *did* see Kirkman at Gail's apartment? What if that person was Tamara Davis, the woman Douglas Hoyte had seen running out of the back of the building?

When Callaway was at Gail's building, he had seen a blanket and some clothes underneath the back stairs on the main level. It was evident that someone slept in that spot.

Tamara Davis was homeless and an addict. Did she also use that very spot to keep warm during cold nights?

Callaway's theory was starting to make more sense.

Someone was blackmailing Scott, and Scott was linked to Kirkman. They owned a production company together. Was this blackmailer using Tamara Davis to get to Scott?

Callaway wasn't sure how this all fit together. What he did know was that he had to find a way to get Kirkman to explain what he did during the time his flight was delayed.

Kirkman would not be willing to talk to him. Callaway was not a police officer, and Kirkman was not a suspect. Even if Fisher agreed to bring Kirkman in for questioning, she would need something concrete to go ahead with that.

As Callaway was trying to come up with a plan, he saw Kirkman exit the office building's main doors. He looked distressed and angry. His brow was furrowed, and his shoulders were slumped. He got in his black Lexus and drove away.

Callaway decided to follow him.

The Lexus drove for several blocks until it entered an alley next to an industrial building. Then the Lexus disappeared around the back of the building.

Callaway parked across the street. He debated whether to proceed further, but the alley was so narrow that only a single car could go through it at a time. What if Callaway went in and Kirkman decided to come out? Kirkman had already seen him, and he would know Callaway was trailing him.

He gritted his teeth.

The Lexus emerged from the alley, got back on the street, and drove away.

Callaway had a feeling Kirkman was headed back to his office. But why was Kirkman here in the first place?

Callaway wanted to find out.

He put the Charger in Park and got out. He walked through the alley and reached the back of the building.

There was nothing but empty parking space. He spotted a metal garbage bin next to the building. He walked over and lifted the lid. He only saw garbage and debris. He was about to shut the lid when sunlight reflected off an object. He leaned into the bin and pulled out a cell phone.

The screen was cracked. Someone had tried to break it, but they had done a poor job. Many of the latest phones were made with high-grade material, which included the front glass.

He pressed a button. To his surprise, the phone was still functioning, but the cracked glass made it difficult to see what was on the screen.

He pulled out the SIM card and placed it in his phone. When he checked the content, he found a list of telephone calls.

They were all to one number.

NINETY-EIGHT

Fisher was inside a small room at the Norton Bridge Toll Center. Three large LCD monitors were placed on the walls. The screens displayed images of the toll booth from different angles.

Security officers were seated in front of smaller LCD monitors. They watched as attendants in each toll booth allowed drivers to pass through once they had paid the required fare. In most cases, the drivers tapped their toll cards and were let through the gates without an incident. Even those who paid at the booth were let through in less than thirty seconds. The system had to work efficiently and effortlessly each day lest it cause a backup.

When Fisher saw the toll pass, it had triggered something in her brain. She drove an hour to the toll bridge to confirm her suspicions. The bridge was the only tollway between Bayview and Milton. If anyone had come to Milton from Bayview, they would have had to cross the bridge. This meant there would be a record of them.

Fisher stood behind a security officer who was typing away on his keyboard. She didn't know the *exact* time of Scott's death, but she had a time frame to work with.

In Jimmy's confession, he said he had left Scott's house after midnight. The limo driver, Mr. Gill, who had discovered Scott's body, said he arrived around 8:00 AM. There was a lot of time between when Jimmy left and when Gill arrived, but Fisher doubted she would have to go through that much footage. She had a feeling Scott's killer had shown up way before Gill did.

She watched as the clock at the bottom of the screen showed 11:35 PM. It ticked slowly. "Can you speed it up?" she asked.

The officer did as instructed.

The booth was not very busy. Night had fallen, and there were not many people driving across the bridge. Whenever a car would appear, Fisher would ask the officer to run the footage at normal speed. When she realized the driver was not who she was looking for, she would ask the officer to speed the footage up again.

This went on until the clock hit 12:23 AM.

Fisher hoped her instincts were correct. If they were not, she had no more cards left.

Holt would return the next day, Jimmy would be let free, and she would have to start her investigation from scratch again.

A Jaguar pulled up to the booth. The driver leaned out of the window and paid the attendant. At that precise moment, the driver's face was clearly visible on the screen. The attendant handed change to the driver, and the Jaguar drove away.

Fisher felt her heart skip a beat. Was this the break she had been looking for?

She asked the officer to fast-forward the footage. She also told him to keep an eye out for that specific vehicle. Fisher was certain the Jaguar would return. There was only one way in and out of Milton, and that was through the toll bridge.

Almost an hour and a half later, the Jaguar returned. The driver paid the fare. Again, Fisher could clearly see the driver's face as he leaned out the window. Then the Jaguar drove off.

Fisher's eyes narrowed. She had just seen Scott's killer. But there was still more work to be done.

"Can you make me a copy?" she asked the officer.

NINETY-NINE

Callaway was not sure whose number was on the SIM, but he wanted to find out.

How am I going to do that? he wondered.

The person on the other end of the line would know just by his voice that it was not Kirkman. Callaway didn't want to spook the other person either. Kirkman was in a hurry to destroy the phone. This could mean only one thing: Kirkman did not want the phone's contents somehow leading back to him. Callaway had tried to access the text messages on Kirkman's phone, but the cracked glass made it impossible. While the call log was saved on the SIM, the text messages were not.

Callaway could take the phone to a nearby electronics store and have them download the information onto his phone, but he wasn't sure what was on the phone or how sensitive the information was. What if the store employees saw something they shouldn't? He didn't want to open something without knowing what was behind it.

He could contact Echo and have her crack the phone's texts. She was good at stuff like that. But he had already bothered her enough. Plus, Fairview was a long drive away. He wasn't going to ask her to come to Milton. He would have to go to her.

He took a deep breath and dialed the number on Kirkman's SIM card. He waited for it to ring before he hung up. He suddenly got cold feet.

That was stupid, he thought. *Maybe I should let Echo extract data from the phone before I proceed further. This number could be my only chance to find out what was going on.*

The phone buzzed. He saw the call was coming from the same number he had just dialed.

He didn't answer.

The phone buzzed half a dozen times before it stopped. Callaway wasn't sure if Kirkman had a voicemail. If he did, there was no way he would ever be able to access it.

The phone then buzzed *once*. He checked and realized there was a text message from that very number. He opened it.

HEY MAN, I TOLD U I AIN'T GIVING U DA MONEY.

What money? Callaway thought. *Maybe I should play along and find out.*

I WANT MY MONEY, Callaway texted back.

I GAVE U UR SHARE.

LET'S MEET UP SO WE CAN TALK.

Several minutes went by with no response.

Maybe I pushed it too far.

OK, MEET AT USUAL SPOT.

Usual spot? Callaway had no idea where that was.

Callaway typed, WHY NOT SOMEPLACE ELSE?

NO WAY, THE TRAIN STATION IS THE ONLY PLACE I MEET U.

What train station?

Callaway didn't want to lose this opportunity.

OK.

He put the phone back in his pocket and frowned. He had no idea where this meetup was.

He saw a man across the street. Callaway got out of the Charger and approached him.

"Sorry to bother you, sir," Callaway said. "I'm not from here. Do you know if there is a train station around here?"

"Sure," the man replied. "The Bayview Central Train Station is about a mile from here."

Of course, that makes sense, Callaway thought. *Kirkman lived in Bayview, so he would meet someone somewhere nearby.*

"Thank you," Callaway said.

He returned to the Charger and drove off.

ONE-HUNDRED

Fisher glanced at her watch and then at the Milton PD's front doors. She was seated in one of the lobby's hard plastic chairs. A laptop was cradled in her arms. She hoped it wouldn't be necessary, but she came prepared just in case.

Ten minutes passed before the woman entered the building. Mrs. Rachel Scott was wearing a long coat, large sunglasses that covered most of her face, a blouse, tight pants, heels, and she wore dark lipstick.

She removed her sunglasses and came over to Fisher. "I hope I can finally take my husband home and give him the burial worthy of a movie star," she said.

"We've completed the autopsy, so I don't see why not," Fisher said.

A smile crossed Rachel's face. "I'm glad to hear that. When you called, I was concerned there was something wrong with Dillon's investigation."

"No, everything is exactly how it's supposed to be."

"That's good to hear. Do you need me to sign any documents?"

"Documents?" Fisher asked.

"Yes, to take possession of Dillon's body."

"We'll get to that later. I was wondering if you wouldn't mind answering some of my questions."

"Questions?"

Rachel looked surprised.

"Yes, just to tie up some loose ends in the investigation."

"Don't you have a suspect in custody?" Rachel asked.

"He's in a holding cell as we speak," Fisher replied. "Please follow me upstairs."

They took the elevator to the second level. They walked through the halls. Fisher noticed how Rachel's heels audibly clicked on the concrete floor.

They entered a room with a giant mirror on one wall. The other wall was bare. There was a metal table in the middle with chairs on either side of it.

"Am I being interrogated?" Rachel asked, suddenly defensive.

"Unfortunately, this is the only room available for us to speak in private," Fisher claimed. That wasn't true. The room was equipped with cameras and recording devices. On the other side of the mirror, an officer was making sure everything was being recorded as evidence.

Rachel almost laughed. "Dillon starred in a couple of crime movies, and this looks awfully like an interrogation."

"Are you not comfortable answering my questions? Is there something I should be aware of?" It was Fisher's turn to get defensive, a tactic she used to disarm an interviewee.

"Do I need a lawyer?" Rachel asked.

"You are entitled to one. Would you prefer to call one while we wait?"

Rachel stared at her. Fisher knew she was wondering where this was going, but she also wanted this over with so she could head home. She figured because they already had someone in custody, she had nothing to worry about.

Big mistake.

Rachel smiled. "No, I don't mind answering a few questions."

"Please have a seat." Fisher took the chair across from her. She placed the laptop on the table and said, "The reason I asked you here was to verify certain things that have come up in my investigation."

Rachel swallowed. "What kind of things?"

"Things that could be minor or irrelevant but need to be addressed before I close the case."

"Okay."

"Where were you on the night your husband was murdered?"

"Oh, that's easy," Rachel said with a smile. "I was at home in Bayview."

"Do you have someone who can corroborate your story?"

"I don't know. My kids were at my mother's house. I think I might have spoken to a friend on the phone."

"Can you give me the name of this friend?"

Rachel thought for a moment. "I could have spoken to my friend a day earlier. I don't remember."

"So, there is no one to confirm you were at home that night?" Fisher asked.

Rachel paused to think. "I guess I was alone," she replied.

"Have you been to Milton before?"

"I've been here several times now."

"I meant prior to your husband's death."

"No, never."

"Not even on the night your husband was found dead?"

Rachel scoffed. "Of course not."

"Do you mind if I show you something?" Fisher pulled open the laptop and pressed a key. An image popped up on the screen. "This footage was taken from the Norton Bridge Toll Center. If you look at the date and time at the bottom, you can clearly see you entered Milton at 12:23 AM—which doesn't really make it the same night Mr. Scott was found dead, but the next morning—but that's not the point here. What's important is that you returned an hour and a half later." Fisher fast-forwarded the footage and pressed pause. "That is you on the screen, isn't it?"

Rachel stared at the image in disbelief.

"Who were you visiting in Milton?" Fisher asked.

"Um… I was going to meet a friend."

"Is it the same friend you spoke to a day earlier?"

Rachel swallowed. "Maybe."

"At this early in the morning?"

Rachel shook her head. "What does this have to do with anything? I thought you had someone who confessed to killing my husband?"

"We have a full written confession," Fisher said. "Now let me ask you about your husband's diabetes."

ONE-HUNDRED ONE

"Were you aware your husband was suffering from Diabetes Heart Disease?" Fisher asked.

"Of course I knew. I'm his wife," Rachel replied. "He wouldn't hide something like that from me. And if you'd like to know, I'm also diabetic."

"I am aware of that. In order to be insured for a movie production, the insurance company looks at a client's entire family history, which includes the wife."

"Okay."

"Can you open your purse?" Fisher asked.

"What? Why?"

"Can you remove a bottle of glucose tablets you carry with you at all times?"

Rachel's mouth dropped. "How did you know?"

"Like your husband, you take insulin injections. But unlike him, you are hypoglycemic. Your sugar levels can fall dangerously low, so low that you have to occasionally take glucose tablets to raise your sugar level. The tablets can be bought at any pharmacy, and most grocery stores. Do you mind pulling the bottle from your purse?"

Rachel reached down and removed a plastic bottle.

"Please place it on the table."

Rachel did as Fisher instructed. "Where are you going with this?" she asked. "I thought my husband died from being hit on the head?"

"Yes and no. He was hit on the head with a heavy object, but he didn't die from that injury. What he died from was a heart attack."

"A heart attack?" Rachel said, feigning surprise.

"Our medical examiner is one of the best in the state, perhaps even the country. She was thorough in her examination of your husband's body. She discovered a tiny wound in your husband's arm. She thought it might be because your husband was using recreational drugs, but when she conducted a blood test, she discovered his blood sugar level was four times higher than normal. The contents inside his stomach did not indicate it was caused by something he ate or drank. It was caused by something else— something that was injected into his body, which would explain the puncture mark on the arm."

Rachel's face turned hard as stone.

"I went back to the crime scene," Fisher said, "and guess what I found? A glass in the kitchen sink. I hadn't paid too much attention to it at first, but when I looked carefully this time, there was a white residue at the bottom. It's in the lab being tested as we speak, but I have no doubt it's residue left behind from glucose tablets that were dissolved in water. The glass is also being dusted for fingerprints, and if my theory is correct, the fingerprints on it belong to *you*."

Rachel's lips quivered. Her eyes turned moist, but she didn't utter a word.

Fisher said, "The first time I met you, I noticed stress on your face. I thought it was because you had lost a loved one and were in mourning, but in reality, you were stressed because you had committed the crime and were struggling to keep yourself together. I also discovered that you are the sole beneficiary of your husband's estate. Even though he was financially struggling, he was still receiving residuals for all the movies and television shows he had starred in. They could add up to millions each year. I also believe you were aware that your husband was unfaithful during your marriage, and that you had heard rumors about what he had done to other women. That he was a sexual predator."

At Fisher's last sentence, Rachel covered her face and broke into heavy sobs.

"He was a monster," she said. "No one saw the real him. All they saw was a hero on the big screen. He was physically and verbally abusive." She looked up at Fisher with anger in her eyes. "I should have left him a long time ago. I hated being married to him, but I knew how being married to him could help me, so I never asked for a divorce. When people found out I was his wife, they would hire me to sell their houses. My real estate firm was flourishing because of who I was married to. *I* was the one who was supporting the family. Dillon hadn't had a hit in years, and the way he spent money was like he was still an A-list actor."

Rachel sobbed.

"And yes, I had heard the rumors, and they ate away at me," she continued. "I'm a woman, so how can I sleep next to a man who does that to other women? I wanted to catch him in the act. I knew he wouldn't be able to help himself when he was on the road shooting a movie. I was certain he would be with another woman that night when I drove to Milton. When I got to the house, I found the door unlocked. I went inside, and I found his body lying on the floor in the living room. I was horrified. I knew something bad must have happened. I thought about calling 9-1-1. I even thought about getting back in the car and driving away. But then he moaned. I could see he was still alive. I don't know what came over me. I thought about taking a pillow and smothering that face of his, but I knew I didn't have it in me." Rachel took a deep breath. "Whenever I get overwhelmed, my sugar levels go down. I went back to the car to get my glucose pills, and I had an idea. I shouldn't have done it, but you can't imagine living with someone like him. He thought he was a gift to the world, like he was someone special. He was nothing but a vile and evil man. I was not going to let this man hurt me or anyone else ever again. I dissolved the entire bottle of glucose tablets in water and then I injected it into his arm. I should have taken the glass with me, but I wasn't thinking straight. I just wanted this nightmare to be over with. I'm so sorry."

Rachel's shoulders slumped. She hugged herself and began crying uncontrollably.

Fisher wanted to reach out and comfort her. Rachel was not only the perpetrator, she was also a victim. Dillon Scott had hurt a lot of people, including his family. Unlike the movies, there were no heroes in Rachel's story.

Rachel Scott would be charged with the murder of her husband, but Fisher would make sure the prosecutor, the judge, the jury, and the whole world knew who the real Dillon Scott was. Maybe that would help Rachel escape a penalty harsher than she deserved.

ONE-HUNDRED TWO

Callaway was at Bayview Central Train Station. He was standing on the platform observing everyone that got on and off the train. He wasn't sure what the caller looked like, but Callaway was certain he would be here. He just hoped he wouldn't miss him.

He glanced down at his watch and then leaned on a pillar as if he was waiting for someone. What if the caller was already here? What if the caller was watching him now?

He shook his head. Like him, the caller didn't know what *he* looked like. They were both on a sort of blind date, but there was a big difference: the caller thought he was meeting Kirkman, so he would be searching for *him* out on the platform.

Callaway had to focus on anyone who was doing just that.

He spotted a man in a hoodie. He was twenty feet away from him. The man had large headphones over his ears, and he was bobbing his head. A train entered the terminal, the man boarded, and the train left the station.

On the other side of the tracks, Callaway noticed a man who was looking at his watch. The man was dressed in a business suit. Callaway doubted the man was the caller. The texts were written in slang. But what if the caller had done that to fool him, to mask who was really sending them?

Callaway kept his gaze on the man. Kirkman was the head of a production company, which at one point was behind million-dollar blockbuster movies. It would make sense for him to meet a man who was properly dressed.

The man looked in Callaway's direction. Their eyes met. Callaway suddenly froze. *Did he recognize me?*

The man averted his eyes. He glanced down at his watch again and frowned. Another train entered the station and blocked Callaway's view. He debated whether he should run down the stairs and go to the other side of the tracks.

The trained pulled away. Callaway caught sight of the man again. He was walking down the platform, holding a toddler. A woman pushing a stroller was next to him.

He was waiting for his family, Callaway thought.

262

Ten more minutes passed before Callaway decided it was time to head back. His trip to the train station had been a waste. The caller must have realized something was up when he didn't see Kirkman.

Callaway was about to leave when his cell phone buzzed. He didn't answer. He looked around the platform.

He spotted a man who had a cell phone to his ear. The man had on a baseball cap, a sweatshirt, and baggy jeans.

Callaway's eyes narrowed. *He can't be the caller.*

Or could he?

He saw the man hang up and type something on his phone.

Callaway's cell phone buzzed again. He looked down and saw a text message.

WHERE U AT?

Callaway looked back at the man. He was staring at the screen, waiting for a response. When no response came, the man mouthed a curse and shoved the phone in his pocket. He then adjusted his baseball cap and looked down the platform as another train entered the station.

The doors opened, and the man got aboard.

Callaway boarded the train as well.

ONE-HUNDRED THREE

Callaway was in the same train car as the man. He had a clear view of him as he played with his phone. Every so often, a girl would walk past him, and the man would look up and grin.

Callaway could not imagine what Kirkman was doing with someone like him. Callaway was not prejudiced in any way, shape, or form, but the man gave off a criminal vibe.

Maybe he was a street thug or drug dealer. Something about him did not look right. Callaway wished he had brought his weapon with him, but his trip to Bayview was solely about digging up information on Gail Roberts's death. He never expected he would be chasing a man who may or may not have something to do with what happened to Gail. However, Callaway had a feeling the man knew something about why Dillon Scott had gone to Yonge Avenue with a bag full of cash.

This man could very well be the blackmailer.

The disposable phone Kirkman had on him could have been provided by this man, and the first text message Callaway received from him was about the money. Was Kirkman in on the blackmail? If he was, it would explain a lot of things.

But before Callaway could jump to any conclusions, he had to see where this man was going.

The train pulled into a station.

The man got off. Callaway followed.

Callaway tailed the man from a discrete distance. The man went down a flight of stairs, never once looking back to see if someone was following him.

The man walked like he was out on a stroll.

This was exactly what Callaway was hoping for.

The man made his way down the street, turned left, and kept walking until he stopped in front of an apartment building.

He disappeared through the front doors.

Callaway debated going after him, but he had a different plan in mind. It was a risky move, but now was not the time to be timid.

He dialed a number, spoke a few words, and hung up. He checked his watch and then spotted an alley across from the building. He walked over to the alley and hid in the shadows. He never once looked away from the apartment building.

Almost an hour later, after making one more call, he sent a text.

I WANT MY MONEY.

After hitting Send, he typed another one.

I'M COMING TO GET IT.

He watched the building's main doors for any sign of movement. Five minutes later, the doors swung open and the man emerged. He was carrying a backpack.

Callaway came out of his hiding place, crossed the street, and approached the man.

"Hey buddy, where you going?" Callaway asked, cutting him off.

"Who the hell are you?" the man replied.

"I'm the guy who's been texting you."

The man stared at Callaway for a moment.

He scowled. "I'm outta here." He turned to leave.

I wouldn't do that if I were you, Callaway thought.

Fisher appeared from around the corner. She had one hand on her weapon, and she held up her badge with the other.

"What's going on?" the man asked, genuinely confused.

Callaway reached over and grabbed the backpack from him. He unzipped the pack and found bundles of hundred-dollar bills inside.

Callaway turned to Fisher. "Does this bag look familiar to you?"

"It sure does," she replied. "If I'm not mistaken, Dillon Scott was seen carrying that exact same bag the night he met his blackmailer in Milton."

"And if we traced the currency to withdrawals from the production company's bank account, do you think we'll get a match?"

"I think we will."

The man looked like he had seen a ghost.

Callaway added for good measure, "Do you suppose he had something to do with Gail Roberts's death?"

"We can charge him and find out," Fisher replied with a wry smile.

She reached for her handcuffs.

The man raised his hands. "Wait! I didn't kill her!"

Fisher scoffed. "Tell it to the judge."

"No, seriously. I had nothing to do with her, but I know who did."

"Sorry. You can't lie your way out of this one."

"Hold on," the man pleaded. "I got proof. It's all in my apartment."

ONE-HUNDRED AND FOUR

Brad Kirkman was led into a room at the Bayview PD. Detective Armen Woodley was in charge of Gail's case, so it was fitting that he bring Kirkman in for questioning.

Fisher and Callaway were behind a one-way mirror. They watched as Kirkman took a seat. Woodley took one across from him.

"Why am I being dragged here?" Kirkman complained.

"I could have arrested you, or you could have come on your own accord," Woodley replied. "You chose the latter, which is why you are not in handcuffs."

"What's this about?" Kirkman asked.

"It's about Gail Roberts."

"Listen, the last time you were at my office, I told you everything I knew. I was on a flight—"

Woodley put his hand up. "I am fully aware of that. You had even shown me your boarding pass."

"Then you know I didn't—"

"Mr. Kirkman, do you know a man named Osman Maxwell?"

Kirkman blinked. "Um… that name doesn't ring a bell."

"Well, he knows you very well."

"I'm not sure how. I would have remembered that name, you know."

"We have Mr. Maxwell in custody. He is being charged for a crime which I'll get to later. In return for leniency, he has provided us with some information."

Kirkman swallowed. "What kind of information?"

"He has audio recordings of conversations between you and him."

Sweat broke across Kirkman's forehead.

"In your conversations, you clearly confess to killing Gail Roberts."

He looked down at the table.

"Would you like to listen to these audio recordings?" Woodley asked.

Kirkman shook his head.

"Do you mind telling us what happened that night, or would you prefer I throw out a dozen theories and see which one sticks?"

Kirkman let out an audible sigh. He shut his eyes and said, "I was only doing it to protect Dillon and our production company. We had money invested in so many productions that even the slightest negative publicity could derail the company. Dillon was involved in certain activities that I didn't approve of."

"What kind of activities?" Woodley asked.

He hesitated.

"Mr. Kirkman, you have far more pressing things to be concerned about than how this will affect your company."

Kirkman nodded. "There were accusations against Dillon. Women were saying he had attacked them, assaulted them, even raped them. Dillon denied all these allegations, of course, but I knew how this could play out, so I worked out a deal with these women. In return for a lump sum payment, the women signed non-disclosure agreements, barring them from ever speaking about these incidents in public."

"How does this relate to Gail Roberts?" Woodley asked.

"Gail found out about these agreements and accusations. She was appalled. She couldn't believe we were condoning this behavior. She wanted Dillon charged and prosecuted for these crimes. Naturally, I couldn't let that happen. I tried to reason with her. I even threatened her with legal action. She was an employee of the company, and as such, whatever was discussed within the company was confidential. She didn't care. She said she was going to do what was right."

"Was Mr. Scott aware of what she was up to?"

"Yes, of course. He knew everything."

"Then what happened?"

"Gail told me she was going to the press to expose all the lies to the world. I was scheduled to fly out the night before she did this. I was grateful for that. I didn't want to be around when it happened. But then my flight was delayed due to bad weather. I knew Gail lived a short drive away from the airport, and I chose to go see her. In hindsight, it might have been a terrible mistake."

"Was your intention to go to her apartment to hurt her?" Woodley was trying to see if it was premeditated. This could raise the charges from manslaughter to murder in the first degree.

Kirkman shook his head. "No, I only wanted to talk to her. I thought maybe I could try to reason with her one more time. I had helped Gail get her apartment, and I had an extra key. I should have given it to her earlier, but I forgot. I knocked on her door but got no response. I then used the key to gain access to her unit. I thought maybe I could find incriminating evidence against her so I could use it as leverage to make her change her mind. I was desperate. I wanted to make this problem go away. I checked her laptop, her personal belongings, but I found nothing. Then I sat down and came up with a plan. I called Gail on her cell phone, and I told her it was urgent that I speak to her in private. I lied that Dillon was prepared to own up to his crimes and that maybe we could put out a statement together. She didn't sound convinced, but she was willing to listen to me."

ONE-HUNDRED FIVE

"I then turned up the heating in the unit and hid inside a closet," Kirkman said. "When she arrived, the apartment was hot. She immediately went and opened the door to her balcony. She then stood by the railing to allow fresh air into the unit. I then got out of my hiding spot and approached her from behind. Before she could turn, I grabbed her by her legs, and I…"

He stopped and bit his bottom lip.

"You did what, Mr. Kirkman?"

Woodley wanted a confession on tape.

"I then lifted her up by her legs and pushed her over the balcony. I heard her scream. I didn't even bother to look down to see if she was dead. I knew she would be. We were fifteen floors up. I then raced out of the unit, and I spotted someone at the elevators. I then took the stairs and exited the building."

"When you took the stairs, a homeless woman saw you leave, didn't she?" Woodley asked.

"Tamara Davis," Kirkman admitted.

"She was a witness who could place you at the scene of the crime, so you hatched another plan, didn't you? This plan involved Osman Maxwell."

"I knew I had to get to Tamara before the police did, so I asked Osman to find her. He was my supplier. From time to time, I bought drugs from him. This business can be stressful at times, and the drugs helped me relax. Osman hustled the streets, so he knew where to look. He found Tamara hiding in a crack house."

"So, when did you get the idea to blackmail Mr. Scott?" Woodley asked.

"I was so angry at Dillon. Gail was dead because of him. If he had stopped taking advantage of those girls, I wouldn't have had to silence Gail. I decided to *force* money out of Dillon."

"But if I'm not mistaken, didn't *you* give Mr. Scott the money to pay Osman Maxwell?"

"Yes."

"Wouldn't it have been easier to borrow or take the money yourself without going through the charade?"

"This wasn't the first time I found myself in money trouble. I had previously siphoned cash from the company to pay off my gambling debts. Dillon had found out, and he was not pleased. He didn't fire me because I knew his secret, but he warned me to never let it happen again, or else he would look for a new business partner. The blackmail was my way of making him squirm. I told Osman how to get in touch with Dillon. I also told him where to meet him in Milton. I needed that money to pay back some really bad people whom I had borrowed money from."

"But then Mr. Scott was found dead, and Tamara Davis was found dead as well," Woodley said.

"I don't know how much Osman told you, but he killed Tamara. He told me so on the phone."

"Do you have any proof of this?" Woodley asked.

Kirkman opened his mouth but then shut it.

"Don't worry. We have already charged Mr. Maxwell with her death. On the day Tamara Davis was found dead from an apparent overdose, a man wearing a ski mask had stormed the crack house and punched an inhabitant in the face when he went to answer the door. The victim provided a description of the assailant. Although his face was covered, the height and build matched Mr. Maxwell. The victim also remembered Mr. Maxwell speaking to Ms. Davis that very morning. Furthermore, we have ordered another autopsy, and I have full confidence that we will know exactly how Ms. Davis died."

Both men were quiet for a moment.

Woodley said, "Is there anything you would like to say that you haven't already?"

Kirkman stared at Woodley, but then he shook his head.

Woodley stood up. He pulled handcuffs from his back pocket. "Brad Kirkman, you are charged with the death of Gail Roberts and the blackmail of Dillon Scott."

Woodley handcuffed Kirkman, took out a card, and proceeded to read Kirkman his rights.

ONE-HUNDRED SIX

Fisher and Callaway watched as Kirkman was led away. They knew he would spend the rest of his life behind bars.

She turned to Callaway. "We work great as a team."

"Better than you and Holt?" he asked with a grin.

She rolled her eyes. "Okay, let's not get carried away. Holt is a detective with the Milton PD..."

"And I'm just a PI," Callaway finished.

"No, it's not that you're just a PI, it's that you don't like to follow the rules."

Callaway shrugged. "I can't argue with that."

Fisher said, "We have Rachel Scott in custody."

"For what?"

"She's been charged with Dillon Scott's murder."

Callaway's eyes widened. "Who? What? When? Where? How?"

She quickly filled him in on what had happened while he was in Bayview.

When she was finished, he said, "Does that mean that...?"

She nodded. "Once I get back to Milton, I will make sure Jimmy is promptly released."

Callaway felt like jumping in the air and pumping his fist, but he was surrounded by police officers, and it would look highly unprofessional.

Fisher looked around and then said in a low voice, "I followed up on the footage from the taxi that Scott and the girl took from Yonge Avenue."

Callaway froze.

"I think I have an idea of what might have happened that night," she said.

Does she know about Becky? he thought.

Callaway swallowed. "What are you going to do?"

Fisher shrugged. "Nothing. We found Scott's killer, didn't we?"

Callaway sighed with relief. "Thanks, Dana."

"No problem. You're lucky Holt wasn't around."

"Is there a way to permanently transfer him out of Milton?"

Fisher smirked. "Not a chance. He loves it here."

Callaway grinned. "What if we get him fired."

Fisher rolled her eyes. "Shut up, Lee!"

ONE-HUNDRED SEVEN

The sun had begun to set. Callaway stood next to his Charger outside the Milton PD. He checked his watch for the umpteenth time.

Why is it taking so long? he thought.

A few minutes later, the doors swung open and Jimmy emerged. He spotted Callaway and came over.

"Hey, kid," he said with a broad smile. "It's good to be free again."

"It's good to see you."

They shook hands. Jimmy reached over and hugged him. In all the years Callaway had known him, Jimmy had never once shown him affection. Jimmy's mantra was "Grown men don't hug and kiss; only wussies and children do that."

Callaway suddenly felt misty.

"Thanks for everything, Lee," he said.

"Don't thank me. It was Fisher who saved your butt. If it was up to me, I would have let you rot in there."

Jimmy continued smiling. "I got the feeling Detective Fisher knows more than she lets on. She's A-okay in my books."

"She's one of the good ones."

"PI's are always better," Jimmy said with a wink.

"No doubt about that."

"While I was doing the paperwork for my release, Detective Fisher filled me in on Gail's case. I knew Kirkman was hiding something. I never imagined he actually committed the crime."

"It's always the people you least expect."

"Just like Rachel Scott."

"Yep."

They were quiet for a moment.

Jimmy said, "Can an old man give you a small piece of advice?"

"He can."

"Don't waste your life like I did. You still got a kid that adores you, and an ex-wife who doesn't hate you as much as she should. If I were you, I would try to spend as much time with them as possible."

"I have an offer on the table to have dinner with Patti and Nina. Right after I leave here, I intend to go straight to their house and take them up on their offer."

Jimmy's smile widened. "I'm proud of you, kid."

ONE-HUNDRED EIGHT

A few days later

The day was bright and sunny with not a cloud in sight. The air was cool and fresh as Jimmy, Becky, and her mom walked through the cemetery together.

They stopped at a grave.

Becky said, "Go ahead."

Jimmy nodded and moved closer to the grave.

"Read what it says," Becky said.

He read the inscription on the headstone.

James Miller. Age 39. A wonderful father, a loving husband, a devoted son to his mother, and a man any father would be proud of.

Jimmy fell to his knees. He began to cry. "I'm so sorry," he repeated between hot tears. "Please forgive me."

Becky leaned down and hugged him.

Jimmy sat next to the grave for a very long time.

He wiped his eyes and got to his feet.

"Do you want to come to our house?" Becky asked him.

Jimmy looked at her mom. She smiled and nodded. "You're family, Jimmy."

He smiled back.

He held Becky's hand as they walked back to the car. He vowed he would spend the years he had left on earth atoning for all the mistakes he had made in his life.

He knew he had a long road ahead of him, but he was ready for it.

Visit the author's website:
www.finchambooks.com

Contact:
finchambooks@gmail.com

LEE CALLAWAY

The Dead Daughter (Lee Callaway #1)
The Gone Sister (Lee Callaway #2)

HYDER ALI

The Silent Reporter (Hyder Ali #1)
The Rogue Reporter (Hyder Ali #2)
The Runaway Reporter (Hyder Ali #3)
The Serial Reporter (Hyder Ali #4)
The Street Reporter (Hyder Ali #5)
The Student Reporter (Hyder Ali #0)

MARTIN RHODES

Close Your Eyes (Martin Rhodes #1)
Cross Your Heart (Martin Rhodes #2)
Say Your Prayers (Martin Rhodes #3)
Fear Your Enemy (Martin Rhodes #0)

ECHO ROSE

The Rose Garden (Echo Rose #1)
The Rose Tattoo (Echo Rose #2)
The Rose Thorn (Echo Rose #3)
The Rose Water (Echo Rose #4)

STANDALONE

The Blue Hornet
The October Five
The Paperboys Club
Killing Them Gently
The Solaire Trilogy

THOMAS FINCHAM holds a graduate degree in Economics. His travels throughout the world have given him an appreciation for other cultures and beliefs. He has lived in Africa, Asia, and North America. An avid reader of mysteries and thrillers, he decided to give writing a try. Several novels later, he can honestly say he has found his calling. He is married and lives in a hundred-year-old house. He is the author of THE PAPERBOYS CLUB, THE OCTOBER FIVE, THE BLUE HORNET, KILLING THEM GENTLY, and the HYDER ALI SERIES.

Made in the USA
Columbia, SC
20 August 2018